Imprisoned by Vampires

Joy Mosby

Imprisoned by Vampires, Daughter of Asteria Series Book 5
1st edition

Copyright © 2019 by Joy Mosby
All rights reserved.
ISBN: 978-1-7325793-6-1

Ruby Gulch Enterprises LLC
P.O. Box 64
Craig, CO 81626

Edited by: A Fading Street

Cover by: Anelia Savova AKA Ann_RS

This book is dedicated to you, my readers
Your enthusiasm for Katie
gave me the determination to finish her story

Chapter 1

Jean tried to move but Natalia was on top of her, and she could hardly breathe let alone move the hundred fifty-pound woman. *I can't lose it now*, Jean thought, twisting her head to one side as far as she could, searching for something to help her move Natalia off her.

"Jean?" Vangel's strangled voice asked before he coughed, and it wasn't a throat-clearing kind of cough. It was a lungs-filling-with-fluid cough.

"Yeah," Jean said, relieved he was alive. She had to get Natalia off her. It wasn't like Natalia would wake up and move. Alex had pumped her so full of lead, she probably died before she landed on top of Jean. Vangel was still alive though, and she had to help him. She got her arms underneath her, pushed up into a low plank and rolled out from under Natalia using every drop of strength she had left. She took a second to catch her breath, now that she was free of Natalia then she got to her knees and took her first deep breath in what felt like years before getting to work.

First, Jean checked Natalia for a pulse, and she sighed, heartbroken but unsurprised when she didn't find one. Then she

1

crawled over to Vangel. "I'm going to roll you over. It might hurt." Not waiting for a response, she used both of her hands, leaned back, then pushed forward to roll the two-hundred-fifty-pound man onto his back. He moaned and coughed as he came to rest on his back.

Jean swallowed back bile as she took in the blood-soaked and dirt-encrusted shirt Vangel wore. There was so much blood she couldn't find the entrance wound until he coughed, and blood foamed on his left side just below his ribs as his lungs tried desperately to expel the blood filling them. She hadn't noticed any blood on his back, which meant the bullet was probably still inside and might be the only thing keeping him alive. She pulled her ghillie suit off and used it to apply pressure to the wound with one hand while her other went to the radio in her ear.

"Man down! I repeat, man down." Jean's voice cracked, and tears leaked from her eyes as she watched the color leave Vangel's face. "It will be OK; we'll get you to the hospital," she tried to reassure him.

"No," Vangel wheezed before another coughing fit began. "Too late for me. Go after Alex, we have to stop him."

"No, I'm not leaving you to bleed out. Alex will get his, just not tonight." She needed to hold it together for Vangel, she had to be strong, but it didn't look good. She hit her radio button again. "Helen, Theron! Vangel and Natalia are down. We need two ambulances ASAP." *Where the hell*

2

were they? She caught sight of Natalia, face down on the ground as a pool of blood slowly grew from under her body. Jean wanted to help her, but she couldn't be in two places at once and Vangel still had a chance.

"What," Vangel struggled to speak. "What happened?"

"I only know what I heard," Jean said, sniffling. "Alex went to check on Natalia, who he thought was Katie. He realized it wasn't her, then I heard a gunshot, and I rushed in to find you on the ground and Alex pointing a gun at me. Natalia tackled him from behind, and they wrestled around. He got his gun back, unloaded it on Natalia, shoved her at me, and I fell and hit my head."

"I fucked up. I couldn't get to the shovel in time and I didn't want to shoot him. Theron wanted him alive," Vangel whispered before the cough came back. "Why didn't he kill you?"

"He said he wanted to leave me alive to tell the story. 'No one double-crosses him,' or something. We almost had him." Jean slapped the dirt floor with her free hand. "Wait, I think I hear someone." She wanted to hide behind the door and be ready in case Alex changed his mind and was coming back for her, but she didn't want to take the pressure off Vangel's chest. She gripped her gun with her left hand, ready to fire it if an enemy came through the door. Her hand was slippery with blood, and she wouldn't be very accurate shooting left-handed, but the door wasn't far away and as long as lead was in the air, there was a prayer.

"Jean?" Helen called before she opened the door.

"Helen." Jean slumped; relieved help had arrived. "Vangel

3

needs to get to the hospital."

Helen rushed through the door, looked around, then knelt next to Jean. "Move your hand; let me see."

Jean did as Helen told her, hoping the bleeding had slowed. Vangel coughed again, and blood foamed. She shook her head. "No, damn it." Jean moved to reapply the pressure, but Helen stopped her.

"Jean, I need you to get Theron. It's the only way to save him." Helen squeezed her hand in a tight grip, forcing Jean to meet her eyes.

"But what about the ambulance? You called for one, right?" She wanted to do as Helen asked, but something in Helen's voice told her it was too late for Vangel.

"We will do everything we can, but he has to want to live." Helen looked down at Vangel then back up at Jean. "Go now, before it's too late." Helen shoved her toward the door then applied pressure to the wound.

"Don't you die on me," Jean called to Vangel, taking one last look before running for the house as fast as she could. She wasn't as fast as Katie, but she would not be the reason Vangel died.

Chapter 2

Vince

Vince paced across the marble floor of the office while Theron sat at his desk, doing who knew what on his computer, and wondered where Jean was. Helen said she would send her to the house as soon as she assessed the situation, but it seemed to be taking forever. He needed her; he had to find out where the helicopter went. Had it landed on the other side of the island? Was he wasting time waiting for Jean when he could be rescuing Katie and killing Lolita? He ran his hands through his hair. Where else could it have gone if it did not land at the airport? He pulled his phone out and checked his messages. Theron's contact at the airport had replied to his text: nothing had landed at the airport since the sun went down.

Goddess, this is all my fault. His job was to stay with Katie, guard her back, keep her safe, and he had failed. How could he be so selfish? He left the love of his life to fight an ancient vampire on her own while he battled the young ones. Now, Katie was with Lolita and who knew what the bitch had planned for her. He cracked his neck. Dwelling on his mistakes would not solve his problems, but he could not stop berating himself.

Katie had been standing on the stage, telling the crowd of vampires that she was the true daughter of Asteria. She had been about to do something—he wasn't sure what—when the doors of the ballroom burst open and Lolita's guards had barreled in with automatic rifles ready to fire into the ceiling, but before they did, they had frozen in place. Vince did not understand what had stopped them until he looked at Katie. She had forced them to freeze like she had when she captured Thomas. Vince had wondered if any of the guests had noticed. Most of the vampires he knew would kill her if they knew what kind of power she could wield. He had planned to talk to her about it after the party; it was not something he wanted spread around.

Lolita had come in after the guards, looking like a dominatrix, and he remembered taking a step toward her before Katie's voice in his head stopped him. *She is mine.*

"Theron, my invitation to your little soirée must have gotten lost in the mail. It's a good thing Geovanni told me about it, or I would have missed it," Lolita had said as the crowd parted for her.

Find your breath, stay calm, he remembered thinking to Katie as she pulled the katana out of its sheath on her back and prepared for battle. She was the most beautiful creature Vince had ever seen as she held her sword in both hands over her left shoulder and waited for Lolita to join her on the stage. He had wanted nothing more than to find a chair, put it at the foot of the stage, and watch the fight about to take place.

"After you sent your man to take over my island, and he failed, I didn't think you would appreciate an invitation." Theron stepped into Lolita's path, stopping her progress to the stage, and Vince wished Theron would kill her; damn what Katie wanted. The sooner Lolita was dead the better.

"Silly, Theron, he was free. He came here on his own and never asked for help. If he had, you wouldn't be standing here blocking my way to the stage. Are you afraid for the little human who wishes to rule us?" She ran one long, glossy, red fingernail down his cheek, and Vince wondered why Theron allowed her to touch him without his permission. If she had touched Vince like that, he would have broken her finger like Katie had with the vampire back in San Sebastian.

"Afraid for her? Never. You have no idea what she is capable of. If you were wise, you would destroy your army and do as the Goddess demands." Theron grabbed her hand and removed it from his cheek before he stepped out of her way and held his hand toward the stage. Vince admired his restraint but wished Theron would take her head off all the same.

"The Goddess? How do you know she's real? And if she is, why wouldn't she want an army?" Lolita climbed the stairs as she spoke, not taking her eyes off Katie before she turned to face the crowd. Vince tore his gaze from Lolita to see how the guests were reacting to her presence. Some had prepared for the fight, smiling, and removing their jackets. Some were backing to the edge of the room, wanting to watch, and others were moving toward the exit, trying not to be noticed.

"I am here to give you all the opportunity to join me in overthrowing Europe. Together, we can rule and turn the humans into our slaves. We have lived in the shadows for too long. It is time for them to bow to us. We are superior to them in every way, so tell me why aren't we ruling the world? I have an army of five hundred vampires ready to do my bidding. If you join me, there will be no stopping us." She brought her hands up to the sky and stared at the ceiling, ending her rant.

"You are wrong, Lolita, you will create a war that will end vampires. Even if you can take Europe, the other countries of the world will stop you, causing a war that will leave our homes in ruin, and vampires living in caves," Katie had said, moving in front of Lolita, and keeping her sword ready to strike. Vince remembered wanting to rush the stage to get between them, but he did not. If he interfered, Katie would never forgive him. He would watch her back while she fought Lolita; that had been the plan.

"Boys, please dispatch the human," Lolita had said, ignoring Katie and inspecting her nails.

"No, Lolita, you brought this fight on yourself," Vince said, moving to the first, still frozen, guard. He pulled a short sword from under his suitcoat and in one smooth motion, took off the guard's head. He could not help his smile as the blood of his enemy showered down around him.

Lolita lunged for Katie, but she spun away before Lolita could touch her. Vince took a step toward the stage. He needed to be closer to Katie while she fought Lolita, but the sound of someone approaching from behind forced him to turn and face another guard. *Katie must have lost her hold on their minds when Lolita attacked her,* he thought.

Vince grabbed the barrel of the gun pointed at his face and flipped it back to the guard forcing him to pull the trigger just as the barrel came in range of his head. The guard fell to the ground, Vince knelt, picked up the guard's head by the hair and used his sword to decapitate him. A bullet through the brain would kill a human, but only slow down a vampire for an hour or two.

He jumped to his feet, ready to storm the stage, but found it surrounded by Lolita's vampires. Some of them were dressed in the black cargo pants and t-shirts of the guards while the others were dressed in rags and smelled of rot. Theron, Helen, and other guests were fighting them. Vince was torn, he was looking forward to a good fight, but he had to get to the stage and watch Katie's back.

Katie looked amazing with her sword held out in front of her, circling Lolita. The blood dripping from the tip reminded him of the rubies in the crown she wore. His heart swelled; his queen had drawn first blood. With a battle cry he rushed the stage, slicing, and cutting whoever tried to stop him. He had forgotten how much he missed fighting to the death; the adrenaline running through his veins making him high, and the thought that one false move could mean the end of him pushed him to cut down everyone in his path.

Vince ground his teeth and pinched the bridge of his nose.

If he hadn't gotten so wrapped up in his lust for killing, he would have easily made it to the stage. Then Lolita would be dead and the only thing they would have to deal with would be her army. Where was Jean? He turned and paced across the floor again. Every second counted

"Theron," Jean yelled, running into the office. Vince stopped his pacing and jerked his head up.

"Jean, what is it?" Theron asked, jumping up from his chair and running to meet her in the middle of the room.

"Vangel, he's hurt bad." Jean looked between them. "Where's Katie?"

"Kidnapped by Lolita," Vince bit out. "What does Vangel need?"

"An ambulance, but Helen said she needed Theron, that she needed his help." Jean crossed her arms over her chest, and Vince smelled the blood drying on her clothes. "I don't know why. He needs an ambulance or better yet flight for life if he's going to survive."

Vince looked at Theron and gave him a nod. Vangel must be mortally wounded if Helen was asking for Theron and not bringing Vangel back herself. If Theron added another vampire to his numbers, the night might not be a total loss. "Go to her. Jean, I need your help." Vince took her arm and pulled her out of the office and down the hall, weaving around the vampires who planned to help them destroy Lolita's army. Theron had invited everyone who wanted to join the fight to stay and help plan the attack.

Depending on what Jean told him, he might need their help sooner than he thought.

"What?" she asked, dragging her feet as Vince pulled her along. "I need to get back to Vangel."

"Theron and Helen will handle it. Can you pull some strings and find out where the helicopter is going?" Vince stopped and turned to her.

"What helicopter and why? I lost my ability to pull strings when Mom tagged me rogue." Jean pulled her eyebrows together in confusion.

"Did you hear the helicopter? It was how Lolita kidnapped Katie." Vince stopped and punched the wall in frustration then shook his hand out. The pain only giving him a moment of peace before reality came flooding back.

"No, I'm sorry Vince I was dealing with my own FUBAR." Jean put a hand on his arm. "Even if I could call someone, they wouldn't do it for me, but I can do better."

Vince stared at her as she spoke, wishing he could force the words he needed to hear out of her. "What?"

"I can hack air traffic control's computers, but it won't do any good without the tail numbers." Jean ran around him and down the hall to her room.

"I have the tail numbers. Where are we going?" Vince wanted to pick her up and run, but he could not, she did not know about vampires.

"To my room, I need my computer. If you have the tail number, and they're still in the air, I will find them."

That was the question though. He had not kept track of the time. When had the helicopter left? Had it been five hours ago or five minutes? It felt like time stopped the moment his feet touched the ground, and the helicopter took off into the night. If they landed somewhere on the island would they still be in the air? "Hurry, I do not know how long it's been."

They picked up the pace, but it was still too slow for Vince. When they reached Jean's room she went straight for her computer while Vince locked the door. He did not want any interruptions. He stood still, forcing himself to keep quiet until she asked for the number. The seconds seemed to pass as hours as Jean's fingers flew across the keyboard. "OK, I'm in. What's the number?"

Vince rattled off the number as if he had known it his entire life. "Where is it?" he asked, moving to stand behind her.

"I'm looking. Keep your pants on." Jean dragged her mouse over the black screen with nothing but neon-green dots moving across it. When she hovered over a dot, a window would pop up revealing the dot's tail numbers. She moved from the ones in the middle of the screen outwards and with each one not matching Lolita's, his gut tightened. Had they already landed somewhere? How would he find them if they weren't still on the island? Was there another airstrip they could use to get off the island?

"Here it is," Jean yelled, bringing Vince back from

his toxic thoughts.

"Where?" he stared at the screen.

"Here." Jean pointed her finger to a dot moving on the upper right of the screen.

"Where is it headed?"

"I don't know but it's over the water and headed toward Africa, how far can a helicopter go on a tank of gas?"

"I do not know." Vince ran his hands through his hair. He was helpless, and he was never helpless, he always knew what to do. The last time he could not help himself, he was a child watching the Romans slaughter his family.

"Where did it go?" Jean rubbed her eyes and blinked at the screen.

"What do you mean? It's gone?" Vince leaned over, searching the screen for the missing dot.

"Yeah, it was right here." She pointed at a black spot. "Do you think it crashed?"

"Goddess, I hope not. They probably landed on a boat." Vince had to believe that was the explanation. Katie had to be alive, but who knew for how long. Lolita did not kill her at the party, and her ego would not allow her to quietly kill Katie. He had to believe Lolita would make a show of killing her or worse, try to turn her into a slave.

"If the boat has radar, I might be able to find it," Jean offered, turning in her chair.

"Do not waste your time. We cannot catch them." Vince was seething; he was so angry he couldn't think. He needed to hit something, kill something. Someone needed to pay for what Lolita did, but the only person who deserved punishment for what happened was himself. He should have had Katie's back.

"Maybe Thomas knows where they went," Jean said.

"We don't need Thomas; I know where they are going." Vince had almost forgotten about their prisoner. "We will go to Venice, rescue Katie, and kill Lolita. It's time to take the fight to her." He opened the door and ran down the hall, leaving Jean without a goodbye. He needed to pay a visit to Thomas.

Chapter 3

Katie

What the hell was going on? I thought to myself. I was lying on my back with my eyes closed, but I wasn't in my bed, it was too hard and too loud, and it was vibrating. I wanted to move, but I couldn't remember where I was or how I'd gotten there, so I left my eyes closed and tried to remember.

I was at the party, fighting Lolita. She was coming at me with a knife; my katana was gone. I needed to break her neck, then I would have time to find my sword and cut her head off. I grabbed her wrist, broke it then held her down. I was about to kick her when something hit me in the back of the head.

Fuck, I thought to myself, *someone hit me from behind, and I blacked out.* Everything after that was hazy. I remembered being carried, then the sound of rotors. We were on a helicopter, leaving my friends behind.

I had to stay calm, if my heart rate increased, any vampires with me would notice. They thought I was unconscious, and I wanted it to stay that way until I made my move. *How am I going to escape?*

I felt out my captors. There were five vampires, no humans.

Which meant theoretically, I could take over their minds, force them to turn around, and take me back to the mansion, but I hadn't been able to make a dent in Lolita's wall before the fight. What would she do when she realized I'd taken over her vampires? Could I command the others to subdue her while the pilot took us back? Would Lolita force us to wreck to keep me from escaping? Could I force the guards to push her out of the door?

I didn't have a choice, every second we moved further away from Vince there was less of a chance of survival. I started with the pilot; he was strong, but I kicked my way through his mental door. Then I moved to the co-pilot and the others in the cabin with me. I had just gotten the last one when Lolita noticed something was wrong.

"Look at her face." She nudged me with her foot. "I think she is playing possum."

"What?" I forced the vampire sitting next to her to ask. "She doesn't look any different to me."

"That's because you're an idiot. Katie, you are going to love what I have planned for you."

I had no idea what I was doing with my face. I thought it was relaxed and hoped it looked like I was still unconscious but breaking into the guard's minds was harder than I thought; maybe I twitched. It was too late to wonder, I had to stop Lolita from whatever she was about to do. *Hold her down,* I thought to the guards surrounding me. The three guards in the cabin lurched forward, trying

16

to stand, but they couldn't get up. *Take your seatbelts off*, I commanded, mentally doing a face palm, who would have thought that vampires would wear seatbelts? They hurried to do my bidding and were almost free when I felt something sting my ass.

"How does that feel Katie?" Lolita asked as my eyes went wide with pain. She looked down at me holding an empty syringe in her left hand while she cradled her right against her chest. Her platinum, almost white hair had been in a slick ponytail before our flight and now long tendrils fell around her almost glowing face, framing her porcelain skin. If I didn't already know she was evil incarnate, I would've thought she was an angel with her ice-blue eyes.

I tried to tell her to fuck off, but I couldn't speak. My muscles wouldn't obey me. *What did she do to me?* I tried to blink to stop my head from spinning, but my eyelids didn't want to work.

Lolita crossed her legs and gave the syringe to the guard next to her. "I hope you like the cocktail I injected you with. I had it designed especially for you. It's a combination of vecuronium, rocuronium, pancuronium, and succinylcholine. It should take care of any special abilities you have and keep you from hurting yourself." Lolita laughed when I was unable to respond but stopped and held her wrist with her good hand as if laughing made it hurt.

Bitch, I thought. How was I going to get away when I couldn't feel my feet? I needed to rest, to conserve my strength, but I couldn't close my eyes, all I could do was stare at the bitch who had ruined my life. My mouth was filling with drool and I could hardly breathe, if they didn't roll me over soon, I would drown in my own spit.

"Stop staring at me," Lolita said looking down her nose. She uncrossed her legs when I didn't move and kicked my head hard enough for my body to roll away from her. Pain exploded across my cheek and I tried to scream but no sound came out. At least the drool filling my mouth dripped onto the floor instead of into my lungs.

I didn't know how long I stared at the guard's feet across from me but eventually we started losing altitude and landed with a bump. I thought we were on the ground at first and wondered where we were, but then we began rocking back and forth.

My eyes were drying out, and I had never wanted to blink more, then the door opened, and I was blasted with a gust of wind causing my eyes to water and giving relief to the desert my eyes had felt like a moment before. Tears I couldn't blink away blurred my vision as Lolita and two guards exited the helicopter. I tried to see beyond them, to get an idea of where I was, but the tears made it impossible for me to focus.

"Madame?" The vampire nearest me asked. "What would you like me to do with her?"

I made out the blurry form of Lolita, stopping and turning with her good hand on her hip and her broken one hanging at her side. "Take her below. The drugs should keep her catatonic for at least eight hours."

Eight hours? I thought before the guard behind me kicked me, forcing my pliant body to roll. I felt him step over me, and the floor bounced as he jumped out. He grabbed my hair and pulled me face first toward the door. It felt like my face was being slowly submerged into boiling water as the rough industrial carpet scraped then burned my face, and hair was ripped from my head. Out of the helicopter, thankfully they didn't let me fall to the ground. I was pulled into the arms of one of the guards and cradled like a baby, except they let my neck flop backwards, and gave me an inverted view of the world.

My eyes cleared and saw that I was on a yacht surrounded by blackness, at least from what I could see. Facing the stern of the boat, I made out an Italian flag, the deck was white fiberglass, and teak deck chairs were scattered around. *At least we weren't switching to a plane.* A boat would give Vince and Theron time to catch up.

"Wait," Lolita said, coming into view. "This is for my wrist." Her fist came out of nowhere and my head jerked as she punched me. Sharp pain lanced up my nose at the same time blood exploded from it, running down my throat and out of my nose, covering my face. Blackness clouded my vision until there was nothing left, and I welcomed it.

Chapter 4

Jean

Jean watched Vince storm out of her room and stared at the empty doorway. She didn't know what to do. Katie was out of reach, Alex was gone, Natalia was dead, and Vangel was dying. She couldn't just sit there doing nothing. Theron and Helen would need help moving Vangel from the shed. She glanced down at the black turtleneck and pants she'd been wearing under the ghillie suit. They were covered in blood and were beginning to harden as they dried. *Who cares, none of the guests from the party will notice.* She raced out of her room and down the hall, ignoring the partygoers loitering there. Most of them had blood on their clothes, and their dresses and suits must have been torn in the fight. Goose bumps pimpled her arms as she ran past them, feeling as if they were staring at her like she was a Thanksgiving turkey, and they had been starving on a desert island for a year. Many had blood on their faces, but she didn't know where it came from since she didn't see any wounds or bandages. She thought about asking a few of them if they needed help, but Vangel was in worse shape than they were.

She made it to the patio door in the great room without being stopped and raced through it, ignoring the eyes on her back.

She slowed to a jog as she reached the trees, searching for the flashing lights of an ambulance or the voices of the paramedics, but it was quiet and dark. Had Helen or Theron called the hospital? Her legs were tired, and she wanted to stop, but she couldn't; if they hadn't called an ambulance for Vangel, then she needed to get back to him, if for nothing else than to say goodbye. The thought of him not surviving made her trip over a branch and she fell hard on her knees. She groaned as pain radiated up to the base of her skull.

She held back tears when she thought of losing Vangel. He was a friend; he hadn't deserted her when he found out she worked for Interpol; he had tried to help her. He couldn't die. She would save him, even it meant hurting Helen and Theron to do it. She slowly got to her feet and moved through the trees more cautiously than before.

She stopped when she heard voices and listened hard, trying to filter out the other noises of the night and concentrate on what was being said. It was Theron and Helen, but Jean was too far away to make out what they were saying. Why were they doing nothing to help the man who protected Katie and gave his life trying to capture their enemy? She creeped to the same corner of the shack where she had listened to Vangel and Alex earlier.

"Vangel, we both know this is a mortal wound," Theron said, his voice more serious than Jean had ever heard.

"Yeah, that's what I thought too," he answered

before he started coughing.

"You have a choice. You can leave this world for whatever comes next or you can become one of us," Helen said, her voice gentle, and Jean imagined her looking at Vangel with sad eyes.

What in the hell were they talking about? Jean wondered. *And why hadn't they called the paramedics?*

"What do you mean?" Vangel asked between wet gurgling coughs.

"We are children of the night. Helen can heal you, but you will become one of us," Theron whispered, and Jean strained to hear him. "You will forever be as you were before Alex shot you, never aging, never falling ill, you will be faster and stronger than you can imagine."

Vangel tried to laugh, but it came out garbled. "What. . . What's the catch?"

"You will be a vampire, a son of Asteria, you will live on the blood of others. Living under the stars never to set eyes on the sun again unless you wish to travel to the afterlife."

"Vampires? I knew there was something about you all that didn't add up." He coughed again.

Jean backed up a step. *Vampires? What was wrong with these people?* Jean thought back to everything she had seen since she met Katie. Jean had seen Katie out in the sun a ton of times, but the others. . . She had never seen them outside during the day, and they were pale, especially when she considered that they lived on a tropical island.

23

She rolled her eyes; how could she believe this? They were never outside during the day because they were night owls, they were sick if they thought they could turn Vangel into a vampire to save him.

Jean had seen some messed-up stuff online, but she never thought she would see it in real life. She thought about when Marios attacked her. She had wondered why he kept going for her neck, but she hadn't seen any fangs. He had moved fast, like faster than Katie fast, and that girl could move when she wanted to. Theron threw him across the room when he saw what was going on… *No, they were all just way into CrossFit or something. Messed up in the head but ripped. Weren't they?*

She took another step back, tripped over something, and fell, landing on her ass. There was no way they hadn't heard her, and she wanted to hide. She didn't want to know what they would do to her now that she knew how demented they were.

"Yes, that's why we don't go out during the day or share meals with you." Helen said, her voice sounding strained. "Vangel you must choose now, or it will be too late."

Vangel, Jean thought scrambling to her feet. *I can't leave him here to die.* She ran for the door and pulled on the handle, but it didn't budge. She needed to call an ambulance and get Vangel away from these people. There was no such thing as vampires. How could there be? "Vangel, hold on.

24

I'll get an ambulance," she yelled through the door.

"Yes, I'm not ready to die." She heard Vangel wheeze before he lapsed into another coughing fit.

Jean banged on the door. "Vangel, no, don't believe them, they're crazy. I'll get you to a hospital." She tried the handle again, throwing all her weight against it as the door opened and she stumbled inside, and fell to her already bruised knees.

Her eyes found Helen and she stared. Jean wanted to look away, but she was frozen in place as Helen bent over Vangel and watched as fangs, that Jean hadn't noticed before, pierced his skin before her mouth sealed over the punctures. "No," Jean screamed, scrambling to her feet, intent on pushing Helen off him, but before she took two steps, strong arms were around her waist, pulling her away. She jerked her head back and forth trying to see who had her. Theron. She wanted to relax, knowing he wouldn't hurt her, but he thought he was a vampire, and they were killing Vangel.

"Help!" she screamed, wondering if anyone in the house would hear her.

"Calm down, Jean," Theron said, squeezing her tighter. "Or I'll knock you out."

Terrified of what he would do to her if she was unconscious, she stopped screaming, and waited for him to tell her what was going on.

Chapter 5

Vince

Vince slid the unlocked door to the barn back hard enough to make the walls shake when it hit the end of the track.

"Vince, what has happened? How can I help?" Argyris asked, running toward him from the other end of the barn.

"Everything that could go wrong tonight, went wrong." Vince stopped outside Thomas's stall and wrapped his hands around the bars. Takis screamed for blood from his cell deeper in the barn while Thomas slowly got to his feet and walked as close to the bars separating them as his chains would allow. He folded his hands in front of him and smiled, pulling his eyebrows together.

"Lolita came for me?" he asked hopefully.

"Lolita came, took what she wanted, and left," Vince snarled. "She probably forgot you existed. Argyris, I need the keys to this cell please." Vince forced himself to be polite. *Lolita, and her army had to pay. Thomas was one of her army. He would pay for the sins of his maker.*

"Do you think it's a good idea?" Argyris asked, pulling a set of keys from his pocket, and fisting them.

"His maker, his mistress, just kidnapped the love of my life and the queen of the vampires. Someone will pay this night." Vince narrowed his eyes at Argyris. "Give me the keys and walk away." Vince held out his hand.

Is he waiting for someone to intervene? Vince wondered, and seeing no one, Argyris handed the keys over and stepped back.

"All I ask is for you to think before you act. Is there not a non-violent solution that will ease your mind? Perhaps meditation."

Vince rolled his eyes. "Violence is the only thing that will make this better." He unlocked the door and slid it open. Deep down he knew violence would not ease his mind, nothing would until Katie was safe in his arms. He stepped into the stall and slid the door closed behind him. "Lock it." Vince passed the keys back to Argyris and waited until Argyris locked the door then held his hand out, waiting for him to give the keys back. "You and I are going to dance," he said, stepping close to Thomas. "Hold out your hands."

Thomas narrowed his eyes but did as he was told. Vince unlocked the manacles surrounding his wrists and let them fall to the floor. Vince offered him the keys. "For your legs." Thomas bent and unlocked the manacles around his legs. "Now throw the keys back to Argyris."

"No." Thomas dropped the keys on the ground. "You do it."

Ignoring the keys, Vince leaped forward, punching

Thomas in the nose, and smiled when he felt and heard the satisfying crunch of bone and cartilage. "What is Lolita going to do with Katie?" he asked, backing up and giving Thomas a chance to wipe the blood from his face.

"How would I know, and even if I did, I wouldn't tell you."

Vince tracked Thomas as he faked a step to the right then sprung forward throwing a round house kick at Vince's midsection. Vince blocked it and followed it up with a punch to the neck.

Thomas fell backwards onto his ass and grabbed his throat, unable to breathe. Not wasting time, Vince moved in, kicking him hard enough in the kidneys to force him to roll onto his stomach. Vince followed him, kicking him in the ribs, the sound of another bone breaking made Thomas forget about his throat and hold his side.

"What is she going to do with Katie?" Vince knelt and grabbed Thomas by the ear, twisting it and forcing him to look at Vince.

"All she told us was that once she had Katie, she would become the most powerful vampire in the world." Thomas whispered; his voice box broken.

Images of Lolita turning Katie into her slave burst into Vince's mind. What would Lolita do if she had the power to break into vampire's minds and divvy out their secrets or even worse, take over their minds to do her bidding? He shook his head, surely the Goddess wouldn't allow it to happen, and neither would Katie. She would die before becoming Lolita's slave. An image of Katie flashed in his mind, broken, bleeding, and dying, using her last breath to tell Lolita to fuck off. A shadow of a smile crossed his lips when he thought about how strong Katie was, but then he thought about her sacrificing her life to stop Lolita. *That was not how Katie's life should end.* The thought of Katie dying, either by her own hand or Lolita's, made Vince shake with rage. He had to get her back, she was the only thing that mattered and not because she would be the leader of the vampires, but because she had his heart, and he could not go on without her at his side.

Vince peered down at Thomas. His mouth was covered in blood. He must have punctured something vital with one of his kicks. It wouldn't kill him, but it would take a long time to recover. Vince shook his head. *This was all Thomas's fault, he told Lolita where we were. Thomas was the one who had been reporting back to Lolita. If it had not been for him, Katie would be at my side and the party would still be raging,* Vince thought, staring at the vampire crawling toward the keys to the cell.

"Where do you think you are going?" Vince grabbed Thomas by the hair and lifted him to his feet. "This is all your fault, if you hadn't come to Crete, none of this would be happening." Vince shook Thomas as he screamed in pain. He was as limp as a ragdoll, so Vince let go of his hair, and let him fall to the ground. "It is time for you to meet your maker. May Asteria have mercy on your soul." Vince knelt and, pushed Thomas onto his back. He cocked his fisted hand behind his head and brought it down hard enough to break through Thomas's ribcage. Thomas's body bowed off the ground and he screamed; his voice box already healed. Vince searched through his chest until he found Thomas's barely beating heart. He wrapped his hand around it and ripped it from his chest with a battle cry. As soon as the heart left his body, he flopped to the floor, dead. The vampire was gone from this world.

"Vince, what have you done?" Helen asked, startling him from his position on the floor. He jerked his head up and looked at Helen through the bars of the stall. Her brown eyes glared at him as she shook her head, causing the body draped over her shoulder to slip before she redistributed her weight to keep it from falling. The sight of her made him remember what she had been doing. She looked pale and worn out, but they probably all did after what they had been through. He stood and glanced at the heart in his hand as it turned grey and began to flake away, the slightest movement causing it to dissolve even faster.

"It was his fault." Vince searched the ground for the keys. Finding them, he dropped what was left of the heart and wiped his hands on his ruined suit pants. The heart disintegrated before it hit the ground. "Would you mind?" He held the keys through the bars and waited while Helen took them, trying not to drop the body he recognized as Vangel.

"We could have used him for hostage negotiation," Helen said, her voice barely above a whisper as she unlocked the stall. "Traded him for Katie."

Vince stepped out of the stall and felt all his energy drain away. *What have I done?* He thought, watching the blood on the concrete of the stall turn to dust. *Did I ruin my chance of getting Katie back in one piece?* He glanced at Helen, his mouth hanging open, but no words came out. He shook himself; he would worry about his actions later. "Here let me, you must be exhausted." Vince took Vangel from her and went down the hall to the cell next to Takis. He laid Vangel on the cot in the corner. He picked up the chain with a manacle at the end and secured it around Vangel's ankle. "Sleep well, Vangel, for when you wake you will be my brother."

Vince exited the stall and locked it, unsure what to say to Helen. Argyris came through the barn door a few seconds later with Natalia in his arms. Had he been so full of rage and vengeance he didn't notice Argyris leave?

He might have lost a bargaining chip by killing Thomas, but he couldn't deny that he felt better after killing him. The inferno that had been burning him up from the inside out was now a slow simmer he could manage until he got his hands on Lolita.

Argyris lay Natalia down in the stall across from Takis and came out with his arms crossed over his chest.

"Will she survive?" Vince asked, looking through the bars.

"Yes, I need to remove the bullets, and she will need lots of blood, but she will come back to us." Argyris stared at the floor as he spoke. "If you will excuse me, I need to get to work on her, and I'm sure you are both needed in the house."

"Argyris, will you alert me when he wakes up?" Helen asked nodding toward Vangel.

"Of course, but it will be a few days," he gave her a sad smile and walked back to his room.

Helen and Vince turned in silence and made their way back to the mansion. With the deed done, and their injured being cared for, Vince allowed himself to think about what Helen said. Would Lolita have traded Katie for Thomas? He almost laughed. If Lolita cared about Thomas, she would not have left without him. He pulled Thomas's phone out of his pocket and clicked it on. There were no missed calls and no text messages. If Lolita wanted him to go back with her, she would have told him she was coming; she had no idea he was their prisoner. At first glance Helen was right, they might have been able to use him as a bargaining chip, but after he thought about Lolita, he knew she would never trade Katie for Thomas. She was too important to Lolita's plans.

Chapter 6

Alex

Alex grabbed the chin of the man slumped on the floor next to the sink of a restaurant's bathroom and turned it back and forth, studying his cheekbones. The restaurant had closed hours before and breaking in had been easy. Alex looked in the mirror and inspected his cheekbones before grabbing a piece of molding clay and stretching it out before attaching it to his skin with glue just below where his own cheek bone protruded. He checked the mirror again before attaching a matching piece of clay to the other side of his face. He looked like a monster from a horror movie with white clay resembling bones protruding from his face and dark circles under his eyes, *but not for long*, he thought as he picked up the tube of foundation.

Finished with his makeup, he looked at his hair. It was matted and sticking up all over the place making him look homeless. Normally, he loved his hair and thought it was one of his best attributes, but he wanted off Crete and shaving it was the only way he would make it through airport security. He took the scissors sitting beside the sink and cut it as close to his scalp as he could then ran hot water into the sink and covered his head in shaving cream. He picked up a disposable razor and was about to begin shaving it off when the man whose face he was stealing stirred.

"Sorry man, you're going to have to sleep for a while longer." Alex took the taser off the counter and zapped the man for the second time. He put the taser on the far side of the sink and began shaving as the acrid smell of urine invaded his nostrils. "You had to piss yourself this time," Alex sneered before resuming his work.

Twenty minutes later Alex studied himself in the mirror, then the passport picture lying next to the sink. It was important for him to look like the photo but not exactly like it. His once ivory skin was now olive thanks to the foundation, and the molding clay thickened his cheekbones making it impossible for him to be tracked using facial recognition software. He smiled, showing his straight white teeth and immediately closed his lips. The passport photo showed gnarly, yellowed teeth, none of them straight, there was nothing he could do about his teeth. He would have to keep his mouth closed unless he could convince the authorities that he had his teeth fixed in — he looked at the passport stamp — the week he had been on the island. *Mouth closed then.*

He picked up his carry-on bag, leaving the tased man on the bathroom floor and took the back door out of the restaurant. The man should wake up about the same time Alex boarded the plane. With a spring in his step, he unlocked the car he stole earlier and drove to the airport. Nothing would stop him from leaving Crete, and no one could pay him enough to return. *What a fucked-up night*, he thought as he drove.

He had had a good feeling about the plan as he drove to the mansion earlier that night. Vangel was on Alex's side, he had no doubt, and even though he had wanted Vangel to take Katie while they had been shopping the day before, Vangel had been right. The vampires might not have been able to catch them, but Theron owned the police and everyone at the airport. They wouldn't have been able to get her off the island without being caught. *Tonight would be different*, he remembered thinking as he parked the stolen car along a deserted stretch of road a half mile from where he had planned to meet Vangel.

He had slowly, and silently, worked his way through the orchard in the darkness, keeping his ears and eyes tuned into anything out of the ordinary. Once he had Katie, they would blow up the mansion and while everyone scrambled to save themselves, Alex, Vangel, and Katie would run for the boat Vangel had secured earlier in the day. Then Alex planned to call Lolita, tell her he had Katie, and set up the drop. Once he knew where to go, he had planned to come up with a way to kill both and Lolita but not until after the money Lolita promised had been deposited in his account.

He hadn't decided if he was going to let Vangel live or not, if he did, he would have to split the money with him. *It would be easier to kill him, no loose ends.*

The straight, vertical lines of the walls of the shack brought him back to the job at hand. He stopped and looked around. He remembered the feeling of someone watching him. Knowing what he knew now, he wished he would've given the place more than a cursory glance.

He ran his hand over his now bald head. If he hadn't been in such a hurry, he could've taken care of the Interpol agent before the shit show started. Alex shook his head as he found a parking space in the long-term lot at the airport, making sure it was far away from the lights and cameras before heading for the terminal and wincing at the pain in his sprained ankle. He snickered at his own stupidity. *How could I have been so careless?*

Everything had gone to hell. Vangel had double-crossed him and he had barely made it out of the shack alive. After he killed Vangel, the woman pretending to be Katie had gone after him. He filled her full of lead and he had pushed her into the Interpol agent forcing them both to the ground. "I'll let you live to tell the story. No one will ever bring me down," he had said, backing toward the door. He had tightened his grip on the empty gun in his pocket. How could he forget to bring an extra clip? He never left witnesses.

As soon as he left the shack, he ran as close to the house as he thought he could without being seen. He pulled the detonator out of his pocket and was about to push the button when the lights of a helicopter blinded him. He tripped and fell, twisting his ankle and had to let the detonator go to catch himself and lost it in the process. He jumped to his feet and winced as pain shot through his ankle. With the detonator lost in the dried leaves and loose dirt he had no choice but to run away as fast as his sprained ankle would let him. Whoever had been in the helicopter had seen him and he needed to be gone before they told Theron there was someone behind his house.

Alex rolled his eyes, *another failed mission,* he thought as he joined the line at the security check point. *At least I didn't lose any money on the C4*, he thought remembering finding the weapons cache in the cave. It was the only good thing that had come from his visit to Crete.

"Boarding pass and passport," a bored-looking guard asked holding out his hand.

"Here you go." Alex handed him his stolen passport and flashed him the boarding pass on his phone. The man looked at the photo then at Alex then back again. Alex stiffened; he swore he could feel the molding clay pulling away from his skin as the guard assessed him. He was about to smile but remembered the teeth just in time and he kept his mouth closed.

"Have a good flight." the guard handed the stolen passport back to Alex and waved his hand toward the metal detectors.

"Thanks, have a good night," Alex said, trying to sound cheerful. He was getting off this rock, but he was far from safe. As soon as he was through security, he went to the bathroom and checked his makeup. Everything was still in place, and he rolled his neck. He needed to calm down. Once he reached Athens, he would take the first flight out of the country he could. He came out of the bathroom, located the cameras within range, and skirted them with his head down before finding an area where he wouldn't be watched. He pulled out the tattered paperback he found in the stolen car and pretended to read while keeping an eye on the terminal.

He had an hour to kill, and he couldn't seem to get his heart rate to slow. He tapped his foot and looked from side to side every time someone came within twenty feet of him. He was paranoid that the police had identified him and would show up any second to arrest him. *Why had I come to Crete in the first place?*

When they finally began boarding the plane, Alex was the first one on board, but he didn't relax until they were airborne. He looked out the window at the blackness of the Aegean far below and thought about how much his life had changed in the past year.

When he first came to Theron for a place to stay, he had no idea vampires existed but as time went by, he couldn't help but notice how few of Theron's people ventured out during the day, and he had never seen them eat food. He confronted Theron about it a few days before Katie had arrived. Theron told him what they were and agreed to let him stay if he promised to never tell anyone about them. Now he regretted the whole thing. If he would have gone to Sanctuary to start with, he never would have met Katie, and he would be with his crew, kidnapping dignitaries and making money hand over fist without a care in the world. Now he was alone, all but broke, and running from two of the most powerful people, well vampires, in Europe.

"Would you care for a beverage sir?" A flight attendant asked, pulling him out of his thoughts.

"What?" Alex blinked, forgetting where he was for a second. "Just water, please." He gave her a weak smile as she passed him a bag of nuts and a napkin before asking the person next to him what he would like.

Alex was ready to get stupid drunk; he was off Crete and he wasn't in a body bag, but he still didn't have the girl. Which meant Lolita would probably come after him, and he didn't know what Theron would do after everything he had done to the vampire.

He didn't know where he would go from Athens, but it needed to be somewhere he could make money, then he wanted to stay off his dad's and Lolita's radar for a while. He believed Zeus when he said he would kill Alex if he didn't start killing vampires, but Zeus didn't understand how hard it was to kill something Alex couldn't get close to. He would take a break, just a few weeks then he would go after Lolita.

He didn't know how he would get close enough to Katie to kill her, and she was on the top of Zeus's list. There had been so many attempts on her life already, he doubted Vince would leave her unguarded for years after what had happened the previous night.

He chugged his water. Damn him for trusting Vangel. If it wasn't for him, Alex would've found a way to capture Katie, kill

41

Theron, Vince, and the rest of the vampires at the party, then the only one he would have left to kill would be Lolita.

The pilot's voice brought him out of his thoughts as he announced that they would be landing soon. Alex closed his eyes, all he needed to do now was get out of the country. Everything else could wait.

Chapter 7

Theron

"Put me down," Jean screamed, pounding on Theron's back. "I don't care what you are. Put me down. I need to call an ambulance for Vangel."

"Not until you calm yourself." Theron rolled his eyes as they entered the great room. He needed a few minutes to speak with Jean privately, but the room was full of vampires who were waiting to speak with him. He made eye contact with a few then looked at the human over his shoulder, indicating that they would have to wait. They nodded their heads and returned to their conversations.

Theron hurried down the hall to his bedroom. He didn't want to have this conversation in his office. He needed undisturbed privacy and his bedroom was his best option with a house full of vampires.

Once in his room, he threw Jean onto the bed then locked the door before she had a chance to run. He put his hands on his hips and watched her struggle to the edge of the bed. *I do not have time for this*, he thought. *I have a house full of vampires who I need to make nice with after the fiasco the party turned into. Katie, Goddess be with you*, he thought praying Lolita would keep her alive long enough for them to rescue her.

Goddess, Jean was a pain in the ass.

She finally made it into a seated position and crossed her arms over her chest with her lips pinched together. If Theron didn't already know how mad she was, he would have thought she was pouting. He crossed his arms over his chest and paced the width of the room while staring at the ground, thinking. He didn't want to tell her about his true nature. How would she take it? She was hotheaded and irrational when the stakes were high, but what choice did he have? He had to tell her, had to make her understand that they saved Vangel. He would've given anything for Thrall to work on her then he could make her forget what happened. He would not be forced to have this conversation with her.

"Jean, I need you to stay calm and listen to what I have to say." He stepped closer to her, ready to throw her back on the bed if she tried to leave.

"What was Helen doing to Vangel?"

"Saving his life," Theron rolled his eyes, of course she couldn't follow directions, but he answered her anyway. "She is making him like me."

"And what are you exactly?" Her voice was flippant, she didn't believe anything he said.

"We are vampires." He let the words hang in the air and waited for her to respond, to either accept or refuse the truth.

"So, you're a bunch of rich guys who like to drink human blood?" She tilted her head to the side. "I don't buy it. There's something else going on."

"Jean, you are so hardheaded when you want to be." He rubbed his temples. He had to prove it to her and the only way he could think of doing it was by showing her his fangs. She would be horrified and would try to run, but it was a risk he had to take. He opened his mouth and pulled his lips back giving her a good look at his teeth. He closed his eyes and took a deep breath. He relaxed and let go of the control he kept in place when humans were nearby.

He let the coppery scent of the dried blood on her clothes take over his mind and allowed his hunger to rise. He felt his fangs descend, and his eyes burned behind their lids. *Food*, not the dried, rotting blood on Jeans hands, but the warm thick, intoxicating liquid flowing just beneath her skin. She would hate him for this, but why should he care? She was only a meal. He opened his eyes, knowing they were glowing red and let her see who he truly was.

Her eyes went huge and she froze. He listened to her fear as her thundering heart began to sprint, readying her body to run. He drew in a lungful of air, her fear making her smell more appetizing than before.

"You're a monster." She scrambled across the bed on her hands and knees then almost fell off before regaining her balance and jerking her head around the room, no doubt looking for an escape. There were no doors except for the one he had locked, and two windows which did not open. She wouldn't have time to break through them before he reached her. *Wait, what am I thinking? I'm not hunting her. I'm trying to tell her the truth and earn her trust.* He closed his eyes and forced himself to lock away the bloodlust begging to take over. He could not make a meal of her; he needed her help. He opened his eyes and ran his tongue over his teeth; he was back in control, and Jean was halfway to the door.

"Jean, wait, don't go." He held his hands up in surrender. Not responding, she sidestepped him, keeping one eye on him and one on her escape route. This would be his only chance to convince her. "Do you really think I'm a monster? What have you seen besides my fangs that would hurt you?"

She opened her mouth then closed it, like she didn't know where to start. "Helen was drinking Vangel's blood. You are monsters. To drink the blood of a dying man puts you and Helen in the monster category." She crossed her arms over her chest and leaned against the door.

At least she's thinking. He sat down on the bed acting as harmless as he thought possible.

"Vangel wouldn't have made it to the hospital, Jean. Helen is turning him into a vampire." Theron rarely talked to humans about what he was, or how he could turn a human into a vampire unless he was offering them the gift. "We gave him a choice death or immortality he chose the latter."

"What happens now?"

"After Helen all but drains him of blood, she will feed him her blood. Then he will sleep for a few days as he transforms. When he wakes up, he won't be himself, but eventually, he will be the man you remember, for the most part."

"Does Katie know?" Jean was shaking, and he could see the exhaustion in her eyes. He wanted to ask her to sit but the stubborn woman would never admit that she needed rest.

"Yes, she has known since Spain. She's special, her mother is our creator."

Jean rolled her eyes. "Please, I'm sure Katie would have known if her mother was the one who created vampires before she came to Spain, and I'm pretty sure you're too old for her mom to have created you."

"Her mother is the Goddess Asteria, a Titan. She came to earth as a mortal but was killed before Katie was born."

"Now that doesn't add up."

"Katie was delivered after her mother died, then she was adopted."

Jean stared at the floor again, and Theron relaxed. She was starting to trust him again. "Can you read minds?"

The question surprised him. "No, why do you ask?"

"Because sometimes it seems like you and Katie, or Katie and Vince are talking about something without saying a word." She pushed herself off the door and moved to the chair in the corner.

"Katie can." He widened his eyes, *and we thought we were hiding it so well.* "Only our kind though, not humans. It is a gift from her mother."

"Is that why she's so fast?" Jean spread her legs, leaned over, and rested her forearms on her knees then laced her fingers together.

"You've seen her move fast?" Theron ran a hand through his hair. *How could Katie be so careless?*

"Yes, and Marios? He moved super-fast too. . ." she trailed off then sat bolt straight. "He wanted to drink my blood." She yelled jumping to her feet. "That's why he kept going for my neck." She paced around the room.

"Yes, I'm sorry about that. I didn't speak to him about you before he arrived." Theron watched as the puzzle came together in Jean's mind.

"Wait." She stopped in front of him and put her hands on her hips. "What will happen now? I'm guessing this isn't something you tell everyone."

"No, it is not." Theron stood and paced the same stretch of the room Jean had. The way the night was going he would have to replace the carpet. "Normally, I would use Thrall and make you forget everything you saw tonight, but it doesn't work on you."

"What? You can brainwash people?" She cocked a hip. "You've tried to brainwash me?" Jean crossed her arms over her chest.

"Yes, and you have no idea how much I wished I could." Theron stopped pacing and met her eyes. He swore he saw a sparkle there, like she was happy about something.

48

"It's not really brainwashing, it's more of a suggestion. 'You didn't see what you saw' kind of thing. It's an indispensable gift."

"What are you going to do with me now that you've told me what you are?" Theron couldn't help but play with her. She was too excited about being immune to Thrall.

"Since I can't make you forget, I could turn you into a slave, but since Thrall doesn't work, I don't know if the slave bond would." He stopped and put his finger to his lips, tapping them. "I could just kill you, but you are not without your uses."

The sparkle in her eyes was replaced with panic. She bolted for the door and yanked on the handle.

"Are you sure you want to go out there? The mansion is filled with vampires." Theron leaned against the wall and checked his nails. It had been a horrible night but messing with Jean was helping his mood more than he imagined it could.

Jean turned around and narrowed her eyes at him.

"Jean, I trust you. I know you want to help Katie, and I don't think you are going to tell the world what we are."

"You do?" Her face brightened for a second before she put her hands on her hips. "How do I know I can trust you? You've all been lying to me since I arrived."

Theron stood silently for a second then moved. He was in Jean's personal space before she could blink. "Do you know how many times I could have drained you already? I could get rid of you and never have to worry about you telling Interpol what we are, and there would be nothing you could do about it." He put his hands on her shoulders and didn't let go when she tried to flinch away. "Jean, trust goes both ways. I'm trusting you not to tell Interpol, and you have to trust me when I say that I won't hurt you."

Jean was silent while she looked into Theron's eyes, likely trying to see if he was lying. She finally blinked. "Fine, we trust each other. Now what?"

"Now, rest. Tomorrow will be a long day of planning. We need to figure out how to rescue Katie."

"Lolita's a vampire too?" Jean asked, finding the lock on the door, and disengaging it.

"Yes, one of the worst. She's old, smart, and devious."

"Katie told me a little bit about her and after what she pulled at the party; I believe you." She looked over her shoulder at the door. "Will the other vampires try to bite me when I leave?"

"They are my guests. They would never feed on a human without my permission. You're safe." Theron bowed his head as she cracked the door and peered out. "Sleep well, we will talk more in the morning." He pulled the door the rest of the way open and Jean leaned out, then looked up and down the hallway.

When she found the coast clear, she glanced back at Theron. "See you tomorrow." She zipped out the door, sprinted down the hall and, as Theron exited his room, he heard her door close and the lock click. He wanted to laugh. She thought a locked door could keep her safe from vampires.

Chapter 8

Katie

I was rocking back and forth. My head was killing me, my throat was dry, and it felt like I'd spent the night before drinking a bottle of tequila. I didn't recognize the room I was in. *Wait, what happened last night?* I tried to look around the room, but I couldn't move, I couldn't even blink. Everything came back then. I was on a boat with Lolita and her men. I had to escape. We were probably headed to Venice, and as we moved closer to her island, my chances of surviving disappeared.

I needed a plan, but my head was so cloudy. I thought about my breathing and slowed my mind. Lolita had injected me with something on the helicopter, and it had paralyzed not only my mind but my body. How long had I been unconscious? I remembered Lolita saying the drug would last for eight hours but she had hit me hard, knocking me out. I could have been out for five minutes or five hours. Since I couldn't move it must not have been more than eight hours since she stuck me.

I needed to burn the drugs out of my system. I wasn't going to get far if I couldn't move. I tried to *see* how many vampires were on the ship, but my vampire sensor wasn't working. The drug was messing with my gifts too. I thought of the labyrinth on Theron's compound; I had burned the drugs out of Vince, Theron, and Helen during my final test and I wondered if I could do it to myself.

I had asked my mother for help that night, then I had run my hands up and down their bodies burning the drug out of their system. How was I going to do it for myself when I couldn't move? *Mom, little help here*, I thought while concentrating on my hands. I focused on them becoming white-hot and able to burn anything that didn't belong out of my body. I still couldn't blink so I unfocused my eyes until everything was blurry and looked inward, visualizing the drug coursing through my veins. My hands continued heating up until they felt like they were going to spontaneously combust, and I would have screamed in pain if I could have. It worked though. I felt the drug sizzle out of my hands and part of the way up my arms. The pain was so intense I thought I would black out, but I held on to my consciousness. With the drug out of my hands I moved the heat into my arms. Once there was no trace of the drug left in my arms, I moved to my legs, then torso. The pain multiplied as I moved the heat through my body. I arched off the floor in pain, terrified that my skin would blacken, and flames would erupt on my skin. Finally, I moved to my head and neck. The fire was so hot; I became dizzy and sick to my stomach, but I swallowed back the bile working its way up my throat and burned through the rest of the poison.

I was covered in sweat and shaking when I finished. Tears stained my face and snot clogged my nose. I wiped it with my arm since there wasn't a tissue handy.

I wanted to rest, to enjoy regaining control of my body. Whatever the drug was, it made me feel more vulnerable than I could remember and being that vulnerable around Lolita was the most terrifying thing I had ever experienced. *I need to get out of here, now.*

Ignoring my fatigue, I closed my eyes and searched for the enemy. There were two vampires outside my door. I knew Lolita wasn't dumb enough to leave me unguarded. There were two more, a few doors down. Above me and to the right there were four more and somehow straight above me, further away from the vampires on my right there were two more.

There were ten vampires on the ship. *How many did she bring to the party?* I wondered. It didn't matter. I was just glad there weren't any more. How was I going to get past them? I could grab their minds, it wouldn't be hard, they were young. I could make them all walk out and jump into the sea, but would they make it before Lolita realized what was going on? Even then, what would I do after that? The captain worked for Lolita and probably knew I was there against my will. What would he do if I killed everyone on board? Would he take me back to Crete? I didn't know how to maneuver a boat this big, so I couldn't kill him. I would need his help.

I stared at the white ceiling and realized I hadn't looked

around the room I was being held in. My hands were cuffed, but I was able to roll onto my stomach then awkwardly push myself to my knees before slowly getting to my feet. It was a small room, probably used for storage when not used as a jail cell. Everything was painted white. It was about five feet wide, by ten feet long, with a seven-foot ceiling. The room was empty except for me, just four walls and a door. The only light came from a bare bulb behind a wire cage above the door. I didn't think anyone, including MacGyver could escape this room on his own.

I stretched my sore muscles the best I could then leaned against the wall and began grabbing minds. They would help me, whether they wanted to or not.

I started with the guards outside my door; they were easy, both oblivious to what I was doing, too caught up in their phones to guard their minds. With the doorways created I let them go and moved on to the guards down the hall.

God, I'm so tired of bagged blood. I hope Lolita will let me have a sip from one of her humans when we get back, the first guard thought while looking at the cards he held. *I wish I could get a few minutes alone with Katie. I bet she would taste amazing.*

"Robert, it's your turn," the other guard said as I slipped out of Robert's mind and made a doorway in his buddy's. *This sucks. I'm so hungry. I wonder if Lolita will give us another bag of blood soon. The fight wore me out.* He looked

56

at his cards then at the card Robert discarded. *We will guard the captain in a few hours, maybe we could each have a sip. No one would know.*

I jumped out of his head before I did something stupid like ask him what time it was or how long I'd been unconscious.

I moved to the vampires to my right who must have been on a floor above me. Three of them stood outside a set of double doors, watching the hallway like a monster would come around the corner at any second. The first guard was hungry and bored. *Jeez, I wish she would at least let us talk to each other. I'll fall asleep if something doesn't happen soon.*

I pulled out of his mind, realizing the vampire I felt on the other side of the door, was Lolita.

I want to go home to Amsterdam. I hope Lolita gives me the city after we take over Europe, the next one thought.

Why does she need three guards? the last one thought. *The girl is drugged, cuffed, and locked in a room with two guards on her door. She isn't going anywhere.*

I jumped out of his mind and took a break. At least he didn't think I was a threat. *OK, two more,* I thought as my head started to pound behind my eyes. I was going to need water and food soon or I wouldn't have the energy to escape.

The two vampires above the rest were in the wheelhouse with the captain. *The sun is so bright if he turns an inch to the left, I'm dead,* the first one thought terrified at the thought of the sun touching him.

I jumped into the other one's mind. *What did I do to deserve this punishment? I did what Lolita told me to do. I made sure no one messed with the helicopter during the party.*

I jumped out of their minds, at least I knew it was daytime and there wasn't any land in sight. We would be traveling for a while. That was a good thing. The longer we were moving the more time I had to escape, and since the captain was human, there had to be food and water somewhere on board.

I grabbed the mind of one of the guards outside Lolita's room. "I'm going for a walk, stretch my legs," I forced him to say as he stood and walked down the hallway. *What the fuck is going on?* he screamed in his mind. *I didn't say that and why am I walking away? I'm going to get in so much trouble.* he thought fighting me for control of his legs.

Shut up and chill out. There is nothing you can do, I thought back to him.

"Are you sure, Sam? Lolita wanted the three of us on the door," Christoph said as I pulled the guard's name from Sam's mind.

Fuck, I thought to myself, *how was I going to work this?* I forced the vampire to stop and look at the others. "What's the worst that could happen? The girl is drugged and handcuffed. Besides you saw her, we all could take her with one arm tied behind our backs."

The others laughed in agreement. "OK, but don't be gone long. Lolita wants us here, and I don't want to make her mad," Christoph said.

"I won't; I just need to walk." I forced Sam to turn and walk down the hall. Once he was around the corner, I made him stop and I took a breath. I had him, but now what was I going to do with him?

You stupid bitch, let me go, he thought, and I laughed.

Why would I let you go? You helped kidnap me. Where is the door outside? I asked, making him walk again as an idea came to mind.

Like I would tell you. But even as the thought left his mind, the image of a door up ahead entered his mind.

Thank you, I thought back to him and forced him to walk to the door.

I can't go out there, I'll die. He panicked when he realized what I had planned for him. He fought me, trying to build a wall in his mind to keep me out, but it was weak, and I tore it down with almost no effort.

No, please I'll do whatever you want, he begged as I made him walk out the door and onto the main deck. I looked around through his eyes, the yacht was huge, over fifty feet, I hadn't seen much of it the night before. The helicopter was sitting at the stern of the boat, not far from where we stood in the shade. There was my way off the boat.

Do you know how to fly that? I asked pointing to the copter.

No, please can we go back inside? I'm smoking.

I made him look down, he was right, small tendrils of smoke were rising from his body even though we were in the shade. *Must be from the UV rays reflecting off the water,* I thought shrugging. *Who knows how to fly it?*

59

I'm not telling you, he yelled at me.

I forced him to take a step toward the sun-drenched deck. *Tell me.*

No, I'm burning. Please stop.

I rolled my eyes. *Tell me who the pilot is.*

Louis, Louis knows how to fly it, he thought, and I let him take a step back into the shade.

Good boy, which one is Louis?

His mind showed me who he was. Sam would be no more use to me, and I couldn't let him go—he knew too much. There was only one option. *Thank you for your assistance. Go with the Goddess.*

What do you mean? Why? What are you doing? he asked as I forced him to step into the sun. He screamed, as fire laced through my mind and I almost let him go to escape the pain. *Why are you doing this?* he begged as I concentrated on keeping him under my power when all I wanted to do was let him go to protect myself.

I held him there, my mind growing numb to the pain the fire caused. Part of me wondered what kind of monster I was turning into, I was letting, no, forcing another being to suffer like a kid with a magnifying glass and an ant hill, but the other part of me felt nothing. This vampire had helped take me away from my friends, and my family. Killing him would get me one step closer to saving myself. I was in a fight for my life and I had to take out anyone who got in my way.

I hadn't thought about what would happen once the flames really got going, heck I had never seen it happen to anyone except in the movies. Real life was not what I expected. He was in so much pain and was so terrified I wanted to cry out, but I kept quiet, aware of the guards below deck. I gasped as the pain spiked and I let him go for a second. He ran for the door, the only place he thought he could find safety. I had to stop him. If he made it below deck, the wood paneling lining the walls would catch on fire and there would be no escape for any of us.

Crap, if he gets inside, we will all die. I forced myself back into his mind, my body shaking as I shared his pain. I forced him to turn around and run for the edge of the boat. When he reached the railing, he jumped at my command, then I left his mind. He would not survive long in the water.

I opened my eyes and took a breath. Burning the vampires alive to escape would be harder than I thought. I was wiped out from controlling him, and I wanted to rest, but I had to find out if anyone knew what happened. I did a quick tour through the minds of the vampires. I blew out a breath, not believing my luck, no one had any idea what happened to Sam. The guys standing guard outside Lolita's door were wondering what happened to him, but not enough to look for him yet.

I rested, staring at the ceiling, and thought about my options. If I figured out who Louis was, I could have him come get me, and I could make him fly me back to Crete. Or I could have the vampires in the wheelhouse tell the captain to turn the ship around. If I went with the helicopter I would have to wait until dark and there was no guarantee Lolita wouldn't come back and give me another dose of her horrible drug before then. If the captain turned around, I could already be on my way back to Crete, but how would I get off the boat? The helicopter sounded like the best route, but then again, would it have enough fuel to get me home? There had to be a way off the boat, I just couldn't see it.

Chapter 9

Jean

Jean leaned against the locked door, closed her eyes, and rubbed her temples. She was so tired. It had been a never-ending night. She believed what Theron told her; that the house was full of vampires and as much as she wanted to believe they hadn't and wouldn't hurt her, double-checking was never a bad idea. She pushed off the door, put the wooden chair from the desk under the handle, and went into the bathroom.

Standing in front of the full-length mirror on the back of the bathroom door she craned her neck from side to side, looking for bite marks. She let out a sigh when she found nothing but unblemished skin. She pulled the collar of her shirt to the side, but it was stiff against her skin. How could she have forgotten that she was covered in Vangel's blood? She locked the door, pulled the shirt over her head, then threw it into the trashcan. She needed to check the rest of her body for puncture wounds, but the pink tinge of her skin made her forget about the chance of already being bitten and worry about cleaning the blood off her body, she didn't want to bait them.

She unhooked her bra, took her jeans and panties off, and threw them into the trash with her shirt. Then she turned on the shower as hot as she could stand. When it was ready, she got in and stood there watching the water go down the drain. At first it was clear, but as the water ran down her body, it changed to pink then red. She picked up the bar of soap and scrubbed the blood off as tears she would never admit to shedding trailed down her cheeks.

She cried for Vangel; she cried for Katie, but most of all she cried for herself. She was a trained Interpol Agent, but she never had watched someone die. Poor Natalia, and that asshole Theron didn't even seem to care.

Jean picked up the shampoo and mindlessly squeezed some into her hand. *Just another human to him,* she thought as she lathered her hair, but then stopped short. *Or was she?* Jean tried to remember if she had ever seen Natalia outside during the day. She hadn't, but that didn't mean much, Natalia had been busy helping Helen and Theron most of the time. Jean couldn't think of a time when they had spoken.

Maybe that was why Theron wasn't worried about her, but how could anyone survive being shot that many times? She rinsed the shampoo out of her hair. *And they just left her in the shed?*

Jean burst into tears again. How could she be so selfish? As soon as she got out of the shower, she would check on Natalia. Jean put conditioner in her hair, realizing that checking on Natalia would mean leaving her room and froze. *I'll just send Helen a text and make sure she wasn't forgotten*, she thought wanting to stay away from the blood suckers.

She rinsed the conditioner out and shut off the water. After she wrapped a towel around her, she hurried to her phone.

Helen, I forgot about Natalia. Is she still in the shed?

Jean tapped her foot on the floor while water dripped on to the carpet and waited for Helen's reply. She looked at the time. *If she doesn't get back to me in the next five minutes, I'll go look for Natalia myself. Vampires or no, we have already lost too many.*

She went into the bathroom, bringing the phone with her. While she dried off and checked her body for puncture marks she may have missed in the shower, her phone vibrated. She picked it up and read the message.

No, she will be fine, Jean. Get some rest.

Jean relaxed and finished checking for bites. When she found nothing but smooth skin, she dressed in her pajamas and got into bed.

They hadn't drank her blood yet, but who knew when they would start. She didn't know how long she lay there waiting for a deranged vampire to crash through the door until she fell into a restless sleep.

Jean inhaled before she opened her eyes and dry heaved. *God, it smells like something died.* She opened her eyes and squinted in the darkness trying to figure out where she was and why it smelled so bad. There were bars on either side of her, but it was too dark to see beyond that.

She turned in a circle but stopped when she found a familiar face. "Dad?" she ran to the man standing in front her with his arms out. She hadn't seen him in her dreams for months, but it didn't matter how much time went by, he still looked the same. Tall with at least six inches on Jean's five-foot ten. He had dark brown hair and eyes to match. He never wore a goatee when he was alive, but when she dreamed of him, he had a short well-groomed one.

"My unicorn," he said, hugging her and spinning her in a circle. "What have you gotten yourself into?"

She couldn't stop the tears as she hugged him tighter. "Vampires," she whispered.

He released her and set her back on the stone floor. "Vampires? Jeanette they are dangerous."

"Believe me I know, but my friend needs help. A bad vampire kidnapped her."

"Ah, that is why we are here." He pointed over Jean's shoulder.

"What?" Jean asked, spinning around to find a body lying on the ground, staring at the ceiling, its eyes open but unseeing. It wasn't until she looked at the dress that she recognized Katie. The once beautiful gown that she wore to the party was now ripped and dirty. Jean shuddered as she took in Katie's skin. What was normally milky white was stained black and blue from her shoes to where the dress covered her, and her poor face was covered in blood.

"Katie?" Jean whispered, afraid that whoever had hurt her would come back.

"Jean?" Katie slurred. "Jean, get out of here before she comes back. She'll kill you." It was hard to understand her, something about her tone made fear trickle down Jean's spine.

"We're coming for you. Just hang on." Jean pulled on the bars separating them, but they didn't budge.

"Jean, go please," Katie whispered. Jean heard the creak of a door opening.

Frozen for half a second, Jean stared at Katie, wishing there was more she could do, but as the footsteps drew closer, she backed away, looking for her dad, but he was gone. She turned and ran.

Chapter 10

Vince

Vince made his way to Theron's office the next morning. The house was full of vampires he should be entertaining but knowing Katie was in Lolita's clutches, he could not concentrate on anything, but the horrible things Lolita could be doing to her.

After he left the barn he went back to his suite and found Vinny pacing back and forth in front of the door. They had left him in the suite because no one wanted the dog at the party. Maybe if they had allowed him to go, Katie wouldn't have been taken. Vince had spent the rest of the night trying to soothe the dog but there was no calming him. Vinny knew something was wrong, and he whined and paced all night.

Vince wove around the few vampires meandering in the hallways, waiting for Theron to call them together to discuss the attack on Lolita's island.

"Vince." The voice from behind him stopped his forward progress. He turned and waited for Livius to catch up with him.

"Yes?" Vince asked, putting his hands on his hips. He did not have the patience to deal with his maker.

"Where are you going?" he asked when he caught up.

"To Theron's office, we have work to do."

"Why? Why not come home with me and let the others deal with this? You are not a leader of a clan, no one looks to you for leadership. Let them handle it. When it is done, you can come back and do whatever you wish." Livius crossed his arms over his chest.

"You still don't get it do you?" Vince shook his head. "Lolita took 'The One,' the prophesized savior of the vampires. Katie has gifts that could be used against us if Lolita enslaves her. We need to get her back and destroy Lolita's army or none of us will be safe."

"I know she can read minds, but what power will Lolita gain with that?"

Vince grabbed his arm and pulled Livius down the hall to Theron's office. It was the most secure place to speak without someone eavesdropping. Vince opened the door without knocking and ushered Livius inside.

"Vince what is it?" Theron asked from behind his desk.

"I am trying to explain why we have to save Katie. What Lolita could do if she was able to harness Katie's powers. I don't want it to become common knowledge yet."

"Good idea, it might make the others feel threatened." Theron got up and went over to the conversation area holding his hands out. "Please sit."

"Tell me what she can do," Livius said after he sat on the couch.

"She can take over our minds and force, make us do her will." Vince was trying to find gentler words, but he couldn't. "We had a prisoner, one of Lolita's guards, sent to spy on us. Katie captured him by taking over his mind and forcing him to give himself up. She even made him talk to Lolita."

"You're serious?" Livius looked back and forth between the two. "Why didn't you kill her? Why would you let someone who could take away our free will live?"

"Because she is the daughter of Asteria. She will not use her gifts for anything other than self-preservation. Once you know her, you will understand." Theron leaned back in his seat.

"Do you understand why we have to get her back now?" Vince stood and paced around the room. "If Lolita turns Katie into a slave, Lolita will be able to not only enslave the humans but vampires too."

Livius sat for a minute, thinking. He started to speak but stopped and crossed his arms over his chest. After three failed attempts he started. "I will help you with Lolita's army but then, I'm gone. I want nothing to do with a human female who can force me to do her will."

"Very well," Vince said. "I will ask you to please keep this information to yourself."

"How long do you think you will be able to keep this from your allies?" Livius asked.

"I'm hoping until after we have Katie back, and we have dispatched Lolita and her army."

"Are you not telling them because you are afraid they won't

help you?"

"Partially. They do not know Katie like we do. Once they realize she will be a fair and just ruler, they will understand and tolerate her gifts."

"What will she do to the ones who do not want her in charge?"

"I believe Katie will let bygones be bygones as long as they do not challenge or harm anyone who is hers."

"Good luck with that," Livius stood and moved to the door. "Now if you will excuse me, I was making time with Pandora and would like to see if she would share my bed."

"Good luck with that," Theron said, relaxing in his chair as Livius left and Helen entered.

Helen took the seat Livius had been in. "We need to talk about last night," she said, glaring at Vince.

Theron looked between them like he didn't know what she was talking about. "What about last night?"

"Vince sent Thomas to the afterlife."

"What?" Theron asked, cocking an eyebrow at Vince. "Why would you do that?"

Vince sank into one of the wing-backed chairs. "I was angry, beyond angry that Lolita took Katie. I wanted to make her pay." He paused for a moment. "I fought and killed Thomas, only realizing my mistake too late."

"Well at least we don't have to worry about feeding him and keeping him quiet anymore." Theron ran his hands through his hair.

"But we lost a powerful bargaining chip," Helen crossed her arms like she was trying to keep herself from lashing out at Theron.

"You think Lolita would have traded Thomas for Katie?" Theron leaned back and laughed. "Lolita cares nothing for her men. Katie was the prize she wanted; she couldn't care less about Thomas. I know I wouldn't. He got himself caught, so why would she want him back? Was any attempt made to contact him or rescue him?" Theron looked at Vince.

"No, there were no missed calls or messages on his phone." Vince could not help glaring at Helen. How dare she give him a guilt trip?

"It might have been worth a try," Helen said, narrowing her eyes at him.

"Helen, I am truly sorry. But he did not deserve to live." It had felt cathartic to pull Thomas's heart out of his chest. It did not help the pain and guilt he felt about losing Katie, but it was better than doing nothing. "What do we do now?" Vince asked, rubbing his chest where it felt like a hole had opened in his heart where Katie used to be. How was he going to get her back? How much will she have changed after being Lolita's prisoner? The longer she was in Lolita's custody the less likely he would get the woman he fell in love with back.

"First, we call Miguel." Theron pulled his phone from his pocket and placed the call.

"Theron, what's going on?" Miguel asked, answering on the

second ring.

"Lolita crashed our party, started a fight, and kidnapped Katie," Theron said, not holding back.

"They escaped in a helicopter," Vince added, closing his eyes, and wishing he could have jumped a few inches higher. "We tracked it. I believe they landed on a boat and are probably on their way back to Venice."

"How could you let this happen?" Miguel roared into the phone. "Lolita has Katie? What are we going to do?" Miguel lowered his voice, probably realizing yelling at them would not get him anywhere.

"We are putting together an army of our own, then we will come for Katie," Theron said, staring into the distance.

"What do you need me to do?" Miguel asked.

"You need to continue as you have been until we strike, then I'm not sure. Once we finalize our plans, I will tell you what we need."

"Protect Katie," Vince snarled. Rage was boiling just under the surface and knowing that Miguel was the reason they were in this situation was making it hard for Vince to maintain control.

"Of course," Miguel said, making it sound like he would do nothing but what was right for the girl.

"But don't jeopardize your position with Lolita. We will need your help when we attack," Theron said, glancing at Vince.

Vince rolled his eyes, Theron was right, but keeping Katie safe was more important to him than anything. Then again, if Miguel blew his cover, Katie wouldn't have any protection. "Just do what you can to help her without getting caught."

"I'm going to have to be the man who raped her in San Sebastian when she arrives. She will hate me and won't believe anything I tell her."

"Find a way, Miguel. She knows you saved us and helped us after the attack on the compound," Helen said.

"I will try, I just hope she'll believe me." Miguel sounded like a heartbroken teenager.

"Good, notify me when they arrive," Theron said, ending the call. "I hope we can trust him."

"We can." Helen crossed one leg over the other. "He cares more about Katie than he does himself."

"I hope you are right," Vince said. "What now?"

The door opened a second later and Jean walked in, holding her computer. "Do you have a printer?"

Chapter 11

Katie

I let my mind drift for a time, wondering what happened after I was knocked out at the party. Did Vangel and Jean capture Alex? I imagined Theron taking out all his anger on him for what he did to the compound and the vampires he lost. Alex wouldn't live through it, and I wished I could be there to watch.

Vince was freaking out and blaming himself for allowing Lolita to kidnap me I had no doubt. I didn't blame him, there was no way to know that one of the guards would bash my head in. He had been busy fighting his own battle, protecting me the only way he knew how. He was probably figuring out how to rescue me as I lay there.

I struggled into a seated position, I couldn't wait around for him to rescue me, I had to rescue myself. Turning the boat around all nice and gentle so Lolita wouldn't notice would be the best plan, I decided, then when night fell, I would make Louis fly me the rest of the way home.

I could do this. I had planned to make everyone bow to me at the party. I could control a couple of vampires at the same time.

I jumped into the mind of the in the wheelhouse who was

terrified of the sun and locked down all his motor skills. *What's happening? Why can't I move?* he thought, panicking.

Calm down, nothing bad will happen to you, I thought to him, wishing there was a way I could make his mind shut up.

Who are you? How did you get here? How come no one else can hear you?

Ignoring his questions, I jumped into the other one's mind while not letting go of the first one. I didn't want him to know I was there until it was too late.

The captain was sitting in a chair behind a control panel with a steering wheel in the middle, reading a paperback. *He must have set the auto pilot,* I thought. He looked like he was in his mid-forties with shaggy, light-brown hair and a well-groomed beard streaked through with gray.

Here goes nothing, I thought before I told the guard to pull his phone out and pretend to answer it.

He fought me, but only for a second, then he pulled out his phone and slid his finger over the dark screen before holding it to his ear. "Yes, Madame," I forced him to say, and the captain looked up from his book.

"Yes, Madame, I will inform him." *Good, now end the call, put your phone in your pocket and get the captain's attention.* He put the phone back in his pocket. "Captain?"

"Yes?" He closed his book and his eyebrows climbed his forehead.

"That was Lolita, she wishes for you to turn around. She wishes to return to Crete." I tried to make him speak with authority, but I felt like I was missing something.

"Really? Let me just call and verify with her." He turned to pick up the hard-wired phone, and I made the vampire lunge forward to keep the captain from picking it up.

"You saw me speaking with her. You don't need to check with her."

The captain eyed him then the other vampire. "If she called, we must do as she says." I forced him to say, beginning to feel the toll of controlling two vampires.

"That's very interesting since we are in the middle of the sea and there isn't mobile phone service this far out, and Lolita asked me to notify her if anyone told me to change our course." The captain picked up the phone.

Fuck, I thought. *How could I be so stupid?* Now, not only would these vampires know something was up, but Lolita would know the drug had stopped working. I could use one vampire to kill the captain, but then who would pilot the boat? If Lolita hired him, it was likely because no one else could do it. The last thing I wanted was to be trapped in the middle of the Mediterranean with a boat full of hungry vampires. I had to do something and fast.

I left the guards in the wheelhouse and jumped into Christoph's mind. "Do you think I should go look for him?" The other vampire guarding Lolita's door whispered as Christoph yelled mentally. *What's going on? Why can't I answer him?*

Who is he talking about? I asked ignoring his questions.

79

Sam, who are you? he thought back.

"No, he will be fine," I answered for Christoph.

"Are you sure? If Lolita finds out he left..." he trailed off as the door behind them opened. Louis spun around to face Lolita and bowed. I forced Christoph to bow, following Louis's lead.

"Louis, where is Sam?" Lolita asked.

"He said he needed to stretch his legs," Louis answered still bent over.

"That little bitch. Come with me now." I was screwed. I remained in the guards' minds as they followed Lolita down the hall to the stairs.

She stopped before going down them and turned to her guards. "Christoph go find Sam."

I stood, frozen. If I let him go and moved to Louis, Christoph would tell her what was going on. I could make him walk into the sun like I had with Sam, but I didn't know if I had time before they reached me. *Forget everything that has happened since I have been with you,* I thought using as much Thrall as I could. *Go look for Sam.*

I moved to Louis, holding my breath as Christoph blinked then bowed to Lolita. "I will find him, and we will catch up with you."

I exhaled, at least something went right. I followed Lolita down the stairs, staying in the back of Louis's mind. I was getting tired, but I had to stop Lolita from drugging me again.

"Get Steven and Robert. We will need everyone to subdue her," Lolita said as we passed the door where the off-duty guards were. I left Louis's mind and prepared for their entrance.

I wouldn't let Lolita drug me again. I looked down at the cuffs circling my wrists. Even if I knew how to pick a lock, there was nothing I could've used to pick them. What was I going to do? I had nothing. I looked at my feet, I still had my shoes and the ice pick heel would work, but could I stab her with my hands cuffed? Could I stab her in the heart by kicking her?

I still had enough energy to grab the minds of the guards. It would have to do; I would not give up. I jumped to Louis's mind, as Steven and Robert exited the room next to mine.

"Do you really think it will take all of us to hold her down?" Steven asked, running a hand through his hair.

"We do what the mistress demands," Robert said as they joined Lolita and the other two guards outside my door.

"Mistress?" Christoph yelled, sprinting down the hall toward us.

"Did you find Sam?" she asked, crossing her arms over her chest.

"No, I searched everywhere and there is no sign of him." Christoph stood at attention, breathing hard. "Do you want me to review the security footage?"

Lolita's nostrils flared, and she narrowed her eyes. I couldn't help smiling. I was getting to her.

"Unlock the door." Lolita faced the door and tapped her foot, waiting. I let out a calming breath, this was it. It was going to take everything I had, but it was my only chance. Who knew what Lolita would do to me if I let her drug me again? I took all five minds and yelled, *Silence!* as soon as they complained. I forced the guard with the keys to do as Lolita commanded and open the door. While she walked in, I made Louis hit her in the back of the head causing her to fall to her knees. "What?" she screeched, jerking around to see who hit her.

Grab her, I thought to the guards on either side of her. Their screams of protest filled my mind, and I blocked them out as I forced their bodies to obey my command and they pulled Lolita's arms behind her back.

"Let me go this instant," Lolita screeched, struggling to free herself, but the guards held their place.

"Unlock my handcuffs," I ordered the guard with the keys. I hadn't caught his name. He moved around Lolita as sweat broke out on my forehead. Holding on to four vampires was harder than I thought it would be.

"So, this is all your doing?" Lolita asked, struggling to free herself but the guards held her tight. "What did you do to Sam?"

I was trying to find the handcuff key as the guard fumbled through them. I needed to hurry.

"Answer me," Lolita demanded, and the guard dropped the keys on the ground.

"Leave them," I said, pushing past him to get in Lolita's face. "I did to him what I will do to you and the rest of your organization."

"What?" She rolled her eyes.

"Sent him to meet the Goddess." I was almost out of energy. I was going to have to do this with my hands cuffed. Not wasting a second I pulled my leg around in a roundhouse kick, but I was too slow, and she saw it in time to jerk out of the guards grasp and move out of range before my leg found its mark.

Keeping the guards frozen with my mind, Lolita and I circled each other. She held a syringe in her right hand; her wrist must have healed. This was not how I wanted to fight her, with my hands cuffed and my energy being sapped away to keep the guards at bay.

"How long do you think you can hold them before exhaustion sets in?" Lolita asked, cackling as I tripped but recovered before I hit the floor, *damn heels*.

She was right, all she had to do was wait until I was too tired to go on, and with the way I was feeling, I might have five minutes before I would have to let them go. "Long enough to kill you." I faked to my right then ran at her and kicked her as hard as I could with my left leg. I caught her in the mid-section hoping the force behind the kick would make her drop the syringe but instead she tried to stab me in the leg with it. I pulled away before the needle could stick me.

I backed away, out of breath and covered with sweat, the guards were fighting me for control, and I would not be able to hold them back much longer. *Get her*, I thought using as much intent as I dared, not wanting to lose them and have them turn on me.

They turned as one and lurched forward, grabbing at Lolita as she rushed me, holding the syringe above her head as she dodged her attackers. I spun away from the needle only to have her sweep my legs out from under me. I fell hard enough to release my hold on the guards and for fireworks to explode in front of my eyes. Freed, they wasted no time and rushed me, each one grabbing an extremity and holding me down.

"Hold her," Lolita yelled as she leaned in with the needle and injected the poison into my arm. "You will pay for that, bitch." She stood and took a few steps away from me.

I tried to grab the mind of the nearest guard, but it was too late. The drug was already paralyzing my body and my mind.

"You not only killed one of my guards, but you forced these vampires, my personal bodyguards, to attack me," she tisked and paced along the wall. "What do you think she deserves for her punishment, Louis?"

"Let us play with her, Mistress," he said, rolling his head from side to side, cracking his neck in the process. "We'll teach her a lesson."

"I will with two conditions." She stopped pacing and ran a hand down his cheek.

"Anything, Mistress." He licked his lips like he would rather spend some alone time with Lolita play with me.

"You can't kill her, and no biting."

The other guards nodded their heads in agreement. "We promise, Mistress."

"I hope you enjoy your punishment, Katie." Lolita strolled through the door without looking back as the guards closed in around me. *Why didn't I close my eyes while I still could?* I asked myself before the first kick hit my midsection.

Chapter 12

Jean

Jean sat up in bed and looked around her room gasping for air. She was safe, *well as safe as I can be in a house full of vampires*. She shook her head. The dream had been so real, but there was no way Lolita and Katie could already be in Venice.

She wanted to help rescue Katie, but what could she offer? Theron and his vampires were all faster and stronger than her. She would probably be more of a liability than an asset in a fight when it was vampire versus vampire. If she couldn't fight them, there had to be something else she could do.

She got out of bed as an idea struck her. She dislodged the chair from under the door and pushed it to the desk. She sat, opened her internet browser, and typed in Poveglia. She might not be able to fight them, but she could make sure her side knew everything about Lolita's island that there was to know before the fight began.

Two hours later she unlocked her door and peeked into the hall. It was early morning, and the hallway was empty. She let out a breath, closed the door behind her, and tiptoed to Theron's office. He had a printer she could use. She knocked softly on the door when she reached it, hoping no one would answer. She wanted to print out the maps and get them ready without any interruptions.

"Come," she heard from the other side, and she cursed under her breath. She was going to have to face him. She opened the door a crack and looked inside. Vince sat in a wing-back chair trying to smile, but it didn't reach his eyes, and his hands were clenched in fists so tight they were turning white. Helen sat on the couch with her back straight and her hands in her lap like they were having tea and talking about a fundraiser for orphans. Theron's eyes lit up when he saw her, and he stood quickly.

"Jean what's wrong?"

"Nothing, I was wondering if I could use your printer. I found a detailed map of the island and blueprints of the buildings. I was going to print them out for you. I thought it might help." She stalked into the room, stopping next to the couch.

"Of course." Theron led her to the desk. "Just unplug mine and have at it."

He moved to guide her around the desk and Jean flinched away. *Why was he being so nice to me?*

"Jean, are you OK?" Helen asked, watching from her position on the couch.

"I'm as good as I can be, knowing what you are," she muttered, sitting down in Theron's chair, and plugging in the printer. She clicked on a few buttons to download the driver. When she looked up, all three of them were staring at her.

"You're going to stay?" Vince asked.

"I want to help." She looked down at her computer, not wanting to tell them about the nightmare.

"Did you have a dream?" Theron asked, taking the seat on the other side of the desk.

She looked up. "I though you couldn't read minds. It's not a big deal, it was only a dream."

"Katie told me your dreams have a habit of coming true." Theron leaned forward and rested his elbows on the desk. "What did you dream?" His voice was low, and Helen and Vince moved to stand behind him.

Jean looked anywhere but at the three vampires across from her. She knew it would make Vince angry, and they weren't going to get Katie back as soon as any of them wanted. *Heck, it was just a dream, they didn't all come true, but Katie was already in bad shape.* She caught Theron's eye, then rolled them to Vince. She didn't know if he could handle it.

"It's fine, we're all adults," Theron said, understanding what she was trying to say. "Tell us."

She took a breath and found a spot on the wall to stare at. She wouldn't be able to get it all out if she had to watch their faces. "I don't think it's happened yet, or even if it will. Katie was in a dungeon; it was dark and smelled vile. She had been badly beaten, she told me to run before Lolita came back."

"Why don't you think it happened yet?" Vince asked as he paced around the room.

"Because if Lolita is taking her to Venice on a boat, they haven't had time to get there yet." Jean looked at her computer. It was ready to restart.

"Do you know when it will happen then?" Helen asked, resting her hands on her hips.

"No, plus I showed up after she'd been beaten." With her computer rebooted she opened the documents she wanted to print and started the process.

"What are we going to do?" Vince asked, running his hands through his hair.

"We come up with a plan to infiltrate the island and get her back before Lolita kills her." Jean went to the printer, pulled the pages off, and labeled them. "Do you have any tape?"

"Top right-hand drawer, why?" Theron asked.

"Because I printed out a map as big as the table over there." Jean pointed to a table four feet by five feet. "We need to be smart about this if we are going to rescue her and kill Lolita's army."

"What can I do?" Vince asked looking at two pages Jean had printed out. "Please give me a job, or I am going to go insane."

Theron looked at Jean. "How long will it take you to put the map together?"

"An hour, maybe two." She took the small pile of paper from the printer to the table.

"Get everyone together. Once Jean finishes the map,

we will strategize." Theron watched as she arranged the pages on the table.

"Come on Vince," Helen said, heading for the door. "I'll help."

With Vince and Helen gone, Jean did her best to ignore Theron and work on piecing the map together, but he hovered behind her. "Could you stop doing that?" she asked blowing a piece of hair out of her face.

"Doing what?" He crossed his arms over his chest as she went back to the printer for more pages.

"Hovering. It's driving me up the wall." She walked to the table and laid out the freshly printed pages.

"Can I help?" he asked moving out of her way.

Jean blew out a breath, it would be faster, but she didn't want to be that close to him. Who knew when he would decide he was hungry? She looked at the work in front of her. "Fine, grab the tape and start taping pages together."

Theron picked up the clear tape from the desk and started taping the pages she had laid out together. They worked in silence until Jean couldn't take it anymore. "Thank you for not killing me." Jean had been thinking about all the ways she had messed things up for him and while it hadn't mattered when she thought he was human, now that she knew what he really was, she realized how lucky she was to be alive.

Theron looked up from his work and gave her a smile. "Thank you for doing this." He nodded to the map. "I would have gotten around to it, but with so many things going on, I haven't had time to make any preparations for the attack."

"Yeah, I have to do what I can to rescue Katie," Jean said, stealing the tape from Theron and taping down the pages on her side of the table.

"We need all the help we can get." It looked to Jean like he wanted to say more but he shook his head and got back to work.

Jean reached for the tape and accidently brushed Theron's hand. She jerked back, forgetting about the tape as a spark moved its way up her hand. She shook her head. *Sparks with a vampire?*

She had to get away from them as soon as possible if she wanted to keep her sanity.

Chapter 13

Katie

It was dark, so dark I didn't know where I was, and I needed light. My head was spinning, and my stomach was doing somersaults. If I didn't find my equilibrium soon, I would vomit and it wouldn't be a good thing, but I couldn't remember why. *Think*, I told myself. *Where had I been before I ended up in the nothing?*

Lolita had drugged me again and gave me to her guards, it came back to me. They had beaten me, leaving nothing untouched: my face, my torso, my legs, my arms, everything hurt, but they followed Lolita's rules: they didn't drink my blood, and as far as I could tell I wasn't dead. I wished I was though. Two of them had held me while the others took turns punching and kicking me. I didn't know what was worse: not being able to flinch away or not being able to fight back. The things they did made me want to dig a hole, curl up in a ball, and never come out again. The worst was when a kick to my lower abdomen forced me to release my bladder. I gave up after that. I couldn't move to fight them or use my mind to control them. What was the point in staying strong when I had no way of fighting back? All I could do was stare at whatever was in front of me and mentally scream in pain as they stuck me.

I had no doubt, Vince and Theron would try to save me, but I knew how they worked. They would plan everything to the nth degree, and it would take forever for them to come after me. They wouldn't make it in time. Vince would feel terrible, so bad he might kill himself, but I hoped he wouldn't. He and Theron needed to execute Lolita's army, even if I didn't survive.

"Katie?" The sound of my name brought me out of my thoughts, and I whirled around, looking for whoever called my name, but it was so dark, and moving my head that fast made my stomach gurgle. "Katie, where are you?"

"Mom?" I asked my words coming out weak and slurred. "Mom, I'm here." *She would make it all better if I could just find her.*

"Are you OK?" She sounded frantic. "Show me where you are."

"I'm right here." I waved my arms around, at least I thought I did, it was so dark I couldn't be sure.

"Why can't I find you?"

"Lolita crashed the party, like we thought she would. I fought her, Mom. I was kicking her ass but then someone hit me on the back of the head and knocked me out. When I came to, she had kidnapped me."

"Can't you escape?" Mom's concerned voice became a cool and calculating one. It was odd in the past, she always freaked out when something like this happened.

"I try every chance I get, but she keeps drugging me,

and then I can't control my body or anyone else's." I strained my eyes, looking for her in the darkness.

"If I could find you, I would burn it out of you." It didn't sound like she was trying to find me anymore though. "Where is Vince and the rest of your court?"

"Probably on Crete looking for me or coming up with a plan to rescue me. Mom, is everything OK?"

"No, everything is not OK," she screamed. "All my plans are ruined. You were not supposed to be captured by Lolita. How could you allow this to happen?"

"I didn't want it to happen. I wanted to kill her," I screamed. "And I won't stop trying to kill her until one of us is dead." What was going on with her? It almost felt like she didn't care about what was happening to me, only that her plan was ruined.

"It is too late for that now," she paused as if she was thinking about outcomes and how they would best suit her. "Your future is set, and I must make my own plans if I am to survive."

"What are you talking about?" I called then waited for a response, but none came.

Chapter 14

Vince

Vince leaned against Theron's desk, standing next to Jean. The guests from the party who spent the night were packed into the office. He knew Zoi, the leader of the Athens vampires, Asher from London, Enzo from Sicily, and Mirko from Macedonia. The rest he would meet soon enough, even though he could not care less who they were as they stood around the table, looking at the map Vince tapped his foot on the ground, impatient for the meeting to begin. The sooner they had a plan, the sooner they could leave.

"Thanks to Jean, we have this detailed map of Lolita's island," Theron began nodding at Jean. She nodded back and Vince briefly wondered what was happening there. Normally the two of them could not have a civilized conversation. "According to our sources, the army is housed here." Theron tapped the middle of the map, bringing Vince's focus back to the issue. "There is a twenty-foot concrete wall around the building keeping them contained. Our informant told me they are living on bagged blood. They are highly trained in hand to hand combat, and they train constantly. They may be young, but don't underestimate their skills or their teamwork. There are two ways we can infiltrate the asylum, we can come in through the only gate, here. Or we can scale the walls." Theron paused while everyone thought about it.

"I don't like the look of the gate," Zoi said, glancing around the room. "It reminds me too much of the battle of Thermopylae."

"I see what you mean," Enzo agreed, staring at the map. "Scaling the wall won't work either though. What if we need to retreat?"

"How will we do it then?" asked the one from Germany, Vince thought based on his accent.

Everyone began talking at once and Theron glared at Vince, silently begging him for help. He rolled his eyes but pushed off the desk and joined the group.

"The solution is simple," Vince said then waited for everyone to be quiet. "We do both. One team starts at the gate while the others scale the wall. Then meet in the middle."

"Still doesn't give the ones who go over the wall a means of escape if we need it," the German said.

Vince peered at him through hooded eyes. "Pride would let you run away from what are essentially adolescent vampires?" There were a few laughs as the German's eyes flashed red, but he stayed quiet.

"Moving on then." Theron winked at Vince in thanks before continuing.

"Lolita's villa is here. We know there will be at least fifteen guards plus her household staff. As you can see from the blueprints, it will be much easier to gain access to her, but she will have her most deadly men with her." Theron pointed at the house.

Vince had already memorized the blueprints. The house was four levels, including a basement which was likely where prisoners were kept. He only found one place to access the basement on the blueprints: a stairway from the kitchen.

On the main floor there was a grand salon, a dining room, and two smaller rooms. There was a front door and a back door. The other two levels, which likely held bedrooms, only had windows, and he would not know until he got there or spoke to Miguel if they could be opened or easily broken to gain entrance.

"While our main force will concentrate on the army, a smaller group will go after Lolita. We must kill the queen to kill the hive."

"Aren't you putting the cart before the horse, Theron?" Zoi asked. "How are we going to show up in Venice without Doge Geovanni finding out?"

"Are we sure he won't be on our side?" Asher asked. "He wasn't at the party."

"Geovanni is a strict Catholic," Maria said, crossing her arms over her chest. "He will be on Lolita's side. He has been dreaming of another crusade for ages. Her plan will be right up his alley."

"Back to my question," Zoi rolled her eyes.

"We will arrive shortly before dawn, and we will attack at dusk. There will be little chance of him finding out we are in town until it's over. Helen, my second-in-command, is arranging transportation and housing. Please inform her of how many of your vampires will join us. Once we have a final count, we will break into teams. If there's a group you want to team up with, tell Helen."

"When are we leaving?" Vince asked. Getting to Katie before Lolita killed her was all Vince cared about. If it came down to rescuing Katie or killing the army, he would go back for the army.

Theron gave Vince a sad smile like he knew Vince would not like the answer. "The soonest we can charter a plane will be tomorrow evening. Before you take off on your own, think about it. Timing is everything, and everyone needs to arrive near the same time, or we risk discovery. We will land and go directly to our lodging, quickly and quietly."

Theron's answer was unacceptable. Vince stomped out without further comment. He wanted to leave as soon as the sun went down. Why were they waiting? It couldn't take that long to secure plane and rent a few houses. He stormed down the hallway to his suite and found Vinny waiting inside the door, whimpering.

"What is it boy?" Vince bent to one knee and wrapped his arms around the dog. "I miss her too, buddy. Don't worry we will get her back." He had to believe she would be OK. He could not let himself think about what Lolita would do to make Katie comply.

"I think he needs to go outside," Jean said from behind Vince, startling him.

He stood and turned to her. He was astonished she was still there after Theron told her about vampires. He knew Katie had thought about running when she had found out what they were. "Probably."

"Come on, Vinny." Jean walked over to the door and opened it. Vinny ran for the door. "I know you want to leave tonight, but there's no point. Katie won't arrive for at least another twenty-four hours."

"How can you be sure?" Vince ran his hands through his hair before settling on the couch.

"It's math. Based on the size of the ship Lolita would have to have for a helicopter to land on it and the maximum speed of the ship. It is a long way to travel, and it will take time." She sat in one of the wing-back chairs and pulled her knees up to her chest. "We have to do this right."

"Why are you still here?" Vince asked, cocking his head to the side, and changing the subject.

"Because Katie needs me. I wanted to leave after Theron told me what you are, but I couldn't do it. She has been nothing but supportive of me. Plus, I owe you guys. I messed up so many things for you. I want to help rescue Katie."

"Thank you."

"She'll be fine, Vince," Jean put her feet down and closed her eyes. "And she will come out of this stronger than ever. Don't give up."

"Vince?" Theron asked, poking his head in.

"Yes?"

"I'm sorry we can't leave tonight, but everyone needs to rest. We want to be at our best when we hit the island. I have some. . ." Theron stopped talking when he saw Jean. "Jean, I didn't know you were here. Thank you for the map, it's making planning the attack much easier."

"Yeah, no worries. I'm going to get Vinny." She stood. "I'll catch up with you guys later," she said, before leaving through the patio door.

"What are you planning to do with her?" Vince asked, staring at the closed door.

"I want her to come with us. We need someone in charge of communications and to run human interference." Theron took the seat Jean vacated. "Helen will stay here to keep an eye on things and help with the new vampires."

"Good idea. Leaving the island unmanned would not be safe with the state of things. The way things have been going it would be overrun with criminals by the time you got back." Vince laughed but stopped. *How can I laugh while Katie is suffering?*

"Yes, and I won't lose my island." He rested his right ankle on his left knee. "I came to tell you I have donors coming tonight. We all need to be at our strongest for this fight. Bagged blood will not cut it, and you need to rest.

"I will rest when Katie is safe in my arms again." Vince drummed his fingers on his knee.

"How will you rescue her when you can barely stand up and are going mad with bloodlust?" Theron put his leg on the ground and leaned forward. "This is war, Vince, nothing like the skirmish we had last night. Lolita has at least five hundred vampires. We must be at our best to win. Please rest." Theron got to his feet.

"Let me know when the donors arrive." Vince growled, knowing Theron was right.

"I will but in the meantime, sleep." Theron rose, leaving Vince to his nightmares of the torture Katie was enduring while he *rested*.

Chapter 15

Katie

I blinked, and moisture flooded my eyes. I blinked again and left them closed for a second. I never realized how good blinking felt until I couldn't do it for hours. I wanted to stretch and work out the cramps in my legs, but I didn't know if I was alone or not, and I didn't want to risk being drugged again. Instead of moving, I turned on my vampire sense and located the vampires. It was working; the drug had worn off, but there were two vampires less than five feet from me. *Fuck, if I move, they will call Lolita.*

My whole body ached from the beating they gave me earlier. The drug wouldn't let me tense my muscles to soften the blows and the pain was immeasurable. I was weak and not just from the beating; it had been hours maybe days since I had any food or water. My mouth was dry, and my stomach was cramping like it was trying to eat itself. I wouldn't make it much longer without water, and I doubted they would bring me any if I asked.

I took the guards' minds, barely able to hold on. *Go get me water and food*, I thought to Steven while to the other I thought, *stay where you are and don't move.*

What? Steven thought, fighting me. *Not this again, the drug was supposed to last eight hours.*

Go, I thought while thinking *stay* to the other guard whose name I didn't know.

You bitch, he thought, trying to get up as Steven went to the door. *Let me go.*

No, now be good, or I'll do to you what I did to Sam. The guard shut up after that, allowing me to concentrate on Steven. *Let's go, Steven, show me where the galley is.*

According to him it was directly above us, but Lolita had placed guards at the stairwell. *What time is it?* I asked.

Twenty-one hundred hours.

Ok we need to avoid the guards, so is there another way to get there? I hated that it was the middle of the night, after what they had done to me, I wanted nothing more than to force them all to walk into the sun and jump overboard. I could still make them do it, but I didn't know if I would be able to without being caught.

No, he thought, smiling to himself, thinking I wouldn't find the other set of stairs.

Thanks, I murmured, sweating as I piloted him to the emergency ladder and forced him to climb while he cursed at me in at least two languages.

We made it to the galley a few minutes later, and I didn't know how much longer I could keep my hold on him. He grabbed a bottle of water and a box of energy bars, then we started the long trip back to my prison while I kept the location of the other guards in my mind. I couldn't afford not to drink water and eat food. It was the only thing that mattered.

Steven was almost back when the others began moving around the ship. I didn't know if they saw him on a security camera or if was time for a shift change. Either way, it wasn't looking good for me. I forced my will on him to move faster.

He made it back before the other guards caught us thankfully. *Put everything next to me*, I thought wishing there was a place to hide it. *Why are they coming this way?*

You're screwed now, blood bag, the guard who stayed with me thought. *It's shift change and I feel your energy fading. Soon you won't be able to control any of us.*

I grabbed the bottle of water and took a sip while trying to grab a hold of the guards outside the door, but I lost my grip on all of them as my strength left me. I was able to put the lid on the water bottle before Steven back handed me, and I fell on my side. "Dumb bitch." He kicked me hard in the back. I tried to get to my feet, but my legs wouldn't hold me. I had nothing left to fight with.

"What's going on?" Louis asked as I closed my eyes and grunted in pain.

"She did it to us again," said the one who's name I didn't know. "She made Steven go get her food and water like he was her servant or something."

"Why didn't you help him?" Christoph asked as Steven kicked me again.

"I couldn't move, the bitch took me over."

"Someone get Lolita, we need another dose of the drug," Louis said, rolling me onto my back. "I thought you would have had enough after your last beating." He leaned over me and licked my cheek. "Maybe if I ask real nice Lolita will give you to me, and I'll show you what kind of fun I like to have."

I didn't want to give up, but I was out of strength and ideas, I couldn't remember a time I felt as helpless as I did in that moment. Hungry, thirsty, beaten, and abused, how could it get any worse?

"What is going on?" I heard Lolita ask, and a shiver slid down my spine at the sound of her voice.

Damn her for making me afraid of her. I would have given anything for my sword and the strength to hold it.

"The drug wore off; we were just coming for you. She needs another dose," Christoph said.

"Very well." It sounded like she planned to leave but stopped. "What is that?"

"She got into my head, Mistress," Steven said, sounding embarrassed. "And forced me to get her food and water."

"She wants food and water, does she?" Lolita asked before her maniacal laughter took over. "Let's make sure she gets what she wants. Get me a hose and tie her down."

I tried to fight them off, but I had nothing left. I wanted to die; I didn't want to give Lolita the pleasure of torturing me again. If I could have ended my life in that moment I would have. Instead, they tied me to a board and strapped my head in place. One guard came back with a hose and handed the end to Lolita. *What was she going to do to me?*

She came to my side and ran a hand down my cheek. "I have ways of making you do what I want, little Katie." She forced my lips open while I kept my jaw clenched tight. "If you were thirsty all you had to do was ask, and I would have allowed you water." She flicked her wrist at a guard and held the hose between my lips. "Have all the water you want."

It gushed in through my teeth and I tried not to swallow, but I had no other choice. With Lolita holding the hose to my lips I couldn't spit it out. I swallowed as much as I could until my stomach revolted from too much water too quickly. I tried to turn my head to the side to vomit but I couldn't because of the straps holding me to the board. I vomited, and the bile had nowhere to go but out through my nose and the side of my mouth. I couldn't breathe as my nasal passages filled with the corrosive liquid. I held onto what breath I had, refusing to inhale the water gushing in my mouth or the vomit in my nose.

I was ready to give up, stop the torture, and here was the perfect opportunity. All I had to do was inhale the water and it would be over. All the pain, all the hurt, I wouldn't have to worry about being kidnapped, or staying in shape. I wouldn't have to watch my back every second of every day. I could finally be at peace.

An image of Vince and Vinny cuddling in bed filled my mind, and tears clouded my vision. What would they do without me? They needed me, and so did Jean and Theron. I thought of my parents. They deserved to know what happened to their daughter.

I couldn't give up.

My vision dimmed and my lungs were about to force me to breathe, whether it was air or water. My body shook as I held on for as long as I could.

Lolita noticed my struggle and pulled the hose away from my mouth. "Shut it off and release her head."

As soon as the hose was gone, I spit using all the air left in my lungs and breathed deep not caring that it was probably more water than air. My head was released, and I turned it to the side, coughing and choking as the water and bile in my lungs forced its way out. When I could breathe without coughing, I sat up and saw Lolita standing over me with the damn needle in her hand.

"When you can be a good girl and do as I say, I'll stop injecting you." She plunged the needle into my arm before I could respond.

"I will never do what you want me to. Just kill me now." My words were already slurring, and I tried to blink, but my muscles ignored my commands.

"What fun would that be?" She looked me up and down, shaking her head. "Untie her except for the handcuffs and leave the food and water where she can see them," she instructed the guards then sashayed out of the room.

Chapter 16

Jean

Jean woke up the next morning excited instead of scared for the first time since she arrived on Crete. She was leaving the island at nightfall. She was going to help Katie, whether Theron asked her to or not. Then she would begin her new life away from Interpol and vampires.

Her mother had tagged her a rogue agent because she refused to turn Theron in or report on his illegal activities. Jean had been terrified at first, but with the help of her friends in Kevó she was going to make a fresh start. She had moved her money to untraceable accounts; and had a new identity with documentation to match. All that was left was to say goodbye to Unicorn once and for all.

She rolled out of bed, grabbed the box of hair dye from her dresser, then went into the bathroom ready to become, *what was my new name again?* She wondered and checked the passport Barkley had made for her. *Sofia Hofer; could be worse,* she thought.

She ran her brush through her pink hair, she would miss her unicorn hair, as she liked to call it, but it was time to grow up.

An hour later Jean ran a comb through her chestnut colored hair, at least that was what the box called it. She picked it because it was as close to her natural color as she could remember. It was so dark; she looked like a different person. With her first chore of the day done, she packed her toiletries and set them on the bed. It wasn't the first time she'd packed up everything from this room, but it would be the last time.

After she finished packing, she sat at the desk and opened her email. When she turned in her badge and her gun, she had also left behind her moniker and all the email addresses she had before. She still hadn't figured out what her new hacker name would be, and she wasn't in a hurry to figure it out. It was one of those things that just happened.

She had a new email address though which no one from Interpol would guess, and she'd only given it to people she could trust. She opened her inbox then did a double take. There was a message from Tad, the leader of Kevȯ. One of her friends must have passed it along to him. She didn't want to read it. She wanted to forget all about Tad and how she had let him down when she gave the soldiers the location of Kevȯ, but ignoring the email was out of the question. If he wanted to talk to her, he would find a way, even if it meant stealing her money or leaking her location to Interpol. She clicked on the email and held her breath as she read.

Jeanette,

I hope this email finds you well. I am concerned that you have not reached out to me about your future. Copperhead and Barkley tell me you have left Interpol and have been labeled a rogue. I am sure you realized that you are no longer welcome in Kevò since your handler knows our location and may search for you here.

That being said, I need to speak with you about a delicate situation. Will you please contact me via Skype? I will be available whenever you are able.

Sincerely,

Tad

Jean re-read the email three times before she believed what it said. Katie had told him what Jean had done, and she thought he would never speak to her again. Now he wanted to talk to her face-to-face? It didn't bode well. Would it be better if she talked to him before or after the attack on Venice? Maybe he could help them with the attack. He never left Kevò, but he could send some mercenaries to help.

The thought of mercenaries made her think of Vangel, and she wondered how he was doing. *How crappy of a friend could I be?* After Theron explained what was happening to him, she just left him, she hadn't even asked how he was doing. *Where was he, anyway?* Jean thought, kicking herself for not thinking of it before. If they were truly vampires, then did they put him in a coffin? None of the ones she knew slept in them from what she could tell. She'd been in Theron's bedroom the other night and there was nothing coffin-like going on in there, plus she couldn't see Katie sleeping next to Vince in one.

Where was he then? She paced around the room. There wasn't a basement, and with all the vampires staying in the mansion all the extra rooms were taken, so it only left one place: the barn.

She wanted to check on him, to make sure he was all right. Who knew when she would get to see him again? It was mid-morning, and the sun was up which meant the vampires wouldn't be able to go outside. She could take Vinny with her as an excuse.

She put her hair in a ponytail, then went in search of Vinny. The hallways were eerily quiet considering all the vampires staying in the house, and she wondered what they were doing behind closed doors. It was ten in the morning; normal people would be up and getting breakfast or making plans for the day, but she felt like she was sneaking around in the middle of the night.

"Jean?" Theron's voice made her jump.

"Yeah?" She turned and put her hands on her hips.

"You changed your hair." He was wearing a pair of black silk sleep pants and nothing else. She tried to keep her eyes on his face, but she couldn't stop them from perusing the hard, pale planes of his pecks and abs. *Vampire, blood sucker*, she reminded herself and made eye contact with him.

"New identity, remember?"

"Of course, it suits you."

"Um, thanks?" Jean didn't know if that was a compliment or not.

"Why are you up so early?" he asked, glancing over his shoulder.

"Couldn't sleep. I'm going to take Vinny outside."

"He should be with Vince in their suite. We are leaving at sundown, make sure you're ready."

"Did you plan on asking me to come with you?" She was peeved, *he just expected her to do as he wished.*

"I'm sorry. I didn't think I needed to. You have been part of the team since you arrived." He paused, put his hands on his hips, and stared at the floor. "It would be a great help if you joined us." He looked up and ran a hand through his hair.

"I'm already packed." Butterflies exploded in her belly as she tried to remain calm, and he could probably hear her heart rate pick up with excitement. Why was she excited that he wanted her to go with them?

"Good, I'm going to go back to bed then. Stay out of trouble." Theron returned to his room, but before he shut the door, she heard a woman's voice ask. "What was the human doing up so early?"

Jean felt her face go beet red, and the butterflies died as she hurried down the hall. Why should she be surprised that Theron took a woman to bed? He was a gorgeous man, well vampire. Who could resist him? It shouldn't bother her, the last person she wanted to be with was someone who wasn't human, plus he hated her, and she hated him, but when she thought of his naked chest and what might be further down, the butterflies rose from the dead in her stomach.

She shook her head to clear it as she reached Vince's room. She knocked on the door and, in less time than she thought possible it opened a crack. "Jean, what can I do for you?" Vince asked, glancing behind her but not opening the door any wider.

"I wanted to take Vinny outside for a while. Vince what's wrong?" she asked, trying to look over his shoulder. Did he have a girl in there with him? If he did, she didn't care if he was a vampire or not, she would kick his ass. Katie had barely been gone two days.

He looked over his shoulder, then back at Jean. "Nothing, I only wish to be left alone." He opened the door inviting Jean in. "Vinny," he called. "Jean is here to take you for a walk."

Jean went inside and he closed the door behind her. "Who are you talking about?" Jean asked, looking for the dog.

"Livius and Maria. Livius seems to think he still owns me, and Maria thinks that since Katie is gone, I need someone besides the dog to warm my bed." He walked back to the bedroom, and Jean followed since Vinny wasn't in the living area.

"Can't you just tell them to back off?" Jean stopped in the doorway between the rooms. Vinny was sitting on the bed with his head between his paws.

"I've tried, but it is not as easy as it sounds." Vince went over to Vinny. "Come on boy, go outside." Vinny whined and wagged his tail, but he didn't move from the bed. "He is waiting for Katie." Vince ran his hands through his hair and stared at the floor. "We both are."

Jean sat next to Vinny. "I miss her too, buddy." She ran her hands down his back. "Don't worry we will rescue her." Vinny rolled toward her so she could scratch his belly. "Well, if there is anything I can do to help." Jean looked over at Vince who was staring at the dog.

"Thank you, Jean, but I think the best thing for me to do is stay in here and away from everyone." Vince snapped his fingers and Vinny jumped down from the bed. "Go outside with Jean now." He pointed to the door as Jean got off the bed and went toward it.

"Come on, Vinny, it'll be fun." Vinny met her at the door and Vince moved out of the path the sun would make when Jean opened it.

"Thank you," Vince said before she and Vinny left him to his troubles.

After Jean played fetch with Vinny, she led him to the barn. She pushed her ear against the door and listened but couldn't hear anything. She wasn't sure if it was soundproof or empty. She looked at the sun shining on the south side of the building, she wouldn't have to worry about burning anyone inside by opening the door on the north side.

"Vinny, stay out here." She bent down as the dog sat and cocked his head at her. "I'll be back soon." Vinny stayed where he was while Jean slid the door back enough for her to get through then slid it back in place.

The barn was long with a concrete floor and had an open, raftered ceiling. The stalls lining the wall were large with wood sliding doors going up about halfway, then iron bars went up the rest of the way allowing whoever was in the stall to have a good look at the room. Jean smelled hay even though she couldn't see any and copper, which seemed out of place until she realized it wasn't copper but blood she was smelling. She wanted to turn back, but she steadied herself. The other vampires she had met acted like humans, so there was no reason to think Vangel would be any different than he was before. If he was alive.

She walked down the hall, looking into the stalls with open doors, but they were empty, and it made her wonder what she would find when she reached the first stall with a closed door. She looked inside, trying to be as small as possible in case something saw her and thought she might taste good.

Inside, Vangel was lying on a cot. He was shirtless but still wore the same black pants he wore the night of the party. The chest she remembered covered in blood was clean and she wondered if he was cold. It didn't feel like there was any heat in the building. *Is he dead?* Jean wondered as she watched his chest for signs of life. "Vangel," she whispered as tears sprung into her eyes. "Vangel are you dead?" she asked a little louder. His hand twitched and Jean smiled. "Oh, thank God you're alive." Jean grabbed the door handle and tried to slide it back. She wanted to be at her friend's side when he woke up, but the door didn't budge. She looked down and noticed the heavy chain strung through the bars and a padlock keeping it closed.

Vangel rolled off the bed, landed on his feet and looked around like he had no idea who or where he was. Then he closed his eyes, stuck his nose in the air and inhaled so loudly Jean could hear him. He brought his head down and locked eyes with her. He rolled his head from side to side as if he was trying to remember her. Finally, he smiled and took a step closer. "Jean?" he asked, narrowing his eyes, and she let out a relieved laugh.

"Vangel, I'm so glad you're all right. What do you need?" She bounced from foot to foot wishing she could give him a hug. The last time she saw him he was on his death bed.

"Thir..." he cleared his throat. "Thirsty," he took another step toward her, but he wasn't looking her in the eye anymore.

"I'll find you some water," Jean said, looking around. There was a faucet with a hose hooked to it, but he would probably want a cup to drink from. "I'll be right back." Jean jogged down the hall, ignoring the other stalls. Vangel was alive, it was all that mattered. She went through the door at the end of the hall. It was dark with no windows. She slid her hand along the wall until she found the light switch. She flipped it on then blinked as her eyes became accustomed to the light.

"Jean?" Argyris asked, sitting up from a cot at the end of the room. "What are you doing here? What time is it?"

Jean stopped in her tracks and stared at him, surprised to see him. She'd met Argyris a few times, but they had never spoken. "Sorry if I woke you. I came to check on Vangel, and he's awake. He said he was thirsty, so I was trying to find a cup so I could get him some water."

Argyris sprung to his feet and grabbed a shirt off a nearby chair. "He's awake?" He pulled the white cotton shirt over his head then sat on the cot and pulled his shoes from under it. "That was quick."

"Yeah, so do you have a cup or a glass or something?" Jean resumed looking around the barren room. There was a set of cabinets along one wall. The cot was against the far wall and a door was next to it. Sitting in the middle was a black, metal desk covered with enough scrapes and dents to make it more chrome than black. Against the other wall was a full-size refrigerator with a sink and more cabinets.

"A glass?" He gave her a sideways glance then went to the fridge. "He will not need a glass." He opened the fridge, took something she couldn't see out then closed it and looked at her, his eyes going wide. "Jean, I'm sorry but you need to leave."

"What why? I want to hang out with Vangel since he's back. Can you unlock the stall so I can go in?"

"No," he shouted then shook his head. "You know about us, and what Helen did to Vangel right?"

Jean took a step back. "Yeah, Theron told me about vampires and how Helen was saving Vangel's life by turning him into one. Why?"

"Did he tell you what happens when they are newly changed?" He looked down at what he pulled out of the fridge.

"No, why? What happens?" Jean took another step back, but she was at the door and had nowhere else to go.

"They are not themselves for a while. You need to go." She thought he was trying to spare her sensibilities, but she wanted to know what was happening.

"I want to stay; a familiar face will probably make him feel better." She crossed her arms over her chest.

Argyris shook his head then shrugged his shoulders. "Fine but stay away from the bars and under no circumstances are you to enter the stall."

"Deal." She moved, letting Argyris lead the way. Vangel was standing near the bars, waiting when they reached him. His eyes were locked on Jean, his mouth was closed, and he was drooling but he didn't seem to notice.

"Welcome to your new life, Vangel," Argyris said, stopping at the stall, still trying to hide what he was holding.

"Thirsty," Vangel replied, staring at Jean through hooded eyes and leaving his mouth open just enough for her to see the tips of his pearly white fangs dripping with saliva.

"I have something that will tide you over for a few hours."

Argyris unlocked the chain from the stall door and opened it enough to slip inside then he slid the door shut behind him. He stepped closer to Vangel and offered him the bag of blood he had been hiding from Jean.

"I want her, not this." Vangel took the bag but didn't take his eyes from her.

"You can't have her, and if you did, when you have control, you would never forgive yourself for hurting her. She is your friend." Argyris stepped between Vangel and Jean, blocking his line of sight. "Do you want me to open the bag for you?"

Jean wanted to move around to watch Vangel drink the blood, but the way he was staring at her made her blood run cold, and for the first time in her life, she understood what being paralyzed by fear meant. She blinked and let out a breath. He couldn't get her, there were bars between them, and they would be locked as soon as Argyris joined her. She listened to the sound of plastic ripping and Argyris moved out of her way in time for her to watch Vangel bring the bag to his mouth.

He sucked on it slowly at first, then as if he was slow to realize that he was drinking the nectar of the gods, he lost control, and gulped it down so fast blood leaked from the corners of his mouth and dribbled onto his naked chest. When the bag was empty, he growled, ripped it in half and licked the insides.

"More," he demanded, his eyes flashed red and

found Jean again.

"No, you will have more in an hour or two, first we will see how it sits with you." Argyris replaced the padlock on the stall door.

"More, now," Vangel lunged toward Jean, she screamed and jumped back as his arm came through the bars reaching for her.

"Go now, there will be no calming him down until you're gone." Argyris took Jean by the shoulders and led her to the door.

"Will he be all right?" she asked, wanting to look over her shoulder but afraid of what she would see in Vangel's eyes.

"Yes, after a time he will be the person you knew from before, if not a little traumatized from the damage that was done to him before his death." He slid the door open for her, staying out of the light. Vinny stood whining outside but stopped when he saw her, then he ran over, jumped onto his hindlegs and licked her face.

"Thanks," she whispered, still in shock over Vangel. Would he have drained her dry if he hadn't been locked up? *He had better get over his bloodlust quick*, Jean thought. She needed him to help her deal with all this craziness.

Chapter 17

Alex

Alex disembarked the plane in Athens, keeping his head down. He wasn't free yet. He was a wanted man in Athens after he stole a lifeboat from the ferry a few weeks before. All he needed was a little time and he could kiss Greece goodbye.

First, he needed to pick up the identity he stashed when he first arrived in Greece almost a year before. The guy he was impersonating would be on his way to the police station soon, which meant Alex didn't have much time before the authorities began looking for him. He had to have enough time to get to his storage locker and change; it was the only way he would be able to escape Greece.

He moved through the airport quickly but not running as he didn't want to draw any attention to himself. Once he was out, he grabbed a cab, gave the driver the address, then sat back and stared at his phone. Where should he go? Where could he hide from both his father and Lolita? His phone vibrated in his hand as if thinking about her caused her to contact him. He clicked on the message; thankful she hadn't called him; he had no idea how to tell her he failed again.

Your services as a bounty hunter are no longer needed. Katie is now in my possession.

"Fuck," he said, leaning his head back, and closing his eyes.

The cab stopped in front of a storage complex ten minutes later and Alex exited the car after paying the driver. He used a code to enter the building and walked down the industrial hallway; the white cinderblock walls and concrete floor could have been anywhere in the world. Between the cinderblocks, three-foot-wide black doors were located every three feet or so. When he reached door twenty-four, he entered his code into the panel and disappeared inside.

When he came out, the next day, it was as if the storage room was a chrysalis. He entered as one person and emerged as someone else. The thick cheek bones were gone, as was the olive skin and the bald head. The man leaving the storage unit pulling a rolling carryon bag was dressed in a charcoal gray suit with a light gray shirt and a black tie. The blond wig was cut close, leaving no need to style it. His pale complexion and square jaw matched the photo on the passport he carried. He ordered a car from a ride sharing app and waited for a ride back to the airport.

Alex still didn't know where he was going but he needed a break from vampires. As he waited, he thought about where he could hide from his father and the rest of his enemies when his phone buzzed from inside his suit jacket. He would never admit it, but he was afraid to look at it. Afraid it was another message from Lolita telling him she was coming for him. *Stop being a pussy*, he thought, pulling the phone out and clicking it on.

Found the woman you've been looking for: Venice

Alex spun around on this heel. Jared found Lolita. *Venice wasn't that far way. I could be there tonight,* he thought, staring at the midday sun. He couldn't do it on his own though. Lolita had an army. A few months ago, it wouldn't have posed a problem but after the expenses of the past year, he didn't have enough money to pay for the equipment or the men he needed. Jared gave him the location as a favor, but he wouldn't help Alex again without payment and he would probably want it in advance.

The car he ordered pulled up, and the driver popped the trunk for him. He stowed his suitcase, closed the lid then got into the back. He confirmed that he needed a ride to the airport then pulled up a travel website on his phone. No matter what he did, he needed to get out of Greece. His luck was running out, and he didn't want to risk someone recognizing him.

The next flight he could buy a ticket for was going to Rome. He didn't know if it was a good omen or not, but he took it. Anything to get out of the country he had come to hate.

While he was waiting to board the plane, he sat near a charging station and, using the airports free Wi-Fi, he checked his favorite job boards for something close to Rome. As much as he wanted to run away from his problems, Zeus scared him enough to at least see if he could raise the money he needed to take on Lolita's army. If Lolita's text was right, and she had Katie, maybe he could kill them both.

There were a few jobs available he could swing on his own, with limited supplies, but Italy was always a tricky place for people in his line of work. Most of the mob's work was done on the inside. The only reason they called in an outsider was if it was too dangerous to risk their own. It was hard to decide if the job was worth the risk.

An hour later while sitting in an aisle seat of a plane headed for Rome, he felt most of his stress melt away as the plane left the ground. He'd made it. He was escaping Greece. There had been times when he didn't think he would make it out alive.

Not very many people who had the head of the Cretan Syndicate after them left alive, let alone of their own volition. He still wanted Theron dead, but he would let things in Crete cool down before he went after him.

"You may not live long enough to kill him," Zeus said from the seat next to him.

Alex jumped then groaned in pain, as the seat belt dug into his lap. "What the fuck? Have you been sitting there the whole time?"

"Do I look stupid to you boy? I want to spend as little time as possible in this tin can, breathing recycled air."

Alex ran a hand through his hair, almost forgetting he was wearing a wig and pulled it off. This was so not what he needed today. "What do you want?"

"To know why you have yet to kill a single vampire." He reclined his seat and stretched out. Alex was surprised the god could fit in the seat with his massive frame. His shoulders were wider than the seat. He was dressed similarly to Alex, with a black suit and tie.

"I've been trying," Alex muttered then glanced at the seat across from him, wondering if they saw Zeus or if they thought he was talking to himself. "You do not understand what I have had to deal with."

"Yes, I do, I've been watching you. You seem to trust the wrong people over and over again." He slapped his hand on this thigh. "Tell me how you are planning to kill them."

"I don't know." Alex was honest with him. "I don't have the resources to launch an attack. All I've done is figure out where Lolita is. It will be months before I'll have enough money to buy the equipment I need and hire people to help me. It may take years."

"That is unacceptable," Zeus roared, and the plane shook. Most of the passengers probably thought it was turbulence, not a pissed-off god from the Greek pantheon.

"It takes money to do things, old man. I don't know how you think life works, but nothing is free."

"How much money do you need?" Zeus asked, in a calmer voice.

Alex did a quick calculation doubting Zeus would be able to help him. If he wanted to scrape by, he could do it for twenty thousand, but all he had been doing was scraping by since the attack on Theron's compound. "To do it right with no mistakes?" He paused, thinking. "A hundred grand."

"That's a lot of money. What will you do with it?" Zeus stroked his beard.

"It will buy me the men and the explosives I'll need to do the job right. I'll blow up the island. Level it so there isn't anywhere for a vampire to hide. I'll do it during the day giving them nowhere to run. It will kill them all."

"Why not hire an army and take them on one on one?" Zeus pulled his eyebrows together. "There would be less noise."

Alex rolled his eyes. "Lolita has a vampire army, even if I could find enough men to fight them, they wouldn't be good enough. If it was just Lolita and a few guards, I could do it myself with a sniper rifle, but my intel says she has hundreds."

"OK, I see your point. I will help you, but if you walk away empty-handed again, I will call our agreement void and you will forfeit your life. No son of mine will disappoint me three times without consequences."

"Fine." Alex tried not to let the threat scare him, but Zeus was serious which meant he could not fail this time. "How am I going to get the money?"

"Check your account when you land," he said a moment before he disappeared, leaving Alex sitting next to an old lady, glaring at him probably wondering why he was staring at her.

"Sorry," he mumbled, then he leaned back in his seat and began forming a plan to level Lolita's island.

Chapter 18

Theron

"It's always a pleasure Zoi," Theron said, before closing the door to his room. He went to the mini fridge and retrieved a bag of blood before limping into the bathroom. It had been a long time since he *played* with Zoi, and looking in the mirror, he remembered why. Long, angry, red welts crisscrossed his pale chest. He ran a finger across one and hissed in pain. Zoi liked her belt almost as much as she enjoyed her cat-of-nine-tails. He turned and looked at the bloody scratches and welts covering his back. He wondered which ones were from her whip and which were from her nails, she liked to dig in as she orgasmed.

He shook his head; thank Goddess he had been able to keep his mouth shut. Thinking, or maybe wishing it had been Jean and not Zoi who brought him to painful ecstasy. He didn't want to know what Zoi would have done if he screamed the name he could not stop thinking about? Although he didn't think Jean would be into playing the dominatrix like Zoi was. He opened the bag of blood and drank while watching himself in the mirror as the welts slowly melted away leaving smooth pale flesh in its place. One of the benefits of life as a vampire was no scars and he healed from superficial wounds quickly. There would be no evidence of the night before on his body by the time he finished the bag. If only there was a way to erase it from his mind.

He had only taken Zoi to bed because he promised her he would after she helped him track Katie down in Athens. It had been a few days before he met Jean and he wondered if he had met Jean first, if he would have been as willing to trade sex with Zoi? Why was he suddenly worried about what Jean thought? He couldn't count the number of times she had ruined his plans. They argued constantly, she hated him, and he hated her more often than not. So why was he wishing he had spent the night with her instead of Zoi?

She was always bouncing around, being an endless thorn in his side. He found her pink hair childish, but her hair wasn't pink anymore. It was a warm shiny brown that made him want to run his fingers through it to see if it was as soft as it looked, then grab a handful and pull her in close to kiss her and test the softness of her lips.

He jerked away from the sink and ran a hand over his face. She wasn't even twenty years old, and he bet she was still a virgin. He hadn't taken a virgin to his bed since he was human and that had been centuries before. He needed to stop thinking about Jean, but his cock jerked when he thought about her lips on his while he slowly made love to her, virgin or not. Knowing her, she wouldn't like it slow though, she would want it hard and fast, probably against a wall. His cock twitched again, hardening more. He stared at it in wonder, how could it be hard again so soon after what Zoi had done to it? *Keep dreaming, you will never know what it feels like to be inside Jean.*

Clearing his head, he got into the shower and washed away what was left of Zoi. When he was done, he packed for Venice. He packed more than he needed. It would be a quick trip. Kill Lolita's army, rescue Katie, and leave, but with his luck there would be complications and he wanted to be prepared if things to not go as smoothly as he planned. *What will happen to my island if I don't survive?* The thought of dying had never crossed his mind until Alex destroyed the compound, and since then it had weighed heavily on his mind. Not that he thought himself unkillable, it was that nothing had changed on his island for so many years it was like they had been in stasis, where the world spun but Crete stayed the same. Then Katie came along and brought him and his island back to life, and where there is life, there is death. He would never blame her for all that had happened but thank her for giving him a mission to complete.

He needed to ensure his island would be safe if something happened to him though. He was already planning to leave the person he trusted most in the world behind while he went to wage war, but he needed to tell her of his wishes if the unthinkable happened, and he didn't return. Finished packing he zipped his suitcase closed and picked his phone up off the nightstand.

We need to meet. Where are you? He sent the message then left his room staring at the phone.

In my room. Are you finally done with Zoi? ;)

Theron rolled his eyes at the jibe, *smartass.*

Why do I put up with you? I will be there shortly.

Theron made it a step into the hall before Jean ran past him, racing toward her room. She was upset about something; she left the smell of panic and fear in her wake.

Damn what did she do this time? He thought, following her to her room while tapping out a message.

It will be awhile. Jean is up to something.
What now?
I don't know. I'll text you when I'm done.

He slid his phone into the pocket of his slacks and followed Jean at a walk. Whatever it was, he doubted it was life or death. She would have told him if it was. She'd learned the hard way not to lie to him. When he reached the door, he knocked, then tried the handle—locked.

"Jean?" he asked through the door. "It's Theron, what's going on?" He listened as her feet stomped across the floor, stopped at the door, then the lock flipped, and she opened it.

"I just—" she sniffled and backed into her room. "I just saw Vangel. He's a monster." She backed up to the edge of the bed and sat down hard.

"You went to see Vangel?" Theron blinked, *she did what?* He let out a breath, closed the door, and sat in the chair by the desk. He needed to stay calm. If he blew up, he would only scare her away, and he needed her. "How did you know where he was?"

"Educated guess." She grabbed a used tissue off the bed and blew her nose loudly. "You lied to me. You said he would be the same person as he was before."

Theron ran a hand through his hair. "I didn't lie to you; I just didn't tell you the whole truth." *Why me?* He thought, staring at the ceiling. He had a million things to do before they left and calming down a human he could not subdue with Thrall was not on his list. "After you are changed, your body needs fuel to replenish its energy. It takes time to level out and become yourself again."

Jean stared at him like he was crazy. "You're telling me that you and Helen and even Vince went through the same thing?" She crossed her arms over her chest and narrowed her eyes at him like she didn't believe him, but her heart rate betrayed her actions, she was calming down.

"Yes, for some it takes months, others take years to overcome it. I'm confident Vangel will master it quickly." He didn't tell her that sometimes they never do, and they had to be sent to the afterlife to keep their existence a secret.

"He scared me, Theron. He was my friend, but in the barn, he would've done anything to drink my blood." She sniffled again.

"I know, I'm sorry. I should've had Argyris lock the door." He stood and paced around the small room. How was he going to earn her trust when he kept hiding things from her? Wait, why did he want to earn her trust? He didn't want her to tell anyone about vampires, but was that the only reason?

"So, you would have rather locked me out than show me the truth?" She jumped to her feet, blocking his path. "Hiding the truth isn't how trust works. How could you keep this from me?" She jammed her finger into his chest.

"I'm sorry. This is a unique situation for me, I rarely tell anyone about our true nature. I have no idea what I'm doing." Defeated he put his hands up. *How am I going to make it up to her?*

"Well, don't worry." Jean sat on the bed and pulled her feet up to hug her knees. "After Venice, I'm not coming back." He opened his mouth to protest but before he could get a word out, she held up a hand stopping him. "I'm going after Alex when this is done. I will make him pay for what he did to all of us and then I'm going to disappear."

Theron wanted to forbid it. She wouldn't last an hour going after Alex on her own, and it hurt him that she wanted to leave him behind. He had to talk her out of it. "Don't hate our race because of me," he said not sure what he was trying to accomplish.

"I don't hate you or your race, but you must understand this life." She held her arms out to the side and spun in a circle. "This isn't life. It's a nightmare. You understand that don't you?"

Shocked, Theron took a step back. "A nightmare?" he asked then thought about everything that had happened since she joined them. Kidnappings, snipers, vampires, shootings, bombs. "Yes, life has been eventful since you joined us, but it's not always like this."

"Are you trying to convince me to stay?" She looked like she was trying not to laugh.

"You could have a good life working for me." *Why am I trying to convince her to stay again?*

"For how long? You don't have the best track record when it comes to keeping humans alive." She crossed her arms over her chest. "Plus, I can't let Alex get away."

She was right, she was the only human who wasn't dead, kidnapped, or been changed since she had arrived. "Agreed, but do you think you can take him down on your own?"

"I will find a way. It feels like there is a knife in my heart that is pushed deeper every day that he goes free, plus I need to figure out who I am without The Syndicate or Interpol breathing down my neck," she said, refusing to make eye contact.

"You will always have a place here, Jean. No matter how much trouble you get into, the vampires of Crete will give you sanctuary whenever and for as long as you need it." Theron took a step closer to her, lowering his voice.

She finally met his eyes and gave him a half smile. "Really? Even after all the ways I screwed you over?"

"Yes, even after all your screw ups." He smiled and shook his head. "You mean something to me. . . and Helen."

"Thanks." She wrapped her arms around his middle. He stood stunned for a moment before he returned the hug. He kissed the top of her head before he could stop himself and froze. He wanted more. He pulled back planning on tasting her lips, but before he moved an inch, she pushed him away. "No, Theron, I won't be one of your harem." She jerked out of his arms and escaped to the bathroom, locking the door behind her.

"What are you talking about?" he asked, standing outside the door.

"I don't know how many girlfriends you have, but I won't be included in their numbers."

Theron stood confused for a second then remembered their meeting in the hall earlier. Zoi had been in his room. Jean must have heard her. "Jean, I'm sorry." He held his hand against the door wishing she would open it. When it didn't, he stormed out, mad at himself for entertaining Zoi. He should've put it off until after the war, then Jean wouldn't have found out about it.

Once he was in the hall, he pulled his phone out and sent a text.

Sorry, that took longer than expected, are you still in your room?

He glanced around then back at his phone.

Yes, I was wondering if I needed to send out a search party.

I'll be right there.

Theron walked down the hall, nodding his head at the vampires lingering in the hallway, his deliberate pace indicated that he was in a hurry and to leave him alone. He was relieved to see everyone ready to leave. They still had hours before the sun went down, but at least they wouldn't have to wait on anyone. When he reached the door he wanted, he knocked once then entered without waiting for permission.

Helen was sitting at the small desk wearing a black skirt-suit. She was holding a stack of papers but looked up at the sound of the door. "Everything is ready to go. The plane will be ready to board at sundown. All you need to do is get to the airport," Helen said, glancing back at the paper. "I've coordinated with the vampires from the other locations who will meet you in Venice. They will arrive within an hour of your group. I set up your house. You will be rooming with Vince, Maria, Jean, Marios, Zoi, and Livius."

"Can you put Zoi somewhere else?" Theron asked, flexing his back at the reminder of the pain Zoi had enjoyed inflicting, and how Jean ran from him minutes before. He would have moved her too, but she didn't know or trust the others. She would probably leave and try to save Katie on her own if he didn't keep her close.

"Yes, but I thought you two were together." Helen looked relieved to hear he wasn't serious about Zoi. He would have been too if their positions were reversed.

"We are not, and I would prefer not to see her for another decade if I can help it."

"Very well, I'll move her. Are you ready?"

"Almost, I want to speak with you about something." He looked at the ceiling then ran his hands through his hair. He hated thinking about it. "If the unthinkable happens and I don't make it

141

back…"

"What are you talking about? You will come home." Helen narrowed her eyes, stood up and put her hands on her hips. "You have to."

"Yes, but if by the will of Asteria I don't, there are some things you need to know." He sat down on the bed and clasped his hands together. "We are going to war, and I will sleep better if you know what I would want."

"Fine but this is ridiculous." Helen dropped into her chair.

"I am leaving everything to you, of course. The repairs to the main house will be completed by May. There is a notebook in the locked drawer of my desk. Here's the key." He pulled a small brass key from his pocket and handed it over. "You will find all my account numbers and passwords in it. I know you have your own money, but it takes a lot to run this island and I want you to use mine before you use yours."

"Theron," Helen started, but he cut her off.

"Let me get this out." He held up his hand to quiet her. "The Syndicate knows you are my second, but to maintain control of it you must rule with an iron fist. You have to win them over; they are what keeps this island moving. If we lose the war and Lolita invades Europe. . ." He shook his head, not wanting to think about what might happen. "If we lose, you need to stay on Crete and protect it, the Syndicate will help. Keeping the people of Crete safe needs to be your number one priority."

"You say that like I would run away and abandon our people." Helen shook her fist at him. "I know our history, and I have experienced enough of it to know what happens when war comes to Europe. I will not rest until Crete and all of its citizens are safe, even if I die, I will not let Crete be harmed."

"I meant no offence, but I'm glad you understand the gravity of the situation. You are a Cretan through and through, and the best second I could ask for. Never forget it." He gave her a tight smile and felt like he should hug her, but that would make everything awkward between them. "With everyone involved, this mission will go off without a hitch, but I want you to be prepared in case there is one."

"Good, now I have work to do since you are leaving me to run your kingdom while you go help save the damsel in distress."

Theron laughed, stood, and went to the door. "It sounds corny when you put it like that."

Chapter 19

Lolita

Lolita stormed into her stateroom. Katie had grown more powerful than she thought. If Katie was at full strength, she could probably tell all her guards to take a flying leap into the sea without breaking a sweat.

She went to the cooler sitting in the corner of the room. She took out a bag of blood and eyed the vial of the drug. It was almost gone. She would be lucky if they made it back to Poveglia before they used it all. What would she do if they ran out before they got there? She could always beat Katie into unconsciousness, but it would be dangerous. Lolita didn't want Katie dead yet. Not after the little bitch kicked her ass in front of the leaders of Europe. No, secretly disposing of her was no longer an option, too many vampires knew about her and her powers.

She had to make an example of the girl. Lolita's eyes brightened as a plan formed in her mind. Katie would help start the war. Lolita went to the dresser and picked up the crown Katie had worn to the party. *Yes, it will do nicely.* She placed it on her head and looked in the mirror before sitting down at her desk and emailing Miguel — she needed him to do some shopping.

When she finished the email, she went for a walk on deck. Being trapped on a boat for days was killing her. She had things to do now that "The One," was in her custody. She breathed in the cool night air and gazed at the stars. She couldn't help her excitement. Her plan was finally in motion. Before the year was over, she would rule Europe and would be making plans to move into Asia and the Middle East. Laying waste to Crete and destroying Theron's empire would be one of the first things on her to do list. She laughed and spun in a circle. After Theron was dead, she would give Crete back to Turkey and let them do whatever they wished with the Cretans.

You have lofty goals for having no special powers. A feminine voice invaded Lolita's mind, and she looked around frantically, wondering where it came from but found no one. It couldn't be Katie; she was drugged and couldn't do more than breathe.

"Who's there?" Lolita straightened her back and narrowed her eyes.

According to you I do not exist. The thought filtered into Lolita's mind and her eyes went wide.

"Then leave me alone. Why are you bothering me?" Her voice trembled as she spoke, and she prayed her guards were out of earshot. The voice terrified her — if it was who she thought it was, she was screwed.

Something hard rammed into her, flinging her through the air. She screamed, windmilling her arms and legs, trying to force herself back down to the deck. She was looking over the inky black water of the sea before she began to fall and she reached out blindly, grasping for anything that would keep her from going overboard. When her fingers found the edge of the boat, she dug in, clinging to the side with all the strength she had.

You captured my daughter and have subdued her. Release her at once or your life will be forfeit.

"Why should I? She doesn't want our race to prosper. She wishes to keep us as we are, second-rate citizens to the humans. She wants our true nature to remain a secret and our numbers small.

And what do you plan to do? The voice asked skeptically.

"I plan on making our presence known to the humans and rule over them as we should." Lolita almost regretted her words. Maybe she should beg for her life instead of revealing her plans for world domination.

Her fingers were becoming slick with the spray from the water below, making it hard for her to maintain her position. They hit a wave hard and she lost her grip. For a split second she thought her time in this world was over as she plummeted toward the water. *At least I'll die at the hand of a goddess and not a human or vampire.* But a gust of wind picked her up and flung her onto the deck. She landed hard on her back then slowly sat up trying not to wince in pain.

What are you going to do with my daughter? The voice asked, and Lolita felt a breeze swirl around her as she got to her feet and checked herself for wrinkles. She couldn't tell Asteria the truth, at least not yet, she needed to win the goddess over, make sure she realized her vision.

"I'm breaking her down, making her forget what it is to be human. I will not be able to conquer the world without her help. I need to harness the gifts you blessed her with to put the humans in their place. They should be worshiping us as their gods and doing our bidding." Lolita walked to the edge of the deck. She crossed her arms over her chest as she stared into the dark churning waters that had almost ended her. She could not let the Goddess know how frightened she was.

You will never be a goddess. A gust of wind pushed Lolita from behind and she gripped the railing tighter.

Fuck, Lolita thought, *what can I say to make the Goddess happy?* "What if they worshiped you?" She might have to do some fancy footwork to keep the Catholics on her side, but she would rather have a goddess on her side than a priest.

Tell me more, the voice said as the wind died.

Chapter 20

Vince

Vince taped the last box of Katie's things closed and Vinny whimpered from beside him. He glanced at the dog then the boxes full of clothes and toiletries Katie had accumulated. He thought about leaving everything in Crete for Helen to do with as she pleased, but then remembered how much Katie hated starting over with nothing. *This time would be different, it had to be different.*

Finished packing, he went into the bedroom and looked at the two suitcases packed for Venice but not yet closed. Vinny jumped on the bed and rested his head on top of the clothes Vince had packed for Katie.

She would want her katana as well, and it broke his heart that he could not give her a working weapon. The sword she had trained with, the one Theron had gifted to her, had been broken in half during the fight. He was bringing it to Venice but the sight of it would break her heart. He would commission a new one, but nothing could replace the one that she had seen so much with.

"Vinny, I miss her too, but you have to move." He put the suitcase on the floor then sat on the bed and pulled the spoiled dog into his lap. "We will save her Vinny, then we will go to Sorento.

No one will bother us there." He ran his hand through the dog's fur, glad only Theron knew about his sanctuary. "I guess you will come with us to Venice. I can't leave you here if we are not coming back. Besides you might be able to help us find her with that nose of yours." He felt like an idiot as he spoke to the dog like Vinny could understand what he was saying, but it seemed to be the only way Vinny would stop whining. Vince wanted to cry with him, but he had to keep his fear and worry locked inside. There was too much at stake to give into his feelings.

He had already called his caretaker in Sorento and told him to make the necessary upgrades to the grounds. It had been decades since he had visited, but he hired a kid the last time he was there to take care of the place and keep everything in working order. Every ten years he would hire an interior decorator to update the paint, appliances, and furniture. His caretaker thought he was crazy since he didn't spend any time there but Vince didn't care, he knew there would be a time when he would return, and he didn't want to live in a construction zone while he waited for indoor plumbing or whatever new modern convenience was installed. "You are going to love it, Vinny." He picked up the suitcases and took them into the sitting room. "There is a huge yard, and the beach isn't far away. There are always birds in the trees for you to chase." He sat the suitcases next to the door. Helen would ship the boxes the next day.

He glanced around the room, making sure he had forgotten nothing, then looked at the time. He still had hours before they would leave, and all he could think about was what Lolita was doing to Katie.

"Come on, Vinny," Vince said, tapping his leg. "Let's go see Theron." The hallway was mostly empty, but Vince could hear vampires in the rooms on either side talking, packing, or fucking. It had been months since he had been around so many of his kind. It was almost a comfort knowing all of them had his back and they were going to help him rescue Katie. They might see it as stopping Lolita but attacking her was the same as rescuing Katie to him.

"Vince," Livius said from behind him, interrupting his thoughts.

Vince stopped and looked over his shoulder as Vinny growled. Vince smiled at the dog's reaction to Livius. He had forgotten that dogs judged a person's character better than humans or vampires could. "Yes? Livius, what can I do for you?" He cursed himself as soon as the words left his mouth. *Will I ever be able to stand up for myself?*

"Come, I want to get in a workout before we leave." Livius nodded and walked down the hall toward the ballroom without waiting for Vince's answer.

Vince followed him without a thought, but then stopped. *Why am I doing what Livius wants? I am my own vampire. I have been free for centuries. If I do not wish to spar with him, I should not have to.* Vince stiffened his back and clenched his fists. "No, I'm sorry you need to find someone else. Theron and I need to finalize our plans."

Vince did not raise his voice as he spoke, convincing himself that he was in control.

Livius stopped, cocked his head, and turned to face Vince. "Did you just tell me no?" he sounded surprised, and Vince understood why, he could not remember ever standing up to Livius before.

"Yes." Vince forced his voice to sound hard and determined, but he broke out in a sweat and fisted his hands to keep them from shaking. Saying no to the vampire who had *owned* him for centuries was one of the hardest things he had ever done, but it was time to stand up for himself. He turned away from Livius and continued walking toward Theron's office. Feeling free for the first time in his life. He had never dared go against his maker before, but things had to change. Vince had more important things going on than being at Livius's beck and call.

His freedom was short-lived though as he heard Livius sprint up behind him, and before Vince had a chance to react, Livius grabbed him by the back of his shirt, slammed him into the wall, and pinned his forearm under Vince's chin. Vince blinked, stunned by Livius as a sliver of fear raced up his spine. *What have I done? What will my punishment be this time?* He crumpled at the thought of the beating he would receive but only for a second. Vinny growled, and Vince heard the distinct sound of flesh hitting flesh followed by Vinny yelping.

"Shut up you mutt," Livius said.

He kicked the dog? Vince awoke from his slavish thoughts. *You do not kick Vinny.* He wrapped his foot around Livius's leg and using the wall for traction pushed off it with his arms extended. Caught off guard, Livius stumbled backward, releasing Vince, and tried to regain his balance but he landed on his back in the middle of the hall. Vince kicked Livius in the ribs as hard as he could. "Never. Touch. Katie's. Dog. We are not yours to abuse." Vince straddled him, pinned his arms over his head and brought his lips to Livius's ear as vampires from the nearby rooms ducked their heads out to see what was going on. "I am no longer yours to command." Vince's voice dripped with intent to kill. "Leave me alone, old man. We don't have time for your dominance games." Vince released him and glided to his feet. "Let's go Vinny." Vince snapped his fingers, and they left Livius on the ground.

"What's going on?" Theron asked, coming out of Helen's room, and looking past Vince.

"Just finishing some old business. I need to talk to you." Vince paused when he reached Theron then continued down the hall with Vinny on one side of him and Theron on the other, ignoring the looks the vampires they passed gave them. Once they were behind Theron's office doors, Vince dropped to his knees. "Vinny, come." Theron went around them to his desk while Vince ran his hands over Vinny making sure he was not hurt.

"What happened?" Theron asked as Vince got to his feet.

"I'm done taking orders from Livius, and now he knows it." Vince felt fifty pounds lighter. He doubted Livius would understand it yet, but Vince had made his decision, and he would live by it.

"Good," Theron said following him inside. "I've been waiting for you to stand up to him for decades. I would offer to throw you a party to celebrate, but why don't we start a war instead?"

"Perfect," Vince grinned but let it go almost as soon as it began. *What right do I have to feel good while Katie is suffering?* Vince slumped into the chair in front of the desk while Theron sat in his. "When this is done," Vince started, not wanting to waste any time. "Katie and I will not be returning to Crete."

Theron nodded his head. "Understandable, not very many happy memories for you here are there?"

"No, and she deserves a break from everything." Vince had been thinking about it since the party. "We will go to Sorento, make it our home base, then she wants to return to America to visit her parents."

"Parents? I don't remember having any," Theron spun his chair around. "She should enjoy them while she can. Is the dog OK?"

"Yes, which brings me to the next matter at hand." Vince looked down at Vinny. "Vinny will be joining us in Venice."

Theron sat up. "What? Do you know how much it will cost to have the plane detailed because of a dog?"

"I don't care, I will pay for it. How do you propose we get the dog to Sorento if he does not come with us?"

Vince rolled his eyes at Theron. "Plus, do you know how pissed Katie will be if Vinny is not there when we rescue her?" Vince put his hand on the top of Vinny's head, the damn animal had grown on him. "He knows her scent and has a better nose than any of us. He will help us find her."

Theron leaned back and stared at the ceiling. "Fine, the dog can come, but make sure he pisses and shits before we leave, I don't want the whole plane stinking."

"Done. That's what Jean is for right?" Vince meant it as a joke, but Theron jerked his chair down and leveled a stare at Vince as his eyes flashed red.

"Don't talk about her like that." Theron got up and paced around the room. "She is not your typical human, don't treat her as such."

"I am sorry, I did not mean to offend. Since when do you care about her?" He could not remember Theron ever defending a human before.

"Since now?" Theron stopped and stared at a painting on the wall. It was of a small Greek village on an island somewhere. The water was turquoise blue, the buildings stark white and the roofs sky blue. "I don't want to talk about it. What else did we need to discuss?"

"How do we know Lolita will be back before we attack?"

Theron went back to the desk and pulled his phone out. "Good question. Let's call Miguel. Lolita is being stingier and stingier with information but surely she would want everything ready for her return." He hit a few buttons and set the phone on the desk between them.

With the phone on speaker Miguel picked up on the second ring. "Do you have a plan?"

"Yes, are you in a safe location?" Theron answered, raising an eyebrow at Vince.

"Yes, Lolita isn't back yet." He spoke in a whisper but still loud enough for Vince and Theron to hear.

"Have you heard from her?" Vince asked.

"Has she told you when she will return?" Theron added.

"She should arrive tonight. I received an email from her last night. I don't know what she has planned but it will be big and involve Katie. She is sending me out shopping as soon as the sun goes down. When will you attack?"

Theron looked at Vince silently, asking if he thought it was safe to tell Miguel the plan. Vince reluctantly nodded then sat back in his chair, praying to the Goddess that Miguel could be trusted.

Chapter 21

Miguel

Miguel put his phone in his pocket and paced around Lolita's office. Katie would arrive before the sun came up. Excitement sent a shiver down his spine. It had been so long since he had seen her. Everything he had done was in hopes of seeing her again and making up for what he had done to her. To earn her forgiveness. The problem was Theron's plan left nothing for him to do except stop Lolita from killing Katie before they arrived. Once the fighting began, he could let his true alliance be known, but until then he had to continue as he had since he arrived, be Lolita's faithful second in command and not care about Katie beyond her gifts. He ran his hand through his hair. Katie would hate him more than she already did.

The alarm on his phone sounded, bringing him out of his thoughts. He pulled it out and glanced at it before cursing. *Time to feed Mark his daily bag of blood.* Miguel went down to the kitchen where the industrial refrigerator was stacked with bagged blood. They kept the blood for all the vampires in the main house where it could be kept under guard. Bagged blood was expensive and when Lolita had over five hundred vampires to feed, every drop counted. The soldiers were kept on a tight diet, Miguel thought they should have more just to be on the safe side, but Lolita refused. She believed that keeping them just on the right side of bloodlust would make them fight harder when it was time.

Only Lolita, Miguel, and a select few of Lolita's choosing were allowed to drink from Lolita's stable of humans who were also kept in the house. It was a good incentive for the men to win Lolita's favor. Miguel would not have stayed to help her if she had forced him to live on bagged blood alone. He had been alive for too long to agree to that.

A wave of relief passed over him when he opened the fridge and saw the tightly packed shelves filled with bagged blood. The weekly delivery had been made. Ever since Theron had mentioned a dream Katie had of the army going hungry, he was afraid something would happen to their supply.

He grabbed a bag of blood for Mark, made sure the door latched closed, and picked up the clipboard hanging on the door. He documented what he took then replaced the board. Every bag removed had to be accounted for, it was the only way to ensure no one took more than their ration.

Miguel went to the door to the left of the fridge and readied himself for the smell of the dungeon before he went down the steps. Mark had no more control over his bloodlust than he did after he was reborn a vampire. Miguel had tried every known treatment to cure Mark of his cravings, but nothing worked, and of course Lolita blamed Miguel for not making Mark strong enough. It was her fault for forcing him to turn Mark. He was a horrible choice for a vampire. Miguel thought everyone knew the two most important abilities a human needed to have to become a worthwhile vampire: a strong mind and excellent self-control. Mark had neither.

It was such a waste of the gift and only to spite Katie but, it would have the desired effect. Katie would feel like it was her fault Mark was changed when really, the stupid human did it to himself. Miguel wondered if Lolita planned on forcing Katie to watch as she put Mark out of his misery. Miguel would never suggest it as it would tear Katie apart, and he wanted to make up for all the ways he had wronged her. That was his Katie though, and one of the reasons why he loved her. Even if she hated someone, she would do anything to keep them from suffering. Reaching the bottom of the stairs, Miguel took his last lungful of clean air then walked down the hall lined with cells. Mark was the only prisoner, and he began screaming for blood the moment Miguel reached the end of the stairs.

"Shut up, or I'll let you starve." Miguel stood in front of Mark's cell with his arms crossed over his chest.

Mark immediately shut his mouth and ran to the bars. His chain was only long enough for him to reach half his forearm through. Miguel placed the bag of blood in Mark's outstretched hand then stepped back. Mark ripped a small hole in the top of then brought it up to drink. *He was beginning to take better care while he ate,*

Miguel thought as Mark drained the bag without wasting a drop. *Maybe I can let him shower and clean out his cell soon.*

"Thank you," Mark dropped the empty plastic bag on top of a pile of empty bags in the corner of his cell. "May I please have another?" His voice was smooth and practiced, he sounded like a wealthy businessman. No wonder Katie had stayed with him as long as she had. He was almost as good at manipulating people as Miguel.

"You know the rules, you don't need another one, you only want another one." Miguel shook a finger at him.

"No, I need it," Mark said as his voice changed from the well-traveled businessman to a ten-year-old trying to talk an adult out of another piece of candy.

What would happen if Mark was free? Miguel thought, *would he go on a rampage? Attacking and drinking the blood of every human he came in contact with, unable to keep the bloodlust at bay? Would he make the existence of vampires known to the world because he had no control? He might be the distraction I need to rescue Katie when the time comes.* "Do you know how much work it is for me to bring you a bag of blood?"

"No," Mark said, sounding confused.

"I have to go into the kitchen which is at the top of the stairs. There is a huge refrigerator up there, you know like the ones they have in restaurants, and it's filled with bagged blood. We just received a shipment in today. The bags almost fell out when I opened the door to get yours. Anyway, I have to pull a bag out for you and write it down, so Lolita knows how much I took, then I have to bring it all the way down here. It's quite taxing." Miguel hoped Mark would remember what he was saying. Sometimes he wondered how Mark remembered to breathe.

"It doesn't sound that hard." Mark thought about it for a minute. "It doesn't sound hard at all."

"Maybe to you, but I'm a busy man." Miguel turned to leave. "I'll see you tomorrow with your blood."

"No," Mark screamed. "Please don't leave, please bring me some more blood. I'll do anything."

Ignoring him Miguel went back up the stairs. *You will do anything won't you?* he thought, smiling to himself.

Chapter 22

Katie

I didn't know how long I had been out, but one minute the world was gone, and nothing seemed to matter, then in the next I was being jostled. I focused my eyes, and tried to blink, but nothing happened. My eyes must not have been closed while I was unconscious. It was an odd feeling, nothing one second then everything the next. I was over one of the guard's shoulders and, based on the white fiberglass floor he was walking on, we were still on the boat. *We must be in Venice*, I thought as I bounced around on his shoulder. *Blink,* I thought. *If you can blink you can escape. Damn it, blink!* But nothing happened, the drug was still in charge of my motor functions.

"Here take her so I can get in the boat," I heard Robert say. Someone grabbed my legs and pulled me off Robert's shoulder. I fell roughly to the floor of what I guessed was a smaller boat given that the stars above me moving back and forth across my line of vision. *Well, at least I have something pretty to look at for a change.* The boat dipped as someone else climbed aboard, then a motor started, and we sped over the choppy water, the stars seemed unmoving in the blanket of darkness above me. Every bump sent a wave of pain through my body since I couldn't brace myself or roll with them. My teeth slammed together, making my head hurt worse than it already did thanks to the beating from the guards and I wondered how far we had to go. At least I had been able to get some food in my stomach and drink some water earlier.

When Lolita was done torturing me, she injected me again, and I had nothing to do but dream about how good one of the protein bars and the bottle of water would be, and how satisfying it would be to force all the vampires to walk into the sun.

I didn't know how long I had been staring at what I wanted most in the world before my hand began moving toward the water bottle, but I stopped before it went too far. My body wanted water more than it cared about being caught. *OK, I have to be sly about this.* I barely had any energy left and I didn't think I could hold both guards' minds even to make them freeze. I remembered thinking that if I didn't get some water and food soon, I would never find the strength to fight my way free.

Somehow I found the strength I needed to force the guards to ignore me while I slowly drank the bottle of water and ate the protein bar. It was the best food and water I had ever tasted. When I was done, I had asked the guard what time it was, thinking that if I had enough strength, I could force one of them into the sun and catch the boat on fire. Christoph told me it was the middle of the night then told the guards outside my cell that I was awake and to get Lolita.

When Lolita joined us, she yelled at them for allowing me to eat and drink. I wished I had the strength to fight her off, but I was still so weak all I could do was lay there as she injected me again. Once Lolita had left, the guards beat me until unconsciousness took me.

The boat hit a wave hard enough that I left the bottom of the boat for a second then slammed back down, forcing me to leave my memories behind. *Mom, I could use some help. Blink,* I screamed inside my head. This would be my last chance. All I had to do was regain control of my body then I could jump overboard and swim for shore. It was no use though. The drug was lingering longer this time, at least it felt like it was.

Eventually the boat slowed then came to a stop. "Miguelito," I heard Lolita say and my mind froze. I didn't want to see the man who ruined my life. "Look, I brought you a present." The boat dipped as someone came aboard.

"Lolo, you shouldn't have," Miguel said as his face interrupted my view of the stars.

I wanted to throw up, I wanted to shrink into myself, more than anything I wanted to knock out his teeth. *Fight,* I told my body, but still it ignored me.

"I would do anything for my little brother. Take her to the dungeon and shoot her up with more of the drug, then meet me in my chambers," Lolita said, and the boat bobbed as someone got off.

"Don't you have any left? I gave you everything I had. It should have been enough to keep her drugged for a week, maybe two."

"No, the bitch burns through it faster than we anticipated."

"I will order some more, but it will take a few days for it to get here."

"Very well, we'll have to come up with a different way of keeping her from using her powers in the meantime. When you are done locking her up, I will be waiting in my room."

Miguel stared at me for a second. He looked the same as I remembered him, a pale complexion, a hard mouth, and his dark brown hair was pulled away from his face. He looked harder but his eyes were sad, like he was sorry for what was happening to me. It wasn't hard to believe what those eyes were saying. If nothing else, so I would have a friend, but then I thought about what he did to me in San Sebastian. He had manipulated me then, when I figured out his game, he raped me. Both Theron and Vince told me how they wouldn't have survived the attack on Crete if it hadn't been for Miguel, but it didn't mean I had to trust him.

"You heard her, take our guest to the dungeon," he said motioning toward the shore

Louis and Christoph managed to get me off the boat without dropping me, and before long I was bouncing around on Christoph's shoulder as he walked along a path. I had no idea where we were going since my only view was of his ass and the grass I could see between his legs.

"I'm so excited that you're here, Katie," Miguel said from somewhere next to me. "We are going to have such a good time." He ran his hand down my ass then under my dress. I tried to jerk away, tried to scream, then tried to fucking blink but still I couldn't move. "As long as my sister lets me play with you that is."

I didn't know what Theron and Vince were talking about. Miguel wasn't going to help me. Everything he had done was only to get me back. He was the same dickhead he had been in San Sebastian. *Blink*, I thought to myself again. It wasn't too late to get away, but if they got me to the dungeon all would be lost. We stopped moving and Christoph carried me down a long dark set of stairs. I heard someone fumbling with keys. *Shit, too late.* I reached out with my mind, but I couldn't feel them. I was completely helpless.

When we reached the bottom someone fumbled with keys and a door with eerily squeaky hinges opened. Then a waft of the worst stench I had ever smelled invaded my nostrils. It made me want to vomit but I forced myself to keep my food down. It was a musty, moldy smell, laced with the smell of rotten blood I remembered from Takis. Were they going to put me in a cell with a new vampire? That would be one way of dealing with me.

He carried me down a hallway with cells on either side from what I could see with my peripheral vision. Someone, probably the new vampire I had smelled, was screaming, and yelling for blood. *Shut up,* I thought but nothing happened.

"Here we are Katie, your new home," Miguel said as I heard another door open.

Christoph took me inside then dropped me on the floor letting the back of my head hit something hard, and blackness faded in and out of my vision. It was dark, so dark that I could barely make out the gray wet stones above me. Miguel came into view again and I tried to shrink away from him, but still my body wouldn't listen to my command. *Blink you idiot. This could be your last chance.*

"Now I'm going to put these manacles on. I need you to be a good girl and hold still," he said laughing to himself.

Fuck off, I screamed in my head. I was so over being drugged. *When I am back to myself you are going to pay for this.* I vowed as he clamped the cold heavy iron around my wrists.

"There's a good girl," he said coming in close. "When I come back, we will have some fun." He came in closer and I felt his tongue lick up the side of my face. "I missed the way you taste." I tried to spit on him, but I had no saliva, and my muscles ignored the command. He laughed again, stood, and walked away.

I listened to his steps fade away, then I heard a door closing. I couldn't tell if was from the direction we came or a different one. The screams for blood from the other cell was my only company and there was nothing for me to do except listen to him scream and tell my body to move when it wouldn't listen.

Chapter 23

Jean

Jean looked around the tarmac. She was leaving Crete and she wasn't as happy about it as she thought she would be. She didn't feel like her mission was complete yet. Katie wasn't safe, which was the only reason why she came to the island, in the first place well that and to arrest Alex.

She hadn't forgotten about him while she waited to leave that afternoon. She had tried to figure out where he went after the shed. Her facial recognition program had tagged him entering a restaurant but not leaving. He wasn't dumb enough to stay there though. He probably left through a backdoor and there weren't any cameras in the alley.

She couldn't prove it, but she doubted he was still on the island. She had received a partial tag at the airport earlier in the day. The man didn't look anything like Alex on the surface, but if she imagined him with a shaved head and some plastic surgery it could've been him. Rescuing Katie was more important than tracking him down though. He would pop up again, and wherever he was, Jean would be ready to take him down.

A car pulled up to the plane as Jean took the stairs to board.

She smiled at the flight attendant waiting inside. "Can I sit anywhere?"

"Yes, if you need anything, use your call button."

Jean bobbed her head and walked down the aisle quickly. The front half of the plane was already full of vampires who had been staying at the mansion, and Jean wanted to get past them before they got any ideas.

When she reached Vinny, she stepped over him then turned and bent to scratch his ears. "We are going to get her back," she whispered then stood and glared at the back of Vince's head.

What the hell was he doing? *We were on our way to save his girlfriend and he's flirting with the Spanish bitch.* Jean wasn't going to take it, Katie deserved better.

"Can I help you, Jean?" Vince asked, twisting to catch her staring at him.

"How…" she started then stopped. She wanted to yell at him, but he was a vampire, and could probably kill her without moving from his seat. "No," she spun and found an aisle seat towards the back of the plane.

Be a bigger chicken, Jean thought to herself, watching Vince's head bend toward Maria's. *He's totally going to cheat on Katie with her.* Jean shook herself; she couldn't let him get away with it.

Marios walked down the aisle, blocking her view and reminded her of other problems. If he tried to sit next to her, she didn't care what he was, she would tell him to fuck off. Luckily, he took a seat closer to the front as did the vampires behind him. Once they were seated, Jean saw Theron standing at the front of the plane with his arms held up waiting for the chatter to stop.

"Friends, tonight we embark on a mission that the world has never seen," he paused for effect, and Jean rolled her eyes. "Never before have so many of our kind come together to fight a common enemy, and in doing so we will make the world safer, ensuring that we stay as we have always been below the humans' notice. I want to thank each of you for your help. As we enter battle remember we not only fight for ourselves, but for everyone in Europe, human and vampire alike. Stopping Lolita and disposing of her army will mean continuing our way of life and ending a war that will destroy the world.

"You all have your lodging assignments and orders for the mission. I cannot stress enough that we go directly to our lodging and not venture out tonight. We can't be seen by anyone, human or otherwise. Geovanni, I have been told has spies everywhere. If he finds any of us before the battle begins, we will face a much more difficult fight." Theron glanced around as if he was making sure everyone understood how important it was, Jean thought. "Any questions?" he asked, raising his eyebrows. "Good, please fasten your seatbelts as we will be taking off shortly."

With his pep talk over Jean watched him start down the aisle, stopping every few rows to have a word with whoever was sitting there. *He knows how to work a room*, she thought. It was no wonder he ran Crete. *I wonder how long he has been in charge.*

She watched him, trying to convince herself that she only wanted to know where he was sitting, so she could stay away from him, but she couldn't seem to tear her eyes away. She expected him to take the first empty seat he came across, but when he reached it, his eyes met hers and softened before he continued down the aisle toward her.

"Is this seat taken?" he asked, reaching her.

Jean blinked. *Why did he have to sit with me?* "There are empty seats all over. Why do you want to sit with me?" She didn't move her legs to allow him to move past her and take the window seat.

"Please, I wanted to use the plane ride to talk about your role. I meant to speak with you before we left, but I ran out of time." He held his hands up in surrender.

Jean had wondered how she would be able to help. She hoped she would be with the team going after Katie. "Fine," she pulled her knees to the side and gave Theron enough room to walk around her to the window seat.

"Actually, can I have the aisle? In case I'm needed elsewhere."

"Seriously?" Jean rolled her head around her neck. "Then sit there." She pointed to the seat on the other side of the aisle.

"It's sensitive information. I need to sit next to you." He crossed his arms over his chest. "You're delaying our take off."

"Oh, my God." Jean undid her seat belt and slid over

to the window seat. "Why am I helping you?"

"Because you love Katie and you know we'll have a better chance of rescuing her together than we would apart." He sat down and buckled his seat belt.

"Whatever. Do you always get your way?" Jean crossed her arms over her chest and caught sight of Vince bending his head toward Maria again. She shook her head and let out a breath.

Theron followed her eyes and shrugged. "Yes, I do." He turned in his seat, so he could get a better look at her. "Don't worry about Vince, Katie has him wrapped around her finger. He is just trying to keep Maria happy. She's high maintenance. If she isn't the center of attention, she gets bored, and when she gets bored, she leaves, and we need her."

"Still, looks pretty bad," Jean said, staring, not caring if Vince caught her.

"Vampires rarely, and when I say rarely, I mean Vince is the only one I know, who only has one lover." Theron looked over at Maria then back at Jean. "It will seem normal to everyone else."

But it didn't matter what everyone else thought. If Katie saw it, she would rip Maria's head off. "Fine, what did you want to talk about?" The plane began to move into position for takeoff.

"I know you want to help, but I want you to do it from a safe distance." Theron clenched the armrests as they picked up speed down the runway.

"Why? I'm a trained. . ." she stopped. She had almost told an airplane full of mythical vampires that she was a trained Interpol agent. "I'm trained to fight."

173

"I know, but you're human, and we aren't fighting humans. You have no experience fighting vampires. Look what happened with Marios," he said, squeezing his eyes shut as the plane shook while they rocketed down the runway before smoothing out as they left the ground.

If he didn't watch it, Jean thought, he would tear the armrest off. She smirked when she realized he was afraid of flying. *The big strong vampire has a weakness.* Her smile faded quickly when sweat broke out on his forehead, he was terrified.

She leaned in close to his ear. "Are you all right?" she whispered as quietly as she could.

He whipped his head around and met her eyes. The cool confident vampire who had been working the room a few minutes before was now staring at her with fear in his eyes.

"Hey, it's OK. I'm right here. You're fine, we'll all be fine." She murmured and reluctantly—he was a vampire after all—offered him a hand to hold.

Theron glanced around then took it. "I've never been on a plane before."

"What?" She didn't know exactly how old Theron was but even if he was as old as he looked, it would've been strange that he had never flown. "Sorry," she whispered when a few heads turned their way. "You've got this. In a few minutes we'll level out and you won't notice that we are at twenty thousand feet."

"Just don't let go." He squeezed her hand a little tighter.

"I won't. Just breathe." Jean watched him close his eyes as his chest rose and fell. *That was why he wanted to sit with me. He didn't want to be alone, but he couldn't let anyone else see him freaking out. Boys and their egos*, she thought, shaking her head, and glancing out the window at the blackness surrounding them. She wondered why Theron had her come if it wasn't to fight. If it was only to keep an eye on her and make sure she didn't interfere, she was going to be pissed.

He was right though, she had no idea how to fight vampires, or how to kill them. *Stake through the heart? Decapitation? Would holy water burn them? What about a cross?* She thought the sun must burn them since they never went outside during the day but knowing that would only help her escape if she was trapped inside during the day. She had a lot to learn before she went out on her own.

The plane leveled out and Theron's death grip on her hand relaxed, but he didn't let go. "Are you up for talking now?" she asked in a hushed whisper.

Theron opened his eyes. "Yes, I think so." He ran his free hand through his hair and turned in his seat to get a better look at her. "Thank you. Can we keep this between us?"

She scrunched her lips together and moved them from side to side like she was debating on whether to tell everyone on the plane his secret. She pushed his shoulder back playfully when panic filled his eyes. "Yes, don't worry. I won't tell your friends."

"Good, thank you. I want you to oversee communications

and surveillance," he said, changing the subject. "As soon as we land, I want you to hack into Lolita's surveillance system and learn everything you can about what we are walking into and report back to me. During the mission I want you to be our eyes and ears. Communicate with the teams and keep an eye on the activity through the security cameras."

"That sounds like the best fit for me. I don't even know how you can be killed," she said, dropping her voice. "You don't have to tell me now, but will you tell me later?"

"Of course, but you are correct, now is not the best time to discuss it." Theron glanced around.

"Right, anyway you aren't giving me much time to hack her network. It's going to be tight." She looked at her watch then calculated how much time she would need versus how much time she had before they attacked.

"Miguel said he would email me everything he could about the system. I will forward it to you when we land."

"Good, let's just hope it's not a closed-circuit system." Jean looked out the window, debating on whether she should pick on him.

"Why?"

"Because, if it is, I can't hack into it remotely. I will need to be on the island or have a relay installed."

"That would ruin everything." He stared at the ceiling. "Let's hope it's not the case."

"No kidding. Hey, do you want to trade seats with me so you can look out the window?" She couldn't help herself.

Theron grimaced and squeezed her hand hard. She gasped in pain, forgetting that he was holding it. "No, I wouldn't want you to miss the view."

"It's dark out, and I can't see in the dark, but you can, right? Why waste a window seat on me?" She tried to pull her hand away, but he didn't let go.

Theron leaned in close and whispered "Why are you constantly challenging me? Do you want me to bite you?" He let go of her hand, reclined his seat, then closed his eyes.

Jean flexed her hand and tried not to shake. Why did she think poking the bear would be a good idea? She leaned back in her seat and scooted as far away from Theron as she could then watched him in case he decided to have a bite.

Chapter 24

Lolita

Lolita walked through her closet, trying to decide on a dress. The shower and fresh clothes were exactly what she needed after a trying week. Capturing Katie had not been as easy as she hoped. All the soldiers she took with her were dead, as were half the guards, but it could have been worse, and she had Katie. After almost a year of waiting, Katie was safely locked away in the dungeon, and Lolita had ended up with the strongest ally she could hope for. The losses hurt, but they had been worth it.

She had a problem though; they were out of the drug that kept Katie quiet and out of the heads of her weak-minded vampires. She cursed herself as she pulled a dress off a hanger and stepped into it. She should've found a few men with stronger minds and turned them, but how was she supposed to know that she would have to deal with someone with mind control?

She smoothed the black bandage dress down and found her favorite MB heels. How was she going to keep Katie under control? *Could she enslave her?* She went into her bedroom and sent her guards a text, she wanted to leave for the club in a half hour. She needed blood but wanted to save the fresh blood in her stable for the coming weeks in case things did not go to plan.

Miguel had enslaved Katie in San Sebastian, and not only had she broke the bond, the little bitch turned it around on him and dropped him like an anvil on Coyote's head in a cartoon. And it had been before Katie knew much about her gift.

Lolita would not put herself at risk and she didn't trust Miguel when it came to Katie. She drummed her fingernails on her leg. She didn't trust any of her guards. Katie would kill them without a thought. Who could she trust to enslave her? A smile slipped from her lips as the answer came to her and someone knocked on her door.

"Come," she said putting on a pair of diamond earrings.

"Katie is secure," Miguel said, sitting on the bed and watching her. "But I have bad news."

"What?" Lolita asked, glancing at his reflection in the mirror.

"The drug is on backorder. I don't know if or when we will be able to buy more."

"How? I thought it was still in testing?"

"One of the components, rocuronium, has become popular as a date rape drug, a squirt in a drink and most people forget who they are and what they are doing for hours. Does Katie remember?" Miguel asked, resting his right ankle on his left knee.

"I don't know, I didn't bother to ask. If she doesn't,

she must wonder where the pain from the beatings came from," Lolita smiled. Anything to make Katie suffer more was a good thing.

"What are we going to do if we can't keep her subdued?" Miguel asked, pulling his phone out and checking the screen.

"I have an idea that should keep her under our control."

"Was our intelligence true?" Miguel tapped a few buttons on his phone then put it back in his breast pocket.

"Yes, the bitch made Sam walk into the sun, then she made Christoph bring her food and water." She would never admit how close she came to being killed.

"What's your plan?" Miguel asked as his eye twitched.

Lolita opened the door of her spare closet. "You can come out now," she cooed. Her pet came bounding out like a puppy seeing grass for the first time and gave her a toothless smile before rubbing against her legs like a cat. Lolita shuttered. "Tonio, stop, you know better." She looked down her nose at the creature, ignoring her command to stop. She kicked him in the side, sending him sprawling across the room. "I said stop."

Tonio yelped in pain, then sat on his haunches as red tinged tears trailed down his pale olive cheek. "That's better. Now if you're a good boy I have a surprise for you."

His tears stopped and he smiled from ear to ear, eager as a boy at Christmas, waiting to see what Santa brought him.

"What does your pet have to do with Katie?" Miguel asked, and Lolita noticed how he could not bring himself to look at Tonio. She shook her head. Tonio was beautiful, and when she thought about how long it took for him to transform and train, she didn't understand how Miguel didn't see him for the beautiful creature he was.

"You will love this. Let's take Tonio to meet Katie." Lolita went to her desk in the corner of the room and took out a black leather leash encrusted in diamonds. "Tonio, do you want to go for a walk?" The creature jumped to his feet and ran to Lolita. She snapped the leash on and waited at the door. "Are you coming?" she asked Miguel, cocking an eyebrow at him.

"Of course." He slowly stood and opened the door for them.

"Good. Grab the keys on your way." Lolita went down the main staircase with Tonio a step behind her and Miguel two steps behind Tonio. She did not trust her brother. She saw the way he stared at Katie. He was going to hate what she had planned. It broke her heart, knowing he would never be able to let Katie go. She had hoped with time and distance he would forget whatever he saw in the human and see her for what she was, a threat to their kingdom and their future. Part of her wanted to lock him up to ensure he would not spoil the plan, but the other part of her thought he would hold it together, and he believed in her vision of the future. It would be a pity to kill him after all these years if he didn't.

"Tell me what happened while I was gone?" she asked, yanking on Tonio's leash when he stopped to smell something on the floor.

"It was largely uneventful. There has been no change with Mark. The blood was delivered on time. Everyone did their jobs and there were no complaints." Miguel opened the door leading to the dungeon and waited while Lolita and Antonio started down the stairs.

Lolita heard him take the keys from the hook as they descended into the bowels of the house. She wasn't sure which was worse, the smell of rotting blood and unwashed skin, or the screaming that never stopped. She shook her head. Mark really was a horrible choice for a vampire. It was too bad Miguel had chosen so poorly. She stopped midway down the stairs and looked back at Miguel.

"Get another bag of blood for your prodigy, maybe it will shut him up for a while." She pulled on Tonio's leash and continued, stopping when she reached Katie's cell. The girl was lying on her back, her eyes open wide. The drug was still working. Katie was too proper to leave her dress around her waist with her legs open wide showing everyone her junction. Lolita wished she had brought her phone; she would have loved to take a picture of this to show Katie later when she would be able to enjoy the embarrassment it would cause her. Miguel walked past her, taking the blood to Mark, and interrupting her thoughts. "Miguel, she can't see what's going on, set her up against the wall when you're done. I want her to meet Tonio."

Miguel fumbled with the keys after he gave the blood to Mark and the basement went blessedly silent except for the water dripping in the corner, then he opened the door to Katie's cell. "Lolita has a surprise for you my sweet," Miguel cooed, picking Katie up and positioning her to lean against the wall in the corner.

Lolita rolled her eyes. He was worse than a lovesick teen. "Katie, I brought someone for you to meet." Lolita stooped and stared into Katie's eyes. "This is my pet, Tonio," Lolita rubbed his bald head and he hummed in appreciation. "Do you remember him? He's the one who helped you escape San Sebastian. Go say hello to Katie, Tonio." Lolita unhooked his leash. "After all she's the reason why you ended up like this." Tonio ran to Katie on all fours and Lolita watched Katie's face for a reaction but there wasn't one. *Too bad she was drugged*, Lolita thought, she almost would have paid to see what Katie thought of the monster.

When Tonio reached Katie, he sniffed around her before his nose found the dried blood on her face from a bloody nose the guards had given her, then, unable to control himself, he straddled her and began licking it. Lolita frowned, Tonio really had no manners. She would never drink nose blood, who knew what else would be mixed with it. "You know why I had to do this to him don't you?" She put her hands on her hips. "He was the only one who knew where you were going when you left Spain. Miguel and I had an argument, and we went our separate ways for a time. I went after Antonio, Vince thought he could trust him to keep a secret, little did he know Miguel had stolen him months before. I thought he would be easy to find but whatever you did to him worked. He was doing everything he could to stay away from vampires. I still don't know if he knew where you went or not, but I enjoyed trying to get him to talk.

"First, I pulled out his fingernails, thank Goddess I had a gag, or his screams would have made me deaf. When he passed out from the pain, I let him rest. When he woke up, I started on his toenails. When he still wouldn't tell me, I got very angry and probably did something I shouldn't have." Lolita looked at his crotch. "But at least you won't have to worry about him raping you. Even after that though, he still wouldn't tell me where Vince hid you, so I pulled his teeth. I meant to put him out of his misery after that but then I had an idea. I always wanted a pet, but dogs and cats have such short lifespans, and since I had broken his mind and made him harmless, I decided to make him my pet. Of course, since he didn't have any teeth before I turned him, he still doesn't have any, but it doesn't stop him from drinking blood." Lolita grabbed Tonio by his collar and yanked him off Katie's lap, noticing that most of the blood on her face had been licked clean. "You see he is like a well-trained dog now. Vampires best friend and he has been a very good boy lately. I think he deserves a reward."

She took his finger in her hand and brought it to her mouth. She bit down until she tasted blood and he squealed in pain. She pulled his finger out and watched the blood well to the surface then run down his finger. He whined again at the sight of the blood. She shushed him, then she dragged him over to Katie and stuck his bleeding finger into her mouth.

Katie didn't even flinch as her mouth slowly filled with blood. When Lolita was sure Katie had absorbed some of the blood, she pulled Tonio's finger out and ran a sharp fingernail down Katie's cheek, causing a thin band of blood to well up and Lolita backed away. "Enjoy your reward, Tonio." Lolita backed out of the cell as Tonio climbed into Katie's lap and began sucking on the cut. "Miguel, come, I'm hungry. Let's give these two some privacy."

Chapter 25

Katie

I had hit a new low and if I thought about what Antonio was doing to me too long, I would throw up and drown in my own vomit. If I ever had motivation to move, it was then. The creature who had once been a man, who helped me so much in Spain, was sitting on top of me, latched on to my cheek like a remora fish on a whale and all I could do was lie there and take it.

I didn't know how long I'd been staring at the ceiling listening to the vampire in the other cell moan for blood. When his moans became screams, I had heard footsteps. *Great, what was Lolita going to do to me now?* I had wondered. The footsteps stopped outside of my cell and I saw three sets of legs in my peripheral vision. I wanted to run for the door when I heard it open or at least turn my head to see who had joined me.

After Miguel had moved me against the wall, I wished I could unsee the creature next to Lolita. He was probably over six feet tall if he had been standing up straight, but he was bent at the waist like he had spent too many years carrying rocks on his back and could not straighten. He was bald and had big brown eyes that seemed too big for his face. He had no eyebrows or facial hair and his jaw wasn't symmetrical. He smiled when he saw me, and I understood his jaw. He had no teeth. His arms hung limply at his sides and there was something wrong with his fingers.

When Lolita told me what she'd done to him, I would have given anything to move, tie her up, and do to her what she had done to Antonio.

The poor man had the worst luck with vampires. First, he was Miguel's slave, then Vince stole him, only to have Miguel steal him back. We all had dicked him around. When he abducted me with orders to take me back to Miguel, I used Thrall for the first time and forced him to take me back to the airport and forget everything Vince and I had said. Then I told him to leave the city and stay away from vampires.

When Lolita forced Antonio's finger into my mouth, I tried to jerk away with everything I had but it was no good. When his blood began filling my mouth, I tried to spit it out, anything to stop her from forcing me to become Tonio's slave but as soon as the first drop of my blood touched his lips, I felt the bond form and with every drop he drank; it grew stronger. I would break it. I had broken the bond twice before, but each time I broke it, it became harder. And the more blood Antonio took, the stronger the bond would be, and I didn't know if I would have the strength to break it when I had my power back. I let my eyes become unfocused and pictured my brain and the weed growing there. I tried to keep the bond from taking root. I tried to burn it out like my mom had taught me, but it was like I had never had the power to start with. My magic was gone.

Lolita had given me one last smirk then left with Miguel on her heels looking over his shoulder. The sick fuck's eyes had glowed red like he would've given anything to trade places with Tonio. He didn't take his eyes off me until the wall broke his line of sight. As their footsteps faded away, the gravity of the situation came down on me, and I panicked. I needed to blink, to pass out, anything to get away from this thing sucking on my face in the dark.

Something fell to the ground with a clink, it was metal and almost sounded like keys. "What was that?" I heard Lolita ask as the footsteps stopped.

"What?" Miguel asked.

"Did you drop something on the floor?"

"No, I don't think so, but I think I heard Mark pulling on his chains."

What was Miguel up to? I wondered. *Did he say Mark?*

"Yes, that was probably it," Lolita said, and their steps faded away until, with the click of the door, they disappeared.

I had tried to shake Antonio off me, I wanted to see where Miguel dropped the keys, but I couldn't move. *Blink, damn it! Was Vince right? Was Miguel on our side?*

I lost track of time after that. I had nothing to do but listen to Antonio suck on my face and moan in pleasure. I thought I had felt dirty after Miguel raped me, but this humiliation was a million times worse. I tried not to cry, I needed to save every drop of moisture my body had. The drug would wear off eventually and then I would get out of there. At some point Antonio stopped sucking and began licking me again and my humiliation was renewed.

"Please, I need another bag of blood. She smells too good; I can't take it anymore." Whoever was in the cell down from me said.

I wanted to tell him to shut up but of course I couldn't move. His voice sounded familiar somehow, even though it was hoarse and broken from yelling.

"God, Katie, why do you have to smell so good? This is all your fault," he screamed, and I realized who it was: my piece of shit ex-boyfriend, Mark. I had seen him leave Lolita's club with Miguel and Lolita when I was tracking her in Crete. At the time I hadn't known if he was dead or if they were changing him. Guess I had my answer.

I wanted to tell him to get over himself, it wasn't my fault Lolita caught him. Whatever happened to Mark was his own fault. I had stopped caring about him long ago. I tried to tune him out as he yelled for more blood, but nothing worked. If I could only plug my ears.

I didn't know how much time had passed when he stopped screaming, but Tonio had finished licking my face clean, curled up in my lap, and fell asleep like a cat. I wanted to push him off me. He didn't weigh much but my legs were cramping. *Blink,* I thought, but there was still nothing. I kept trying to blink until a sound pulled my attention away. It sounded like metal being dragged across a stone floor.

"Yes," I heard Mark whisper, then heard chains rattling. Had Miguel really dropped the keys? Why hadn't he dropped them where I could reach them? What good was helping Mark escape going to do?

Damn I needed my voice, I needed to talk to Mark. The sound of a cell door creaking open filled me with hope as I tried to shove the sleeping creature off my lap, but nothing happened. I tried to call out to Mark as he stopped outside my cell.

If I would've passed him on the street, I wouldn't have recognized him. I couldn't tell what color his shirt was originally, but it was stained a dark rust color. His eyes looked hollow and his nostrils flared as he stared at me. His hair had grown out, probably too lazy to find a barber between binge drinking sessions. It was shaggy blond, but so stained and covered in dirt it looked brown. His black pants had both knees ripped out giving me a glimpse of pale knees covered in grime.

"Don't you have anything to say to me, Katie?" he asked, glancing at the keys in his hand.

Stop being an ass and let me out, I thought to him with all my might, but I wasn't getting through to him. I couldn't feel him.

"You're trapped with a vampire creature on your lap, and you have nothing to say to the man holding the keys to your freedom?" He shook his head as he flipped through the keys.

You bastard, I thought, *don't you think it's strange that I'm not begging you for help?*

He pushed a key into the lock and turned it till it clicked.

Move, I screamed to myself. This was my chance to escape. The cell was unlocked, and if I had control over my body, Mark would already be dead, and I would've been halfway to the door. Instead the sound of the cell door opening roused Antonio from his nap. Mark took a step inside, and Antonio scrambled off my lap and stood between us.

"You've got to be kidding me, dude," Mark said, laughing at Antonio. "Do you really think you can protect her from me?"

Blink, I thought, Antonio had nothing to fight Mark with and besides, Mark was going to save me, right? The last time I had seen him I wasn't very nice, and he was in the middle of bloodlust. What was I going to do? *At least if he killed me Lolita wouldn't get to do whatever she had planned.*

Mark leaped around Antonio and lunged toward me. I tried to jerk away but I still couldn't move, Antonio sprang into action though, sweeping Mark's legs out from under him and kicking him in the head when Mark went down.

"What the hell are you?" Mark yelled, scrambling to his feet.

Antonio howled and ran at him, punching and kicking him until he was out of the cell. Antonio slammed the door, reached through the bars, and took the keys out of the lock.

Give them to me, I thought as tears ran down my cheeks. I was so close to my death or my freedom I couldn't stop them from falling. Something had to give.

Antonio ignored me and threw them at Mark then stood guard in front of the door with his arms crossed over his chest.

"I like your new boyfriend." Mark laughed picked up the keys and started toward the stairs. "I hope you will be very happy together."

Shocked I watched my jailer and my savior stand guard until the door at the top of the stairs clicked closed. Antonio came back to me, sat down beside me, and pulled me into his arms. He petted my head and mumbled nonsense, trying to soothe me while I stared at nothing and added one more vampire to the list of people who needed to die.

Chapter 26

Vince

"Maria, please, I appreciate the offer but if I shared a room with you, I would exhaust myself before the battle," Vince said as they waited to disembark the plane. Vince had spent the entire trip ignoring Maria's advances while trying to keep her happy. She wanted Lolita to come to an end just as much as he did, but if she got bored, she would leave, and they needed her and her vampires if they were to win.

"You have truly changed, Vince, and I'm not sure it was for the better. All you seem to care about is rescuing your human and killing Lolita," she huffed. "Do you remember that night in Madrid when we dined on a group of high school students from America then spent the day locked in my bedroom?"

Vince looked at his feet as they shuffled toward the exit. He remembered the night very well, but even as he thought of it, he felt he was betraying Katie. "Yes, Maria, it was a long time ago." He finally made it to the exit and took a deep breath as he stepped out. The air was crisp, and fog hung in the air so dense he could not see the stars or more than a few feet in front of him.

"You are no fun," she pouted behind him.

"I like to have fun, Maria, but not while the queen, my lover, is being held captive. Who knows what Lolita is doing to her?" Vince descended the stairs, wishing for solitude. "Welcome to Venice, Vinny." He scratched the dog behind the ears. *Vinny is the only company I want*, Vince thought. *He never has anything to say.* Vince followed Theron to their water taxi. The others were friends, but they were quickly becoming the most annoying vampires he had ever known. He did not wish to talk to anyone unless it was about Katie.

"Sit, Vinny," he said, after boarding and finding a seat near the bow. Vinny jumped into the seat next to him and laid his head on Vince's lap. Vince ran his hand absently through the dog's fur and stared out the window into the fog. *Katie, I am here. Do not give up. We are coming for you;* he sent the thought out into the night, hoping it would find its way to her. He should be going after her, not sitting on a boat going to a house to wait some more. He ran a hand through his hair as he felt the boat dip and he resisted the urge to see who joined them.

"Hey," Jean said eyeing the empty seat next to Vinny. "Can I sit there?"

Vince closed his eyes. She would be better than Maria or Livius. "Yes, but…" he trailed off. Vince thought Theron was making his move on the plane and figured Jean would sit with him and share his bed for a while.

"But what?" Jean asked, sitting down and petting

Vinny.

"I thought you would sit with Theron."

Jean laughed and looked over her shoulder then down at Vinny. "After that flight I'm ready for some alone time. Besides it feels weird being here and not going after Katie."

"I agree, I wish we could attack now." The boat dipped again and, glancing over his shoulder, he saw Maria huff when she saw Jean sitting next to him. He let out a sigh of relief, at least he had a break from her.

"Do you think she's all right?" Jean met his eyes and her expression tightened at seeing the worry in his eyes.

"Yes, she has to be. If I think she is anything but OK, I will go to her now and ruin everything."

"Good point. She's Katie, the toughest, most badass woman I know. She's fine, she knows how to handle herself," Jean said before they both lapsed into silence, and the boat pulled away from the dock.

Jean was right, Katie was the most badass human woman he had ever known. She wouldn't give up, no matter what Lolita did to her. Katie would bide her time and wait until an opportunity arose, but if Miguel was correct about the drug, she would be helpless and could not escape if the opportunity came. She needed them to rescue her. He clenched his fist. Waiting was the hardest thing in the world, but it was all he could do.

The boat slowed down, pulling Vince from his thoughts. Vinny sat up and looked around. The house they arrived at resembled the rest of the houses on the block, and Vince hoped they had heavy curtains, otherwise they would spend the day avoiding the windows.

"Welcome everyone," Theron said, standing up and grabbing onto a truss in the ceiling and holding on to it to keep his balance. "The final conference call is scheduled for seventeen hundred hours. Until then, do as you please, but please don't leave the house. As we've discussed, being discovered now would make this fight infinitely harder."

The taxi driver tied the boat to the dock while Vince and Vinny prepared to disembark. Vince grabbed the two suitcases he brought with him, one for him and one for Katie, and left the boat to go inside, happy to be the last one in. The foyer was empty and by the noise coming from above him everyone had gone up to pick their rooms.

He walked around the first floor, looking for a place away from everyone, there was a living room filled with modern furniture, a dining room, kitchen, and den. Vince put his hands on his hips, he was hoping to find a bedroom on this floor.

Vinny went to a door he had not inspected yet and scratched it. Vince opened it and let the dog into the courtyard. It was filled with roses and vines and had a fountain in the middle. Under different circumstances it would be beautiful. Vinny ran around lifting his leg on the bushes while Vince dreaded the thought of finding a room on the next floor.

Vinny trotted back to Vince, and they paced around

the first floor while Vince tried to convince himself to go upstairs. *The house is old and at one point it probably had servants' quarters,* he thought. He went back to the kitchen, remembering two doors he had not checked. The first door led to a pantry. There were shelves on each side, but it was long and narrow. *It will work if I cannot find anything else.* He shut the door and opened the next one.

It was perfect. The walls were bare, and there were no windows. A single bed was shoved into a corner, covered with white bedding. There was a small desk in the opposite corner with a stool under it. Vince rolled the suitcases into the corner, closed the door, and lay on the bed. Vinny whined from the floor and Vince snapped his fingers.

Vinny jumped to his side and lay down next to him. "Don't worry we will save her in a little while," Vince murmured to the dog as he closed his eyes and willed himself to relax. He needed to be at his best for the battle.

"How could you let this happen?" Asteria yelled as a whip came down on Vince's back. He didn't know where he was, it was black, so black he couldn't tell if his eyes were open or closed. His arms were above his head and he tried to lower them but found them chained. The whip cut into his back again and he winced. "Answer me."

"You are right, Goddess; she was in battle with Lolita and I was fighting one of Lolita's vampires. I should have never left Katie's side." The whip came down again, and he breathed through the pain. Pain he deserved for letting Katie take on Lolita in the first place.

"Do you know what they are doing to her? Do you have any idea the pain and suffering she has endured because you failed to protect her?" The whip came down again.

"No, Goddess, I can't imagine what Lolita has done to her."

"What are you doing about it?" She materialized in front of him, holding a long bull whip in one hand.

"We will rescue her tomorrow night." Vince knew better than to ask her any questions. She would only answer him with the whip.

"Lolita plans to kill her, Vince," Asteria whispered, looking at her feet. "My only human daughter will die by the hand of my creation. The consequences will not only affect you but the entire world. This was not how I wanted things to go, but I cannot fail."

"She will not die," Vince yelled, yanking on his restraints. "I will not allow her to die, and if she dies, then I do as well."

"I wish I could believe you, Vince." Asteria met his eyes and cocked her head. "But I cannot risk losing her again."

"You will not lose her." Vince hung his head in shame. "But do what you will to me. I deserve no better. It is my fault they took her."

She gave him a sad smile then moved behind him. He prepared himself to feel the whip on his back, but the pain never came. "You and her protector have done all you can. I have to ensure my victory now."

Vince was about to ask who Katie's protector was and how she would ensure victory, when a pounding on the door jerked him awake. Pain pulled at his back as he sat up from where the whip had struck, and he was half tempted to check a mirror to see if the pain was imagined or real, but the pounding resumed, pulling him from his thoughts.

Chapter 27

Miguel

Miguel studied his sister from the corner of his eye as the boat bounced over the choppy water on their way to the club to celebrate capturing Katie.

Lolita didn't seem to think anything was wrong which made Miguel relax a hair, but if Mark did what Miguel hoped he would, everything would change.

When they went down to the dungeon, Miguel had made a point of grabbing the keys off the hook so Lolita would know they were where they were supposed to be. Everything had been going to plan until he dropped the spare set he'd had made, making more noise than Mark's screaming.

She won't be able to blame me, he thought, wrapping his hand around the other set to ensure they were still there. *It will be fine. She can't blame me if I have the keys, right?*

What if Mark used them to access Katie's cell? The thought crossed his mind. *Why did I copy all the keys? The poor girl is still drugged up and can't defend herself. Tonio is with her, but he is the weakest vampire I have ever seen. He doesn't have a chance against Mark. What if Mark sucked her dry? Tonio had no teeth and Lolita starved him before she changed him. All his muscles had atrophied, and he can barely walk. Asteria please keep your daughter safe.*

He hated the way he had to act around Katie, the moment he saw her he wanted to drop to his knees and beg her for forgiveness, then take her in his arms and run back to Spain, or anywhere that was away from his sister. Instead he had to be the asshole who still lusted for her and, now that he had her, he had to make his sister think he only cared about Katie's gifts and what they could do to help Lolita's cause.

After they arrived at the club Lolita led him to the main floor instead of going straight to the VIP section. "What are we doing?" Miguel asked as they moved between the people waiting at the bar and standing at tables. Lolita never spent time in the main section, she always sent one of her guards to select her meal.

"We are celebrating little brother. I wanted to pick my own meal tonight. We are on the eve of a new world," she said, stopping to scope out the crowd.

Miguel tried to look excited, but the thought of going to war with Europe terrified him. He didn't think Lolita understood how easily the countries of Europe could kill them all. "Of course, let's celebrate." He gave her a smile then looked over the crowd.

"Good, now go find yourself a meal and meet me in the VIP section. We aren't sharing tonight."

"Thank you, sister." He didn't want to share either.

He watched Lolita stare at a woman on the dance floor. She moved slowly to the beat of the music, caressing her body with closed eyes as if her hands were the hands of a lover. Her long blonde, curly hair fell halfway down her back like a waterfall and her shirt rode up, showing the world a diamond stud in her belly button. She was Lolita's type and as he watched, Lolita went behind the woman, put her hands on her hips and whispered in her ear. The woman leaned back and ground her hips into Lolita's.

Miguel rolled his eyes. He hated watching Lolita pick up women. He turned and took in the rest of the patrons. There were lots of men and women in attendance, but none of them looked very appetizing until he saw a woman sitting at the end of the bar. She had long black hair and an hourglass figure. She was sitting by herself with a half-empty glass of wine in front of her. Most women alone in a bar would have been staring at their phone, but this one wasn't. She was watching people. He smiled to himself, she actually looked interesting.

Miguel moved to the empty stool beside her. "Is this seat taken?"

She looked him up and down before speaking. "No, help yourself."

Miguel took the stool, ordered a glass of wine, then watched the woman in the mirror behind the bar while he waited for his drink. He was intrigued and the last woman who had intrigued him had been Katie. He opened his mouth to speak but closed it, unsure of what to say. He felt like a teenager trying to find the courage to talk to his crush. He used to be good at picking up women, but that was before Katie.

"Are you waiting for someone?" he finally asked, turning on his stool to face her.

"No just enjoying an evening out." The woman bit her bottom lip and fluttered her black eyelashes at him.

"Do you live nearby?" Miguel could not get over how this woman made him feel. Like maybe he would survive without having Katie as his lover, maybe he could be happy after all.

"No, I'm here on business. I return to Rome tomorrow. I'm Terrassa." She offered him her hand.

He took it, brought it to his lips, and kissed it before letting it go. "It's a pleasure to meet you," he said, savoring the sweet taste of her skin, imagining it was what honey would taste like. It took all his control to let go. "I'm Miguel."

"Do you live in the city, Miguel?"

"For the moment, but I will return to my birthplace soon."

"Where is that?"

"San Sabastian, Spain. Have you been there?"

"You're kidding?" Her eyes went wide. "My next job is there. I leave next week, and I'll be there for a month."

"Then you must call me, and I will take you to dinner." He wasn't sure what it was about her, but he wanted to spend time with her, get to know her.

"Miguel," Lolita called, stepping beside him with

the woman she had been dancing with hanging on her arm. "Are you ready to go to our table?"

Terrassa clutched her purse like she was ready to leave. "Wait," he grabbed her hand keeping her on the stool. "This is my sister Lolita. Lolita this is Terrassa."

"Nice to meet you." She gave Lolita a shy smile. "I thought…"

Lolita looked her up and down then rolled her eyes. "Come have a drink with us in the VIP section." Lolita turned and pulled her *date* behind her through the crowd without waiting for an answer.

Terrassa checked her watch like she was debating on whether or not she should go with him. "Please," Miguel said pulling a card out of his pocket. "I would love to talk somewhere with fewer people around, here is my card. It has my phone number and address, so you can look me up while you're in Spain."

"OK, one drink." She grinned and took his hand allowing him to lead her to the VIP section. "I've never been in a VIP section before."

Miguel's mouth watered when he thought about how good this woman's blood would taste on his tongue, but something was bugging him. He wanted to see her again, he hadn't been lying, but would taking her mind and making her forget about what he was about to do to her taint their future?

He stopped and pulled her against the wall. "I want to see you again."

She raised her eyebrows. "OK, I promise I'll call you when

I arrive in Spain."

"Thank you. I'm sorry but I'm going to need you to forget about everything that's about to happen," he said using Thrall

"OK," her voice sounded faraway, and Miguel cursed himself. The first woman he was slightly interested in since Katie and he had to fuck with her mind to slake his thirst.

He pulled her through the crowd, thinking about how hungry he was but if he had his way, he would take Terrassa home, seduce her, and drink from her while making love. Not in a booth with his sister looking on.

When they reached the table, Lolita was kissing her date while the waiter stood by staring at the floor. "Go ahead," Miguel said to Terrassa holding his arm out toward the booth. Her face had gone red after witnessing Lolita caress her date's breast. "What would you like to drink?" Miguel asked, sitting next to Terrassa, and snapping his fingers to get the waiters attention.

"Pinot?" she answered, but it came out as a question.

"Make it two." Miguel nodded to the waiter, and he began to back away from the table when Lolita stopped him.

"Be a dear and lower the curtain, would you?" she asked, before resuming her primal make-out session.

"What's going on?" Terrassa asked as Lolita's hands disappeared under the table.

"Just a little privacy," Miguel whispered in her ear before kissing his way down her neck.

"What are you doing?" she tried to push him away, but he stopped her.

"You're fine, you like me. You like the way I kiss," he said thankful that Thrall worked so well.

"I do," Terrassa said, melting into his arms as he resumed kissing her neck. Her skin tasted so good he could hardly wait to taste her blood. He found the spot he liked, at the junction of her shoulder and neck, then bit down. Blood flooded his mouth, and it reminded him of the first time he had drank blood. Somehow it was even better than the sweetness of her skin. He wanted to describe it as a bottle of wine: full bodied with hints of honey, walnuts, and chocolate. He didn't think he would ever get enough. He found his hand moving over her breast then between her thighs as she moaned for more. He rubbed her on the outside of her panties as he drank, imagining what it would feel like to be balls deep in her while drinking her blood. His cock stiffened at the thought. He brought her to a climax then reluctantly pulled away from her neck as she came down from her high. He tried to push everything about her from his mind to make his cock go flaccid before he did something stupid.

He looked across the table, Lolita was still drinking, and he hoped she wouldn't take it too far. The last thing he wanted to do was get rid of a body because Lolita couldn't control herself. She pulled away a few minutes later, licking her lips and Miguel relaxed. Lolita snapped her fingers and the privacy curtain lifted.

"Here are your drinks, ladies," Lolita said as the waiter stepped forward with a tray full of glasses. "That was amazing." Lolita leaned back in the booth and played with the blonde's hair as they made goo-goo eyes at each other.

"I agree, you're amazing," the blonde leaned in to kiss Lolita but was pushed away.

"How was she, Miguel?" Lolita asked, ignoring her date now that her desire had been satiated.

"More enjoyable than I thought possible." It had been a long time since he had tasted someone so sweet.

"I can't remember the last time I came that hard," Terrassa whispered in his ear. He smiled and patted her leg.

"It's good to know you can still please a woman." Lolita laughed then looked at her watch. "Would you look at the time? The bar will close soon."

"It's time to go, Terrassa," Miguel said, again using Thrall. "Remember what I said earlier."

"Leave," Lolita said to her date as Miguel rose from his seat and helped them both out of the booth.

"Until we meet again." Miguel kissed Terrassa lightly on the lips before she turned to leave.

"Now that the celebration is over it's time to get back to business," Lolita said, pulling a flask from her purse and adding a few drops of blood to each of their wine glasses.

"What is the next step in your plan, now that we have Katie?" Miguel asked, taking a sip of his wine.

"I wasn't sure until I had time to think about it. With

her ability to control us, I only see one way to handle her." Lolita swirled her glass of wine watching the liquid create a whirlpool as if all the secrets in the universe would bubble out of the center.

"How is that?" Katie had enough power to rule the world if she wanted to. He shook his head. She would never do it though. She didn't want power, but if Lolita figured out how to control her, it would be another matter.

"You're thinking about the possibilities too." She took a sip of her wine. "It's too late for us. She won't bend to our will like I had planned in San Sebastian. Vince and the others poisoned us to her."

Miguel nodded. He agreed. Katie would never come around to Lolita's way of thinking, but it wasn't Vince's fault it was theirs. They mistreated her badly, and now they would pay the price for it. "What's the solution?"

"I will absorb her powers." Lolita drained her glass.

"How?" It took everything Miguel had to stay calm, he would not allow his sister to kill Katie, he didn't care if he blew his cover, he would not allow it to happen.

"By drinking her blood of course. If I do it on Facebook and what do you call it? Post a live feed? After I'm done, I will announce that I'm the head of the European Vampires and we will begin the takeover."

"What if you don't gain her powers? I didn't gain any of her powers when I drank her blood in Spain."

"It won't matter, everyone will think I have them, and everyone who followed Katie will know she is dead. If they don't do as I say, I will threaten to kill them by forcing them to walk into the sun."

This was a nightmare. There were so many things wrong with her plan, but he knew better than to try to talk her out of it. He needed to call Vince. They needed to rescue Katie as soon as possible. Miguel couldn't do it on his own, but if Vince didn't make it in time, he needed to have a plan to save her. "So, it begins. When are you planning to do this?" he asked, playing his part.

"Tomorrow night. As long as Tonio can keep her from causing any more trouble." Lolita's phone vibrated from her purse. She pulled it out and clicked the answer button. "This had better be important."

"Madame, I don't know what happened, but the vampire in the dungeon escaped, he drank all the blood in the refrigerator and now we can't find him," Miguel heard Christoph say.

Miguel forced himself to stay calm and look concerned. He had almost forgotten about the keys to the dungeon and Mark.

"What about Katie?" she asked, and her frightened eyes met Miguel's for a moment. "How did he escape?" She looked at Miguel with raised eyebrows.

"Katie is still in her cell with Tonio. I don't know how he escaped, his chains are on the floor, the door to his cell is wide open and the keys are missing."

Miguel tried not to let the relief he felt show on his

face. Thank the Goddess, Mark had left Katie alone.

Lolita narrowed her eyes. Miguel was so fucked; she would kill him. "Very well, we will leave shortly." Lolita ended the call and got to her feet. "Let's go, Miguel."

Miguel followed Lolita to the boat with the guards flanking them. He put his hand in his pocket and grasped the keys like they were his only chance for survival.

"Are you sure you didn't drop the keys before we left the dungeon?" Lolita asked as she boarded the boat.

"Yes, I thought I put them back on the hook, but wait, here they are." He held the keys out for Lolita.

She snatched them from him and inspected each one. "I wonder how he escaped then," Lolita asked as their boat picked up speed and headed back to the island and Miguel let out a sigh of relief. She believed him.

Chapter 28

Katie

It felt like it had been hours since Mark left. The bastard was going down, assuming I wasn't paralyzed. Had they double dosed me? It seemed like this round was lasting longer than the others. Hadn't Lolita said it would last eight hours? A lot could happen in that time, and I needed the use of my body and my powers.

I wondered what Vince and everyone else was doing. I prayed they were on their way to rescue me because I wasn't getting out of this on my own. I was so weak; my stomach was cramping from dehydration and starvation. Even if I was able to command my body and take the minds of vampires, I didn't know what to do with them. What could I make them do? Now that I had time to think, I wondered why Lolita made Antonio enslave me. Was she hoping he could control me with the slave bond? Or was it out of spite, just to show me who was in charge? Maybe it was only to show me the horrors she was capable of.

As I looked down at the mangled creature in my lap, I knew I wouldn't be able to endure the same torture. I would end myself before then. *Vince, please hurry.*

I blinked and turned my head to look up and down the hall.

What am I going to do? Wait, did I just turn my head? I blinked and turned my head again, then I flexed my feet. *I could move*, a sob escaped me, disturbing Tonio's sleep. I stilled, not wanting to wake him. *Thank Goddess, it's finally wearing off.* I closed my eyes as tears filled them, making them burn with relief.

I opened my vampire sense wanting to know how many were on the island. I jerked, smacking my head against the stone wall at the bombardment of so many thoughts and so many emotions flooding me, there were hundreds. I brought my hand up and rubbed the sore spot but smiled. I could move! And I had my powers back!

I was so thirsty, my mouth tasted like I had eaten a mouthful of sand where an animal had died and rotted in hundred-degree heat, but I could fight now. Antonio stirred on my lap, reminding me of what I needed to do first: get rid of the slave bond.

I closed my eyes and found it growing like a weed in my brain. It had been a long time since I had to pull one out, but I hadn't forgotten how much it would hurt, but it was only pain. I couldn't remember what not being in pain felt like. What was a little more?

I tugged on the weed, slowly dislodging it from my brain, it felt like someone drove an icepick through my head with each strand I removed. There were so many of them it didn't seem right. We had only exchanged blood once, how did it get so big so fast? I pushed the thought away; it wasn't important. My head pounded like someone was using a jackhammer from the inside trying to break through my skull to escape but I didn't give up. I pulled the last strand out and I held the weed-like bond in my minds hand. I touched a spark to it and it exploded as pain blasted through my head, becoming worse with every beat of my heart until everything faded to black and darkness claimed me.

"Katie, you are alive," Mom said from the dais of her temple.

"Mom?" I asked, staggering. *She doesn't look happy to see me*, I thought, trying not to fall over with exhaustion and pain. Destroying the bond had weakened me even further. I slumped to the ground but never reached the floor as Mom caught me before I met it. "Mom, I'm sorry. When they drug me, I can't do anything. I'm so weak, I don't have the strength to fight." I closed my eyes and let her rock the top half of my body.

"Fight, daughter," she said, pulling away from me as I struggled to stay sitting up.

"I have nothing left. Removing the slave bond from Lolita's creature took everything I had." I could feel it in my bones. I wanted to sleep, and I didn't care if I ever woke up.

"Do you know what will happen if you give up?" Mom put a hand on my shoulder and shook me. I opened my eyes halfway. Didn't she understand how tired I was?

"Vince and Theron will save me. Then, when I'm better, I'll finish it." I said as the room began to spin.

"Look, daughter," she said, leaning forward and resting her forehead against mine. "This is what will happen if you don't find the strength to fight."

I closed my eyes, wishing the world would stop spinning. When I opened them, I was flying above a city on a starlit night with a full moon above me. I blinked, trying to figure out what I was seeing. It was Venice, with the canals and buildings seeming to grow out of the water, but something was wrong. There was smoke everywhere and I could hear the faint sound of people screaming. Something squeezed my hand startling me and I looked to my right, Mom was next to me and I relaxed.

"What is going on?" I asked, looking back down at the city where people were running down the sidewalks as if they were trying to outrun a monster, pushing others into the canal to escape whatever was chasing them.

"I will show you." We lost altitude until we were flying twenty feet above the water, speeding down a canal while people ran in the opposite direction. They were terrified, and I didn't understand why until we came to a large square with a towering cathedral overlooking it. On top of the steps Lolita stood, speaking into a microphone while her army of vampires stood ready to charge a line of police dressed in riot gear.

"Vampires have sat back and watched the human race destroy the planet, afraid of making ourselves known because our numbers were too few, but it is time for humans to pay for their sins against Mother Earth and the vampires they hunted and killed out of ignorance. We are the apex predator on earth, and it is time for us to take our place as the rulers of the world."

As she spoke, the vampires charged the line of police, slaughtering them, drinking the blood that ran from their throats like a river, bathing in the crimson fountain that flowed as they decimated the humans, bullets and batons doing nothing to slow the vampires down.

"But the humans will stop them," I said as we gained altitude and left the city.

"Not until it is too late, and Venice will not be the only city under attack."

One minute we were flying away from Venice and the next we were in Rome, with Vatican City looming in front of us. When we reached Saint Peter's Square the same scene as in Venice was playing out, only with a different vampire speaking instead of Lolita. Then we were in Paris and we found the same.

"You can't allow this to happen, Mom. Do something." I turned to look at my mother, the Goddess, the Titan, surely there was something she could do to stop this.

"It's not how I wanted things to end, but if you give up, I have no other choice." She let go of my hand and I realized we were back in her temple on Delos.

"But what about Vince, Theron, and Helen? They will stop this from happening." I followed her toward the dais, she stopped and turned to me, placing her hand on my temple.

"Watch." I closed my eyes, and the darkness morphed into Lolita's island. Vince and Theron were fighting the army trying to rescue me. They were covered in blood with cuts on their faces and down their arms. They stood back to back, each holding a katana. They blocked and parried but with each soldier they killed, two more took their place. It was a battle they couldn't win. Before long I couldn't see my saviors, only the soldiers surrounding them. Twin cries rose up from the middle and I felt their spirits leave me. I cried out, falling to my knees as tears sprung into my eyes. "Noooooo," I yelled into the night. I turned to Mom. "No, this cannot happen."

"Then you must fight, Katie, you can't give up. If you do, everything you've been trying to stop from happening will happen, this is my prophecy." Mom put her hands on my shoulders and shook me. "Only you can stop this. Find the will to fight."

"How?" I asked, feeling hollow inside. I was alone, surrounded by the enemy with no food, no water, no energy. I needed something to give me the strength to go on.

"Help will come from an unexpected direction, do not throw it away." She pushed me hard, and I fell backwards but instead of landing hard on my back, I just kept falling. My arms and legs flailed as I tried to slow my descent, but I never seemed to reach the ground.

Chapter 29

Lolita

Lolita rode back to the island in silence; nothing anyone could say would help the situation unless the guards caught Mark and threw him back in his cell before she arrived. Allowing Miguel to change him had been a mistake. How could Miguel think he would be a good candidate? He had none of the qualities she looked for when selecting someone to change. She shook her head, there was nothing she could do about it now, the deed was done, but who had let him out was another question entirely and where were the guards when it happened?

Had Katie discovered who was screaming for her blood? Maybe she helped him, but how? Even if the drug wore off, and she took him over there wasn't anything in the cell he could have used to pick the lock. And if she did, why didn't she free herself? Katie might have magic, but Lolita doubted it would give her the power to magically unlock manacles and the locks on the cell door. Again, why wouldn't she free herself? Tonio might have been able to stop her, but only if the slave bond stopped her magic from working on him. She shook her head. She had to get to the bottom of this, there was a traitor among them. She had to find whoever it was and get rid of them before they ruined her plans.

She looked at Miguel from the corner of her eye. She had heard something fall on the ground as they were leaving the dungeon and when Christoph told her the keys were missing she'd been ready to tear Miguel's heart out; she didn't care how many humans witnessed it, but then he had the keys in his pocket, and why would he drop the keys where Mark could reach them and not Katie? Why hadn't Mark killed Katie and Tonio? If he could get out of his cell, he should've been able to open Katie's.

I will have the answers I need soon enough. She leaped off the boat as they pulled up to the dock and sprinted to the house, leaving Miguel and the guards behind. It was out of character for her, but they had a vampire in full bloodlust on the loose, and she had to find him before he found a way off the island. She smelled the spilled blood a quarter mile from the house and wondered if it was because Mark had used the same path or if it was because she was downwind. She kept her eyes open for any sign of life as she approached the house. She needed this situation taken care of before the sun came up.

When she reached the clearing surrounding the house, she slowed to a walk, searching for clues. She circled the house. There had to be a clue to where he had gone. She was about to give up when she found a set of bloody footprints. She followed them through the backdoor and into the kitchen. Christoph was leaning against the counter and Louis was standing with his arms crossed. They were trying to keep themselves in check, but their eyes flashed red and their fangs distorted their profile, giving away how close they were to losing the battle against bloodlust. Lolita rolled her eyes and held her breath. *Didn't they know how to stay in control?*

The once white kitchen with stainless steel appliances looked like a red room of pain. Blood covered the floor, while streaks of white broke up the blood where either Mark or the guards had slipped in it. The walls and ceiling looked like they had been spray-painted red.

"What have you found?" Lolita barked, opening the refrigerator, and finding it empty. The idiot had wasted more blood than he drank. It was almost like he did it on purpose. Empty bags littered the floor, some were opened with fangs, others were ripped in half.

"After he finished here, he went upstairs and broke into your stable," Christoph said, not making eye contact as he spoke. "They are all dead, necks broken."

"Where were you when this happened?" Lolita whirled around, her spiked heel losing purchase on the slick blood covering the floor for a moment before she recovered and stared the vampire down.

"I was at my assigned station, Madame, in the guard shack outside the barracks. Everyone was in their assigned locations."

Lolita wanted to be impressed that he stood his ground, but she needed answers. "You're telling me that while you guys sat on your asses in the guard shack, Mark broke out, drank all the blood, killed everyone in my stable, and you heard nothing?"

"No Madame." He looked down at the floor for a second before finding the courage to meet her eyes. "We didn't know anything was wrong until the patrol came by your house as they do every two hours and noticed the back door open."

Lolita glanced at the ceiling, thinking, *Goddess save me from stupid people.* Her gaze found Miguel, and she wanted to blame him. "Why are you just standing around? Find someone to clean up this mess and take care of the bodies." She walked to the door of the dungeon. "The rest of you look for Mark. If he finds a way off the island and starts terrorizing the city, Geovanni will kick us out and we have nowhere else to go."

Leaving them to do her wishes, Lolita went to the dungeon. Katie had some explaining to do. She stopped at Mark's open cell door and inspected the lock then the manacles he had been chained with. Nothing was damaged. In fact, it looked like someone had unlocked the door, then him. There was no sign of foul play or evidence of who helped him escape. Frustrated, she spun on her heel, and went down the hall to Katie's cell. Katie looked the same as she had before they went to the club. The drug was lasting as long as it should for a change.

She looked at Tonio curled up in Katie's lap like a cat. Why didn't anyone else see Katie for who she was? Katie wanted to keep things the way they were for vampires: stay hidden from humans, continue to play by human rules, even though vampires were superior, and all to avoid a war. *The only way to live was to take what you wanted. Dominating and enslaving the humans was the next logical step in the world's history,* Lolita thought. *Why did so few of us see it?*

She unlocked Katie's cell door and pulled it open. Tonio sprung to his feet and ran to the corner, cowering like he would be in trouble for sleeping on the job. Katie on the other hand didn't move.

Grabbing Katie by the hair Lolita pulled her to her feet, trying to ignore the smell, she must have pissed and shit herself somewhere along the way. "Where did Mark go?" she asked, looking into Katie's glazed eyes, and getting no response. "Did you help him escape?" Lolita shook her, but she still didn't respond. Lolita dropped her back to the floor. "Tonio, my pet, let's get you to bed."

Tonio tiptoed to Lolita, then she locked the door and led him upstairs. He was acting like he did something wrong, but he had done what she asked, even if he fell asleep in the bitch's lap. Lolita almost hung the keys to the dungeon back on the hook but thought better of it and took them up to her room. Mark would be easily dealt with, but if Katie got away, everything would be ruined. Wheels were in motion that Lolita could not stop.

She put Tonio to bed in the closet then changed from her dress to her leather pants, corset, and ass kicking boots. Dressed in her hunting gear, she went to her computer and reviewed the security footage. She didn't have any cameras in the house, but

225

there were plenty on the grounds and mounted on the exterior of the buildings. She backed the feed up to when the guards found the door open. She noted the time, 00:30, then moved backward until she watched Mark run backwards from the woods to the house, she looked at the time. 22:30. Mark had two hours to run before they realized he was free. She looked at her watch, it was now 01:30, three hours before anyone started looking for him. *At least we are on an island.* Lolita picked up her phone and sent a text out to Miguel and Christoph.

Check all the boats on the property, I want a guard on them until we find him.

Lolita left the house to begin her own search. Mark had not bathed in months and was covered in blood, so she should be able to find him easily by smell alone. It would be such a waste to kill him, but what choice did she have? He wasn't going to get over his bloodlust as quickly as she needed him to. She had seen it happen before and killing the young ones always made her heart hurt. At least she hadn't given up any of herself on him. It was all Miguel.

She followed the trail, by the smell until it ended at a small pond. *Mark wasn't as dumb as he looked and having his fill of blood had probably sharpened his mind.* She walked around the water looking for anything that might tell her where he went after his bath. She found what was left of his tattered, blood-stained clothes in a pile on the edge of the pond. They were so caked with blood the smell would never come out, so he left them behind. *Now he was naked too*, she thought, kicking the pile. Her phone vibrated in her pocket and she pulled it out, finding a message from Christoph.

The rowboat is missing.

Lolita cursed and checked the time. It was a half hour till dawn, and she wondered where the time had gone. There was no point searching anymore.

Meet me at the house, she sent back to him then headed home.

She spent the walk back to the house trying to find her calm. She couldn't afford to kill any of her men. She couldn't kill them for allowing Mark to escape, but she could make sure they were on the front line when the war began. By the time she reached the house she was back in control of herself. She met Miguel and Christoph in the kitchen which was now clean and smelled like bleach.

"I'm sorry Madame, I should have sent out a search party as soon as we found him gone." Louis stood at attention and Lolita mentally applauded his ownership of the situation, but it changed nothing.

"Too little too late. Get back to work. We will go live with our intentions shortly after sundown tonight. Then we will take Venice. Make the necessary arrangements."

"Yes Madame, but may I ask a question?"

"Please," Lolita said, watching Miguel stare out the window, he did not seem to have a care in the world.

"What are we going to feed the army?"

Lolita closed her eyes, *fuck,* she hadn't thought of that.

227

"None of us will eat until the war begins. It will make the first battle that much quicker. Now go."

His eyes went wide as she spoke, but he didn't question her before leaving to do her bidding.

She turned, went into the grand salon, and stopped at the fireplace to warm her hands. She wasn't ready to speak to Miguel, and the humid night had left her with a chill. He was making her angry by acting like nothing was wrong.

"What are we going to do about Mark?" He moved to stand beside her.

"He's your begotten, it's your problem." Lolita had enough to worry about with planning Katie's execution and the coming battle, plus she was tired of holding Miguel's hand when it came to Mark.

"You're the one who forced me to change him. I told you he would not make a good vampire," Miguel yelled and slapped his hand against his leg.

"Watch your tone, Miguel. I forced you to change him because you refused to add to our ranks. You did this to yourself. You figure it out." Lolita turned to face him, astonished he would raise his voice to her. He had not sounded this angry since they lost Katie in Spain.

"I'm done watching my tone with you, sister. I tried to get Katie back on my own. After I lost her, I came back to help you in your quest. I have gone along with your plans; I did as you asked and changed Mark, even after I explained to you that he wouldn't make a good vampire. Now, you will call Geovanni, and notify him about Mark. Have his people be on the lookout for him. We don't have a choice." Miguel put his hands on his hips and glowered down at her.

"You have a backbone after all, I thought you left it in Spain." Lolita purred then narrowed her eyes. He had been such a bore since he joined her. It was good to see the fire back in his eyes. "I will do this for you, but I expect you to make sure it never happens again. Next time I need you to change someone, do it." Lolita spun away from him and went to her room. Her trust in Miguel was waning and with Katie under the same roof she needed to ensure he would not run off with her. She typed a quick text to Christoph. It was time to put the house on lockdown.

Chapter 30

Jean

The boat ride to the house was one of the coldest and most miserable rides Jean had ever experienced. They were in a cabin but there was no heat and her light coat did nothing to keep the chill out. It didn't seem to bother anyone else, but they were vampires, the cold probably didn't affect them like it did her.

She squinted into the foggy darkness and wondered how their captain could see where they were going. Everyone was quiet. She wondered if it was because they were tired or if it was because they didn't want the local blood suckers to find out what they were.

When they arrived at the house Theron stepped onto the dock then helped Jean off. "Thanks," she said then went to the stern to get her messenger bag and suitcase. She was exhausted, but she wanted to corner Theron and get the IP address and network information for the island before she got a few hours of sleep. Unfortunately, the slut Maria was talking to him in rapid Spanish and Jean couldn't follow it. It was too cold to wait outside, so she went inside, and everyone followed her.

"The bedrooms are on the second and third floors, first come, first serve," Theron said from behind her as everyone but

Vince gathered around. "Tomorrow night will be a long one, I suggest you spend your time tonight and tomorrow wisely." He stepped around Jean, headed for the stairs.

"Theron, wait." Jean jogged to catch up with him.

"What is it Jean?" He glanced at her without stopping.

"I need the Wi-Fi password, and did you receive the information about the network yet?" she asked as they reached the second story, but Theron continued to the next floor.

"Jean, can you give me five minutes to settle in?" he snapped, running a hand through his hair when they reached the third floor. The stairs went up another flight, but Theron started down the hall. "Pick a room, and once I'm settled, I'll bring you up to speed." Theron stopped at the first door he came to and went inside without waiting for a reply.

"OK, yeah of course," Jean stopped. *What crawled up his butt and died?* Jean stood in the hallway staring at Theron's door like an idiot for a second. *Choose a room*, he had said. She didn't want the room right next to him, but she didn't want to be too far from him either. She hated admitting it, but she felt safe around him, especially in a house full of vampires.

She chose the room two doors down and across the hall. It was small with one small window overlooking the courtyard. There was a cross over the full-size bed and a painting of the Virgin Mary hung on the opposite wall above the dresser. The room was too small for a desk and Jean almost went to find a bigger room, but she heard footsteps coming down the hall and voices speaking Spanish. She couldn't make out who it was or what they were saying but she wanted to stay away from the unfamiliar vampires.

She put her suitcase on the floor and pulled her computer out of her bag. She sat on the bed with her back against the wall and booted it up. Jean looked at the nearest Wi-Fi networks then chose the one with the best signal to hack into. She had just gotten in when there was a knock at her door.

"Who is it?" Jean shut the lid and moved to get off the bed, cursing herself for forgetting to lock the door.

"Theron."

She relaxed. "Come on in." She opened the lid on the computer. *He'd better have the information I need.*

Theron came in and shut the door behind him before glancing around the small space. "The owners must be very pious."

"Yeah, all that's missing is a pew to kneel on." Jean laughed.

"No, they want you to kneel on the cold wood floor, a cushioned pew would not do at all." He laughed, and it amazed Jean how normal he could be. Theron sat at the foot of the bed and glanced at his phone.

"What?" Jean asked not liking his tone.

"I have the IP address for the island, but I have bad news." Theron handed his phone to Jean.

Theron here is the IP address for the network on

233

the island: 11.234.765. This is the best I can give you right now. She recently increased the security. I have no idea what the password is, and I don't know how much help it will be. The surveillance system is on a closed-circuit, Lolita had it hard wired in and the computer it is connected to isn't hooked up to the network.

I don't have the time or the knowledge to get what you need to access the footage remotely. I wish there was more I could do.

Miguel.

"Fuck. What are we going to do?" Jean asked, giving the phone back to Theron.

"Do we have a relay?" Theron put it in his pocket.

"No, hardly anyone uses closed-circuit systems anymore. I don't even know where to find one." *Shit, the whole reason for me to be here is gone.* She looked at the home screen on her computer. It so wasn't fair. She wanted to help rescue Katie. "What are we going to do?"

"I don't know. Going in blind is a huge risk but we don't have a choice." Theron stood and paced the five steps to the wall then back to the door.

Jean agreed it was dangerous. "Let me hack her network, maybe I'll find something."

"OK, but make sure you get some rest and don't get caught."

"I will." Jean stretched her fingers then moved them back and forth, she was excited to prove to Theron that she could still be of use. "Night."

"Good night." Theron left, hesitating in the doorway for a second but didn't turn around. Jean watched him shrug his shoulders and leave, closing the door behind him. She put her computer on the bed, got up, and locked the door. She didn't want to worry about someone interrupting her.

Two hours later she looked at the clock. It was late, and she still hadn't been able to access Lolita's network. She had tried everything to break in, but it was like there was a five-foot-thick, fifty-foot-high firewall around the network. *Maybe I shouldn't have sent her the virus when I took down Katie's hit.* She had to get in; there had to be a way for her to help. Sighing, she realized that she couldn't do it on her own. She clicked over to her email and stared at her list of contacts, they would all offer to help her, but who had better skills than her?

She paused at Tad's name. He had asked for her help, and she had completely forgotten about it with all the drama going on. He might be the only one who could help her. She pushed the video call button, forgetting about the late hour, and waited.

"Jean, is everything alright? Where have you been?" The flawless, pale skin of Tad's face filled the screen. Jean smiled. It felt like she had been among strangers for years and seeing Tad made her gut tighten with a pang of homesickness.

"I'm sorry to call so late, and that I waited so long before returning your email. Life has been a little crazy. What did you need?"

"Wait, first tell me what is going on with you and Katie." He leaned back in his chair and laced his fingers together.

She didn't know how much to tell him, but she would tell him everything if it meant he would help her. "Katie was kidnapped by Lolita two days ago. We are in Venice to rescue her, but I need help."

"Jean, you know better than to ask this of me. There is nothing I can do to help you from Kevó." Tad leaned forward, his voice becoming angry.

"We aren't doing this only to save Katie, if we don't stop Lolita there is going to be a war that will ravage Europe." Jean was losing him. How could she make him understand how much they needed his help without telling him about vampires?

"Again, you know we only handle cases that have been approved by the committee and since you are no longer part of Kevó you can't request help." He ran a hand through his hair.

Jean couldn't blame him; it was her fault they were almost found. What right did she have after what she had done to them? But then she thought of Katie and how none of the things that had happened to her were her fault. *I could tell him the truth,* he was an honest man, and he knew how to keep a secret. He probably wouldn't believe her, but what did she have to lose?

"Look, the people who have her aren't really people,

they're vampires and if we don't stop them, they're going to take over Europe. Their surveillance system is on a closed-circuit, but I was hoping I would be able to find something if I hacked their network. The problem is I keep running into a wall. I know it's hard to believe, but vampires are real, I found out a few days ago. There are good ones and bad ones. I'm working with the good ones to stop the bad ones. Please help me, Tad. The fate of Europe is on the line."

Jean held her breath as Tad went silent. She watched his face as she told him about the vampires, looking for any sign that he thought she was crazy, but he sat as still as a statue while she spoke. If Tad didn't change his mind, maybe she could sneak onto the island, find the password for the network, and find a way to wire the surveillance system to it. Theron would be pissed when he found out, but without eyes on Lolita's army, it would be insane to fight them. Jean stared at her monitor, waiting for Tad to reply, he probably thought she was having a mental breakdown. No sane person believed vampires were real. She shook her head, how was she going to tell Theron that she couldn't get in? She opened her mouth to tell Tad never mind then he began speaking.

"Send me what you have, and we will look at it. How soon do you need it?" He drummed his fingers on the desk.

Jean smiled, relieved. If Tad and the team in Kevó couldn't get in, then no one could, and Lolita could make trillions selling the program on the black market.

"Thank you, Tad. The attack begins at dusk. The more time I have in her system the better chance I have to find a way to

237

monitor the situation."

"Why didn't you contact me sooner? This is going to take time." He rolled his eyes.

"It couldn't be helped. I only received the information two hours ago."

"Very well, I will contact you when we are done."

"Thank you, Tad, you are really helping to save the world. What did you want to talk to me about?" she asked now that she had what she needed.

"Oh, nothing that can't wait. When this is over, call me, and we'll talk about it." His hand went to his keyboard and before Jean could ask him anymore, he ended the call.

She closed her laptop and climbed under the covers, relieved that she had help, but guilt swamped her when she thought about Katie, and she wondered where she was sleeping.

Jean regretted breathing through her nose the moment she inhaled. *Not* again, she thought, realizing she was back in the dungeon where she had dreamed of Katie the night before. She heard grunts coming from nearby but didn't know what was making the noise. She crept as quietly as she could down the hall to investigate, stopping when she found the source, and she stared.

A monster. She didn't know how else to describe it. It had two legs and arms, it was bald and dressed in a loincloth with a collar around its neck and was sitting on top of Katie. Jean yanked on the door to the cell. She had to help her friend, but it was locked. She made eye contact with Katie, but she looked at Jean with vacant eyes.

"Katie, what are you doing? Stop him. How can you just sit there and let him do that to you?" Jean yelled, trying to get their attention; anything to make the creature stop. They ignored her. "Oh God, Katie, I'm so sorry. We're coming for you, we'll save you. Tad is even helping. Just hold on." Jean ran down the hall. *There had to be a set of keys around.* If she could open the door to the cell, she could pull the monster off Katie and get them out of there.

She ran up a set of stairs ending at a closed door and pushed through it searching frantically for keys, but she was no longer in the dungeon. She was in her childhood bedroom. She turned to go back. She had to help Katie, but where a door had been was now a wall. She pushed on it, even kicked it, but all she found was a smooth wall.

Frustrated, she crossed her arms over her chest and glanced at the rainbow-painted walls and the stuffed unicorn her dad had brought her when he came home from a trip. The thought of seeing him again made her forget about Katie and run to the door. She pulled it open and skidded to a stop. Instead of the hallway lined with family photos and painted a light blue with thin industrial carpet, she was looking into the blackness of the universe. Galaxies swirled down in paths only they could follow, and stars shone bright around her. She tried to turn back to her room, but she hit a wall. She looked behind her and found her room was gone. She was floating in space. *I'm dreaming*, she finally realized.

"There's my unicorn," a deep voice she would recognize anywhere said from somewhere nearby.

"Dad?" She spun to face the man whose face looked so much like hers, with a sharp nose and bright blue eyes. "I miss you." She tried to run to him, but she wasn't moving fast enough. She kicked her feet then pushed her arms in front of her and pulled them back like she was swimming. Finally, she reached him and hugged him tight. There was something on his back though, sticking out. She looked over his shoulder and found black feathered wings. She pushed away. "Are you an angel?"

"It's not important right now." He flapped his wings, and they moved through space quicker than she thought possible as the stars and galaxies sped by. Everywhere she looked something made her gasp in awe at the beauty of the universe, but she shook her head. *Katie.*

"I need to go back to the dungeon; I have to help Katie." She glanced at her dad with pleading eyes.

"What's done is done. You can't change the past, but your actions will help shape the future of humanity." He made a sharp turn, flying toward a spiral galaxy.

"What do you mean?" Jean asked. He was always cryptic in her dreams, but this was worse than usual.

"Tomorrow's fight will determine not only your future, but the future of the human and vampire races. You have to do the right thing, Jean."

"I'm doing everything I can all ready. I can't fight

vampires. What is the right thing Dad?"

"Trust him, he won't lead you astray."

"Who are you talking about?" she asked suddenly feeling coldness at her back. She looked behind her, expecting to see her father but instead found herself alone. Without her dad and his wings to guide her she began to fall toward the spiral galaxy closest to her. She sped up with each second. *How can I be falling? Space doesn't have gravity*, she wondered as the stars and galaxies rushed past her. Then she was falling toward a blue dot that was growing larger as she came closer, it was Earth, she was falling to Earth. Her heart rate increased, if she didn't slow down, she would burn up entering the atmosphere. She closed her eyes and thought of her bed. She needed to wake herself up. She started to panic and the nothingness that had been rushing by her turned to wind, and the cold turned hot. Her whole body began to sweat as she moved closer and closer to the ground. *Wake up!* she screamed.

Chapter 31

Alex

Alex stepped out of the terminal at the airport in Venice and stretched. It had been a long night but worth it. After he had landed in Rome, he checked his bank balance and almost yelled in delight. Zeus had made good on his word and then some. Instead of giving Alex the hundred grand he asked for, his old man had given him five hundred grand. After Alex went through customs, he found a chair and stared at his phone. He thought about taking the money and disappearing, going back to the states, and settling in some no name town and never thinking of Crete or vampires again. But would he be safe? Would Zeus be able to reach him on the other side of the world? Would Lolita come to America looking for him? Would it be worth it to be looking over his shoulder for the rest of his life?

Decision made, Alex had dialed a number from memory and headed toward the exit. "What?" the man on the other end of the line answered.

"Are you ready to make some cash?" Alex asked, joining the line for a taxi.

"Alex? What the fuck?" Jared asked. "I thought you were

broke."

"I recently came into some money." He laughed as he got into a cab, nodding his thanks to the attendant. "Take me to the closest hotel," he said to the driver in broken Italian. "Call it an inheritance of sorts."

"What's the job?"

"I can't talk about it now. I'll call you in a few hours," Alex said, meeting the cab driver's eye in the rearview mirror. Alex didn't trust anyone.

"Fine, I will wait, but if you are dicking me around, I swear to God."

"I'm not, just let me get somewhere secure." Which was how Alex had found himself outside the airport in Venice late the next morning, looking for Jared.

"Good to see you," Alex said, offering Jared his hand when he found him waiting near a water taxi.

Jared took it. "Yeah, I better get paid this time."

"I already wired half the money to your account. You'll get the rest when we're done and there's nothing left of the island." Alex looked out the window at the gray sky. Nothing would get in his way this time. "Who else were you able to round up?"

"Todd *the bod* is waiting for us at the hotel and Randy arrives in an hour and a half." Jared glanced at his phone to check the time.

"Did you hack into the security system?" Alex asked while typing a text to the local arms dealer confirming their meeting.

"Yeah, but it wasn't easy I had to sneak onto the island and set up a relay, it's a closed-circuit system. I didn't think anyone used those anymore."

Alex looked up from his phone slack jawed. "You did what? Do you know how dangerous that was?"

"Relax man, I didn't see anyone, and no one saw me. Are you sure there's anyone on the island?" Jared laughed and tapped his phone screen.

"It's full of people but they only come out at night." Alex almost said they were vampires, but Jared wouldn't believe him. Telling Jared about vampires would make him question Alex's sanity, and he might change his mind about helping. His phone buzzed, and he read the message. The meeting to pick up the explosives was a go. All they needed to do was pick up the boat and meet the dealer at the coordinates in the message.

"This is a weird hit," Jared said, still tapping on the screen.

"I know, I just want to get it over with. Let's pick up Todd and the boat, then it will be time to pick up Randy. We will barely have enough time to meet with my arms guy, go over the plan one more time, and execute it before sundown." Alex looked at his watch; it was just past nine in the morning. He was glad he'd spent the night in Rome, he would need all his energy to make it through the day.

"I don't understand why we are doing this in the middle of the day. It seems like it would be easier to get caught."

Alex rolled his eyes. "Did you not hear me say that our

targets only come out at night? These are bad motherfuckers, so believe me when I say we want to do this during the day."

The cab pulled up to the hotel and Alex paid the captain while Jared took Alex's suitcase and got off the boat. Then they went up to the suite Alex had arranged the night before.

"Where's Todd?" Alex asked, putting his suitcase on the bed. They had just enough time to pick up the boat he'd reserved they needed to pick up Randy.

"Alex, the man with the money," Todd said getting up from the couch as Alex came back into the living room. "Sorry I was in the crapper when you came in."

Alex clasped his hand. "Good to see you. Are we ready to roll?"

"Yeah, and I have everything you asked for." He held up a gym bag and Alex nodded.

"Let's hit it then." Alex headed for the door.

"Hey, you guys might want to grab a coat, there's a big storm coming our way." Todd said, pushing his arms through the sleeves of his coat.

Alex shrugged. "I didn't bring one. I'll survive." As they left the suite Alex thought about how lucky he had been to find help at such short notice.

The day before, after he had checked into his hotel room in Rome and had taken a shower, he had called Jared back to go over the details of the hit.

"I take it the information I sent you was what you were after?" Jared had asked.

"Yeah, exactly what I needed," Alex said. "Now I need your help."

"Giving you the information was a freebie. Anything else will cost you. What's the job?"

"I need you to run surveillance for me and we need two guys to help. If they have explosive experience all the better. I lost everyone's contact information when my phone went for a swim in the Med." "How much?" Alex asked, knowing it would not be cheap.

"Twenty grand."

"No way, it will be easy, five." Alex hated negotiating and even though he could pay twenty, he couldn't let Jared walk all over him. They bickered over the price for the next ten minutes before they finally settle it.

"Fine, ten grand, half now and half when it's done."

"Fine, but if you don't come through this time, I'll make sure no one ever works with you again."

Alex had leaned back in the crappy hotel room chair and had taken a sip of the overpriced hotel mini bar whiskey. "Yeah, but at least I know you're paying attention. Here's the deal: first I need you in Venice ASAP. Then I need you to hack into the network on Poveglia, it's an island owned by our primary target."

"When were you planning to make this happen?" Jared had asked.

"Tomorrow. I arrive at eight thirty from Rome."

"That will be tough. You're lucky I'm on holiday in Florence. Let me see who else is around and interested. What about my half up front?"

"Send me your account information and I'll wire you the money. I need you to go shopping too, I'll send you a list of supplies to pick up too."

"It's really short notice if you need me to buy the C4," Jared said, sounding condescending.

"Not the C4, I already talked to my contact in Venice. I need some household stuff to make it neat."

"OK, let me see what I can do, and I'll get back with you." Jared ended the call, and Alex enjoyed the rest of his overpriced drink in silence then went to bed and slept like the dead for the first time in weeks.

"Randy," Alex called as the tall black man stood outside the arrivals door looking out of place wearing a tank top and shorts when everyone around him was in winter coats and hats. When he saw Alex standing next to the boat, he smiled, showing off his white teeth and made his way over. "Long time no see."

"Thanks for the half up front," Randy said, clasping his hand. "I heard about what happened on Crete last summer."

"Not the way I like to do business." Alex let go of his hand and motioned to the small seventeen-foot fishing boat. "Do you need to stop anywhere before we meet with my arms guy?"

"Nope, everything I need is in here." He tapped his duffle bag. "Jared my man, Todd The Bod, good to see you again." He threw his bag in the corner of the cabin then shook everyone's hand.

"All right, let's move out." Alex went to the console and entered the coordinates into the GPS. As he drove, he watched his small band put their heads together over a map of the island and talk about how the mission would work. He couldn't hear what they were saying over the engine, but it didn't matter to him. He wanted them to be as familiar with the island as possible. The more they knew, the quicker they would be on and off it.

Alex looked at his GPS, then out the window. They should be getting close to the meeting place. The weather had not improved since he landed, and an icy breeze was working its way into the cabin, making him wish he had brought a coat. He steered the boat around an outcropping and found the boat he was looking for waiting on the other side. Alex glanced at the GPS and smiled. *This will be a walk in the park.*

Alex checked his watch as he pulled away from the arms dealer's boat. *Right on time*, he thought. It was just past noon they had plenty of time to get to the island, set the explosives and get off before the sun went down.

He set a course for Poveglia and wondered how Katie and Lolita would spend their final hours. While the guys were busy unpacking and putting together the C4. So far everything was going to plan, and it seemed like it had been a very long time since things had gone to plan for him.

When the island came into view Alex cut the engine and set the anchor. He wanted to have everything ready before they arrived.

When they finished distributing the bundles of C4, Alex looked at the map. "These are the buildings that need to be leveled." He pointed to the main house and the asylum. "And when I say level them, I mean reduce them, and the earth they are sitting on, down to the water table."

"Are our targets in them?" Todd asked.

"Yes, and believe me this is the best way to take them out. The house should be easy. Jared hasn't seen any evidence of a ground patrol during the day and there aren't any proximity alarms. We should be able to place the charges and go. The asylum on the other hand," Alex tapped on the map, "is another story. The surrounding walls are ten feet tall and based on the recon Jared did this morning, there are proximity alarms set up along the top. Any ideas on how we work around them?" Alex had a few ideas, but it would take a lot of time.

"No problem." Randy went over to his duffle bag, picked it up and sat it on the table. He unzipped it and pulled out a drone. "Are there any alarms on the roof?"

Jared and Todd laughed, and Alex smiled, God, he loved the merc community. Give them short notice and one of the hardest places in the world to access, and they jump on board with guns blazing and the latest tech to get the job done.

"Not that I've seen. That should work perfectly." Jared fist bumped Randy.

"Are we ready to go?" Alex asked, pulling the straps of his C4 laden backpack over his shoulders.

"Let me put the cameras on a loop and we will be." Jared went to the computer sitting on the table. "You guys have your radios, right? Let's do a radio check."

Everything was ready when they approached the island. Todd would rig the three boats on the island, while Alex placed his explosives on the house and Randy rigged the asylum. The house was the most important to Alex since Lolita and Katie would probably be inside. It was the easiest way to take care of them, but he couldn't help wishing that he could watch the light go out of their eyes as they took their final breaths.

They jumped off the boat as soon as they hit land then pushed it back out. Jared would come back for them when they were done setting the charges.

Alex studied his GPS, then took off toward the main house at an easy jog, going through the trees that reminded him of a rainforest in the Congo except for the chill in the air. He keyed his mic as he ran. "Good luck guys. Let's get this done and get out. No screw ups, I've missed this bitch too many times."

"Roger, we got this," Randy said.

"Like stealing candy from a baby," Todd said.

When Alex reached the clearing bordering the house, he stopped to catch his breath and looked it over. It wasn't as big as he imagined, especially compared to Theron's compound or the mansion he had moved into after Alex had destroyed the compound. It wouldn't be as hard as he thought, but there were a lot of windows and if it was like Theron's they would be UV protected, which meant anyone could watch as he placed the explosives.

He took his pack off and pulled his balaclava out, not wanting to be recognized. He pulled it over his head and stuck his hands into rubber gloves. No mistakes meant no fingerprints.

Ready, he walked the perimeter of the house, finding that the north side had the fewest windows. He sprinted to the wall, staying low to the ground. When he was safely against it, he pulled out the first charge and a roll of black duct tape, then taped the C4 to the wall. Then he sidestepped, staying tight against the house as he worked his way around it, placing the rest of his charges. Rain began to fall as he taped the final charge.

"Todd, what's your status?" Alex asked, sprinting back into the trees then slowing to a jog as he headed toward the shore.

"Just finishing up. Will be on the way to the rendezvous point in less than five minutes. Randy are you done playing with your drone?"

"Yeah, placing the last package now."

"Good, let's get out of here. This rain is cold." Alex sped up ready to get back on the boat and into the cabin where it would be dry, if not warm. "Jared are you ready to pick us up?"

"Already on the way."

Twenty minutes later, Alex stood shivering in the cabin of the boat while they moved a safe distance from the island. For the first time in a year everything was right with the world, and nothing had gone wrong. He would finally complete his mission and be able to take a vacation with the rest of the money Zeus had given him. He opened a pocket on his backpack and pulled out a garage door opener with one large button. "Let's get this over with." He turned and looked over his team. "Thanks guys, I couldn't have done this without you."

He squinted through the windshield covered in drops of rain and stared at the island with his men behind him ready for the fireworks to begin. He depressed the button on the remote detonator and waited.

Chapter 32

Jean

Jean blinked and sat up in bed, forgetting where she was for a second. Her hair was wet with sweat and her heart was racing from the dream. At least she had woken up before she caught on fire, she thought.

It was just a dream. She pushed the covers back and glanced at the clock. It was early, but she had a lot of work to do before the vampires left to rescue Katie.

She grabbed her makeup bag and a set of clean clothes then went down the hall to the bathroom. The house was eerily quiet when Jean thought about how many vampires were sleeping in it.

She locked the door then Jean turned the shower on and waited for the water to get hot. After her shower she would feed Vinny then let him hang out in the courtyard while she checked in with Tad. She was still toying with the idea of sneaking onto the island. She needed access to the video feed more than anything. It would make the mission so much easier. Theron would kill her, but then again when did she ever do what she was told?

After her shower, she made some eggs she and let Vinny out of Vince's room and put him in the courtyard. When she finished eating, she set up shop in the dining room, or the command center as she thought of it, since Theron had stacked all their equipment for the mission in the room. Hard-sided boxes with weapons from Serafeim covered the floor while radios, and stakes were piled at one end of the table. She sat down at the other end and clicked on her email, praying for an update from Tad. "Yes," she whispered when she found one waiting.

> **Jean, we hacked her network. Here is the link. I did some poking around and your intel was correct, the surveillance system is on a closed-circuit, however someone already set up a relay. Here is the link. I don't have time to send a team to assist you but if there is anything we can do remotely to help let me know.**

Jean typed out a quick reply thanking him and everyone else for their help and hit send. She opened the link Tad included in his email and was about to check out the feed from the closed-circuit feed when the doorbell rang. Jean blinked and glanced at the clock. It was just past nine in the morning, the last thing she needed was someone bugging them.

She got to her feet and took the Walther PPK Theron gave her out of her waistband. She pulled back the slide making sure it was loaded then tiptoed to the door. She looked through the eyehole and held in a gasp. *How in the hell did she find me?* Jean took a breath. She wanted to ignore the unwanted guest, but she knew better. If Jean didn't answer it her mother would probably pick the lock, or worse call in the SO19.

Jean unlocked the deadbolt, cracked the door, and aimed the gun at her mother's head. "What do you want?"

"Is that any way to greet your mother?" her mom asked, pushing the barrel of the gun out of her face. "Really Jeanette, where are your manners? I'm glad you fixed your hair." She tried to push the door open and invite herself in, but Jean stopped her with her foot on the other side.

"You're not coming in. What do you want?" Jean held the gun close to her chest so her arms wouldn't get tired.

"I came to bring you home." She put her hands on her hips and blew a loose hair out of her face. The wind was picking up and Jean saw dark clouds brewing in the sky behind her mom. "Do we have to do this on the street?"

"Yes, and I'm not going back." Jean moved to close the door. She was finished with her mother and Interpol.

"Wait, I just want us to be a family again." She ran a finger under her eyes to catch a lone tear.

"You blew that when you made me a rogue." Jean studied her. Something wasn't right. The only time she had seen her mother cry was at Jean's father's funeral. The only time Jean got a hug from the woman was after she was sworn into Interpol. "Why haven't you?"

Jean's mom stared at the ground for a minute as if trying to find the words. "Everyone thinks you're deep undercover. I'm buying you time. You must come to your senses. Your new boss,

Theron, told me what you are doing for him. I'm proud of you Jean, but I want you to come home. I want us to be a family. Ever since your father died, I feel like we have become strangers."

Jean almost dropped the gun at her mother's words. Theron had spoken to her mother? He was the reason why she hadn't been tagged rogue? She blew out a frustrated breath, *he probably used his vampire magic to make her back off.* She couldn't think about the other things her mom said. None of it was true, and it would be incredibly stupid for her to consider it. "I have to go, Mom, leave me alone." Jean slammed the door, locked it, and stormed up the stairs to Theron's room.

How could he go behind my back like this? He had made my mom back off? What right did he have to interfere with my life? She didn't stop when she reached his door, walking in without knocking. She didn't care what he was, he had some explaining to do.

Chapter 33

Theron

"Jean what's wrong" Theron sat up in bed ready to spring into action. *Had Geovanni found out they were in town without permission?* He felt his fangs inch out and his eyes go red.

"What did you do to my mother?" she asked in a calm voice that didn't match the way she stomped into the room, folding her arms over her chest so he saw her gun peeking out from her waistband. She looked him up and down, blushing. "Put away your fangs and stop doing that with your eyes. It's creeping me out and I don't need much of an excuse to shoot you right now."

Theron glanced down. He was in bed shirtless with the sheet pooling around his waist, which was a good thing or else he would embarrass her even more, some things never changed whether he was human or a vampire. He schooled his features and forced his fangs to retract. Blinking a few times, he calmed down and his eyes went back to their normal brown.

"Are you going to answer my question?" Jean asked, tapping her foot on the wooden floor.

"Jean, you woke me from a dead sleep. Can you please repeat it?"

"What did you do to my mother?" she ground out.

Fuck, Theron thought, running his hand over his face, *she wasn't supposed to find out about that.* "I told her she should act like a mother, and a mother would never tag her daughter a rogue. I told her to love you. How did you find out?"

"She was just at the fucking door, begging me to come home with her." Jean put her hands on her hips. "I knew it was too good to be true. My mother was actually crying because she was worried about me. You're an asshole."

Theron shrugged, why was Jean upset? Theron couldn't make anyone feel something they didn't want to. Deep down Jean's mom must really love her. "It should wear off soon. I just wanted to give you a chance to create a new life before she tagged you; if she tags you at all. The important question now is: How did she find us and who else did she tell?"

"She works for Interpol. She probably had an alert set up on her facial recognition software. She's a pain in the ass but she knows how to find mo a I don't think she told anyone. She told the powers that be at Interpol that I'm deep undercover." Jean let her arms fall to her side and stared at the floor. "Why did you do it?"

"Because you deserve to live the life you want, not running from your mother because you don't want to do what she tells you." Theron wanted to go to her, take her in his arms, and make her forget about what he did, but he still wasn't in control of his cock, and he wasn't sure she would want his comfort.

"That's why she followed Vangel and Katie that day isn't it?"

"Yes, I believe so. Thrall worked a little too well on her which is interesting because it doesn't work at all on you." He looked at the bed. "I won't take back what I did."

"Stay out of my personal life, vampire," Jean said, but the words weren't angry, it almost sounded like she wanted him to do the opposite but then she stormed out of the room and slammed the door behind her. *Why am I worried about what she thinks of me?*

Theron lay back in his bed and stared at the ceiling. He was starting to look forward to her barging in on whatever he was doing to yell at him or give him news. He didn't know what to do about her though. He didn't think she would want to become a vampire, and he hadn't had a woman who wasn't a slave, a human he could make forget or a vampire since before he was changed. He had never wanted to deal with romance and wooing, but after they solved this problem with Lolita, he might have to start.

Chapter 34

Alex

Alex pushed the button on the detonator and waited for the explosions to send smoke into the sky, but nothing happened. "You've got to be kidding me," Alex said to himself and pushed the button again holding it down longer this time.

"What's wrong?" Jared asked, looking over Alex's shoulders.

"It's not fucking working," Alex growled, wanting to throw the detonator into the lagoon, but he couldn't, it was the only detonator they had. There had to be a way to fix it.

"Here let me see it." Jared held out his hand and Alex handed it over. Better Jared look at it than him. He would probably break it.

Jared sat at the table and pulled a screwdriver out of his pocket. Alex wondered if he always had one handy or if this was a special occasion. Jared removed the screw then pulled the back off the small box.

"Those dicks," Jared said, getting up and grabbing the gym bag Todd had brought along.

"What? Can you fix it?" Alex looked at the two pieces of

plastic on the table as the boat bobbed up and down in the water. He didn't know what he was looking at but there was a motherboard and a bunch of wires.

"Yeah, it's an easy fix. We need two triple A batteries."

"You mean they didn't include the cheapest part of this thing?" Randy looked over Jared's shoulder. "Do we have any?"

Alex stood over Todd as he went through the contents of the bag. The pitter patter of rain hitting the roof drew his eyes up. It was going to be a heck of a storm and he wanted to be finished before the water got any rougher.

"I'm not finding anything. Looks like we need to find a Radio Shack." Todd zipped the bag up and threw it in the corner. "Unless one of you brought your pocket rocket and haven't killed the batteries yet."

"Fuck." It was past three. By the time they got to town, bought batteries, and came back it would be close to dark, but what choice did they have? "Let's go, before the storm gets any worse."

Jared made the boat go as fast as he could but the cresting white caps kept him from flooring it. It was a rough ride and Alex's teeth had slammed shut enough times to give him a headache. When they reached the closest store Alex and Todd jumped out of the boat. "Go fill up with fuel and come back for us," Alex said, not wanting to take any more chances. Everything had been easy so far but not having batteries for the detonator had his stomach twisting into knots.

"OK, we'll be back in ten minutes," Randy said as Alex pushed the boat back and Jared idled down the channel.

"Let's get this done," Alex walked into the store with Todd trailing behind him. The corner store had a little of everything from produce to underwear. They split up looking for batteries but came up with nothing. Alex was about to ask for help when he found them next to the register. He grabbed a four pack of two brands and joined the line.

"It only takes two batteries," Todd said cocking an eyebrow at Alex.

"What if one batch is bad? I don't want to do this again." Alex turned around and noticed a rack of neon yellow rain jackets. "Wait here." He went over to the rack and grabbed four then went back to the register.

"Aren't you being a little paranoid?" Todd asked as they waited inside the door for Jared and Randy to return.

"Not at all," Alex pulled the tags off one jacket and gave another one to Todd. "You don't understand how many times I've gone after this target and failed." He pulled on the jacket and zipped it up. "I'm. Not. Going. To. Fail. Again." Alex was almost shouting by the time he finished, and he forced his clenched fists to relax. He looked at his palms, relieved that he had cut his fingernails otherwise his palms would have been bleeding. "There's the boat. Let's go."

They ran through the pouring rain and ducked into the

cabin of the boat. "Fucking rain," Alex said, opening the bag. "Here, I got these for you guys." He gave Jared and Randy the other coats then pulled out the batteries. "What are you waiting for?" Alex looked up at Jared when he realized they weren't moving.

"They issued a small craft advisory because of the storm. We can't leave the city limits with this boat." Jared backed up and put his hands up as if he expected Alex to hit him.

"You've got to be fucking kidding me." Alex spun around and looked out the window at the horizon, praying for a break in the storm. "What are our options?" he asked, turning back to Jared.

"We have to be within two hundred yards of each charge for the detonator to work. We will only be able to do it from the water, and with the storm we will probably have to be a lot closer than that. We should wait for the storm to pass but doing so would give them time to find the explosives and we can't risk that. We could try to outrun the police with this boat, but I think our best option will be to get a bigger boat, blow it up and get out of town."

Alex watched Todd and Randy as they nodded their heads in agreement. "Then what are we waiting for? Let's find a bigger boat."

Chapter 35

Katie

Goddess my head hurt from where Lolita had pulled me up, but I didn't let myself move until I heard the door at the top of the stairs close. I didn't want anyone to know the drug had worn off yet.

Alone for the first time and able to move I rubbed my head gingerly, touching the spot where she grabbed me. The hair was still attached which meant no bald spot; it was something. I stretched my arms over my head hating the manacles around my wrists. I didn't know how long I had been in the same position, but my body was telling me it had been too long. I flexed my toes a few times, surprised I still had my shoes from the party. I wanted to stand up, but I had to take the shoes off first. I didn't know if my legs would hold me while I stood flat-footed; I doubted I could walk in my heels.

Once I had the shoes off—which took triple the time it should have—I braced my arms on the wall behind me and ambled my back up the cold stone. Once I was vertical, I leaned against the wall and worked the pins and needles out of the lower half of my body.

After feeling had returned to my legs and feet, I pushed off, putting all my weight on my legs but ready to fall against the wall if they gave out. They held, and I walked around my cell, using the wall as a crutch. After a few minutes I stretched and moved through one of my katas, using my arms as much as the manacles would allow, reminding my body to do what it was told. I could barely stand by the time I finished it. Hungry and thirsty, I slumped to the ground with my back against the wall and looked myself over for the first time since before the party. How long had it been, two days? Three days? Or a week? Lolita's drug had done a number on me if I couldn't keep track of the time.

The once beautiful dress was stained with blood, urine and who knew what else, the skirt was torn in too many places to count. My legs were covered in bruises, my arms too were more black and blue than their normal pink. I was afraid to look at my chest and stomach. They had kicked me so many times in the midsection it still hurt to take a deep breath. I smelled. I didn't think I had ever smelled worse in my life.

You're not dead yet, I thought to myself and closed my eyes. If I wanted to stay alive, I needed to find a way out of there. I opened my vampire sense and jerked, hitting my head on the stone wall. I rubbed the spot and stared at the other wall. There were so many. The emotions and feelings that poured into me were overwhelming. Everything was so jumbled and mixed together, my stomach turned over, and I went lightheaded. I let go of them, not ready to jump into their minds yet; I didn't know if I had the strength to handle all of them. They were hungry, not starving like they had been in my dream, but hungry.

Knowing what I was working with and as back to myself as I would be while starving and being dehydrated, I needed to figure out how to get out of there. Lolita thought I was Tonio's slave; I could make that work for me. If I acted like a mindless twit, she wouldn't know I broke the bond. In a perfect world I would grab all the vampires' minds and force them to kill each other, but I didn't know how many I could grab in my weakened state, and if I did it in small groups, Lolita would catch on to what I was doing and since she was out of the drug, she would probably beat me until I passed out to stop me.

For my plan to work, I would have to grab all their minds at once and force them to walk into the sun as one. Once they began burning, I could let go of them and let them burn the place down. It would work but there were too many variables. I would need to know what time it was, and I needed a way out of my cell, or the house would burn with me trapped inside.

There had to be a better option. What if I had Tonio kill Lolita? He was her pet, she kept him close. I wondered if she kept him chained. He couldn't talk, I could jump into his mind and just look around, but to do that I would have to find him among the hundreds of others. *What am I going to do?* I felt tears prick at the corner of my eyes, but I refused to blink and let them fall. I couldn't give up yet, but I was tired, and if I didn't get some water soon, it wouldn't matter how many minds I could grab, I would be too weak to make them do what I told them to do.

The door at the top of the stairs opened, and I stiffened. I slumped in my spot and stared at my shoes, sitting against the wall opposite from me. *Fuck*, I thought. *I should have put them back on.* What would Lolita do when she found out the drug had worn off? Should I prepare to fight her? Did I have enough strength to beat her? Maybe she wouldn't notice the shoes and think the drug was still working. I wanted to know who was coming down the stairs, but I didn't have the strength to filter the thoughts of all the vampires out.

"Katie," Miguel breathed, standing outside my cell. I almost screamed; he was the reason I was there. Everything I had been through in the past year was his fault. He was the one who told Lolita about me, tried to control me, and when he couldn't, he raped me. Now he was staring at me like I was a dog who had been beaten and left on a chain to starve, like I needed to be put out of my misery. I kept up my charade by staring at the wall, doing the only thing I could at the moment: Ignore him.

"I'm sorry. You will never know how sorry I am. I will never forgive myself for messing up what we could've had together."

How do you yell at someone when you agree with everything they say? I stayed quiet, but I couldn't help noticing how different he was acting than when he was around the others. Who was the real Miguel? The asshat who grabbed my ass while I was paralyzed or the remorseful shell of a man standing outside my cell?

"Look, I'm trying to help you. I know it doesn't seem like it when Lolita and the others are here, but I have a part to play. I will do anything to keep you safe."

I almost lost it then. How was this keeping me safe? He must have a very different definition of safe than I did.

"Here's some water and a sandwich, I know it's not much, but we don't keep a lot of human food around." He looked up and down the hall as if someone was waiting for him to blow his cover. After he made sure the coast was clear, he set a water bottle, and a sandwich wrapped in a napkin on the ground inside my cell. "Don't eat it or drink it too quickly or you'll be sick. When you're done just shove the trash down the drain in the floor." He stood up and looked at me with sad eyes again. "Vince and Theron are coming tonight, but they will need your help. Save what strength you have. You'll need it."

I wanted the water so badly my hand shook, and I ached to reach for the bottle, but I wasn't ready to talk to him yet, and if I moved, he would make me talk. He said everything I needed to hear: he was sorry for what he did to me, Theron and Vince would rescue me soon, he would protect me. *Miguel, the master manipulator,* I thought, thinking about my time with him in Spain. Did I dare believe him? I wanted to with all my being, but I had to be smart and that meant not depending on him or anyone else to save me.

"I have to go but be ready when they arrive. Nice shoes by the way." Miguel said before he ran up the stairs making almost no sound.

Fucking shoes, I thought, waiting until I heard the door close and lock before I crawled over to the water and the food. I picked up the bottle and looked at the lid. Were they trying to drug me with something else? The safety seal hadn't been broken thank Goddess, and I twisted the lid off then forced myself to only take a small sip instead of chugging the entire bottle. I grabbed the sandwich next and took a bite. Peanut butter and jelly, it was perfect, I didn't know if it was drugged and I didn't care. I needed food and water more than I needed air.

I felt better when I finished the sandwich. Without my stomach reminding me of how much my life sucked, I put my shoes on and went back to my place against the wall of my cell and got to work. Mom said I had the power I needed, and it was time to see if she was right.

Chapter 36

Vince

Vince lay in bed, staring at the ceiling. It was the only thing keeping him sane. He had hours before they could leave for the island, and every time he thought about what Lolita might do to Katie, he wanted to hit something.

He sat up. Meditating on the peeling plaster wasn't working. He needed to do something. He looked at the dresser where his katana and knives sat. He went to his suitcase to dress. He put on his leather pants and a tightly woven, white, long-sleeve silk shirt. He grabbed his knives, katana, and sharpening stone.

Vinny and Jean were up. They weren't the company he wanted, but he no longer wished to be alone with thoughts of Katie as his only company. He stopped in the doorway of the dining room, and Vinny lifted his head from where he lay on the floor next to Jean. She was staring at her computer and must not have heard him. He knocked on the doorjamb to get her attention.

"Morning," she said, looking up, unsurprised to see him then looked back at the screen and resumed typing.

"Morning. Mind if I join you?" Vince moved to a seat that would give him plenty of room to lay out his blades.

"No, but why are you up? It will be hours before you can leave."

"I want to make sure my blades are sharp." He sat, placed his weapons on the table, then unfolded the cloth around his sharpening stone.

"Good idea." Jean nodded, watching him over her screen for a second before returning to her computer. She was acting out of character, and Vince wondered if something happened or if she was always this calm when she worked. She always seemed to be bouncing off the walls with endless energy, and he had never seen her this focused before.

"What are you working on?" he asked, testing the sharpness of an eighteen-inch blade with his finger. *It could be sharper.*

"I hacked Lolita's server, with some help from Kevo, and now I'm checking it out."

"Were you able to access her surveillance system?" Was there a chance that Lolita had a camera wherever they were holding Katie? Maybe he could get a look at her. *Wait, am I prepared to see her? Yes, if nothing else to make sure she is still alive.*

"It's complicated, and I'm working on it." She looked at him with sad eyes.

"What is it?" He put down the knife and gave her his full attention.

"I had another dream," she said, keeping her eyes

on her screen.

"What was it about this time?" Vince growled, as his anxiety picked up. Jean's dreams had a habit of coming true. Vinny got to his feet and went to Vince. He buried his hand in the dog's fur. It was almost like Vinny knew Vince needed his calming presence.

"Katie."

"Tell me, please," he said, forcing his voice to come out softer.

Jean looked up and must have seen the desperation in his eyes because she closed her computer, laced her fingers together, and rested them on the lid. "She was in the same cell as she was in last time only this time, she wasn't alone. I think Lolita drugged her because she would never allow what was happening to her to happen without a fight."

"Jean, you are scaring me. Tell me what you saw already." Vince tried to keep his voice calm, but Jean was trying his patience.

"There was this creature licking her face, and it was like she didn't care, she just stared straight ahead with a blank expression. I tried to save her, to wake her up, but she couldn't hear or see me. She looked bad, Vince, they beat the crap out of her, but she was still breathing."

Vince swallowed hard and looked at his hand fisted in Vinny's fur. He forced himself to let go and stroked the dog's back. He would make Lolita pay for what she did to Katie, for every bruise he found, he would give Lolita two, for every broken bone he would break three of hers.

Jean put her hands up in surrender. "Hey, I'm sorry Vince, it was just a dream. It probably wasn't real." Jean's voice broke as the words left her mouth, and she refused to make eye contact with him.

"But it is, isn't it?" he asked through clinched teeth.

Jean looked down at the table then up at him with tears in her eyes. "Yeah, I think it is."

"Did you see where she was being kept?" He wanted to have as much information about Katie as possible before he went in.

"The same place as my last dream, a dungeon only somehow it smelled worse than last time."

"Did you see anyone besides Katie and the creature? Did you see any of the entrances?"

"No, I ran up a set of stairs looking for keys, but I can't guarantee the door was there, my dream took me somewhere else after I went through it."

"I have to rescue her, Jean." Vince looked down at his stone.

"We will get her, let me do my part. The more intel I can gather, the better prepared you will be."

Vince nodded and began running the knife's edge over the stone as they lapsed into a comfortable silence.

"Yes," Jean said, causing Vince to wake up from the hypnotic rhythm he fell into while sharpening his katana. He wasn't sure how much time had passed but the katana was the last blade he needed to sharpen.

"What?" Vince dropped his sword and looked at Jean expectantly. *Had Katie escaped?*

"I'm in." Jean typed on her keyboard then moved to her mouse.

"What do you mean? I thought you were already in." He cocked an eyebrow, waiting for her to explain.

"I hacked the network, but the surveillance system is on a closed-circuit and I had no way to access it, but Tad found a relay someone set up. Now I have eyes on the ground."

Vince jumped from his chair so quickly he sent it flying into the wall. "Can you find Katie?" he asked, looking over Jean's shoulder at the squares of video taking up the screen. He counted twenty-five cameras.

"No, it looks like they are all exterior cameras except for one." Jean clicked on a square, and it expanded to take up the whole screen. Everything was white, the floors, the walls, even the desk sitting in the middle of the room with a vampire sitting behind it made it look sterile, like a lobby of a hospital.

Vince cursed under his breath then went back to his chair and sat. He wanted proof of life. Something to set his mind at ease that Katie was still alive. He picked up his katana and double-checked the edge.

"This is strange," Jean said. Vince cocked an eyebrow and watched her squint at the screen. "It looks like the cameras are on a loop."

"Why would they be on a loop?" Vince asked, setting his katana down gently, and going to look over Jean's shoulder again.

"See this bird," she pointed to one of the squares. "It flies away here." They watched the bird fly off to the right. "And now," she said after a minute. "It's back without flying in." The birds head popped back on screen. "This is a loop."

"You are right. Can you get around it?" Vince asked. *Why would they put the cameras on a loop?*

"Why? I thought vampires couldn't go outside during the day?" Jean twisted in her seat, waiting for him to explain.

"We can't, but what if someone else is going after Lolita?" Theron needed to know what was going on. Vince headed for the door.

"Oh shit." She started typing again then looked up. "Where are you going?"

"To get Theron. This could change everything."

"His room is the first door on the right on the third floor," Jean said, not looking up from her work.

"Thanks. See if you can get around the loop," Vince said, breaking into a run and flying up the stairs. He stopped outside Theron's door and knocked.

"What is it now?" Theron growled, opening the door. "Sorry, I thought you were Jean. Come in." Theron backed into the dark room. He was naked from the chest up and his leather pants reflected the light from the hallway.

"Jean found access to Lolita's security cameras. Someone put them on a loop." Vince sat at the foot of the bed and watched Theron pull a shirt over his head.

"How? And why would it be on a loop?" Thoron tucked his shirt in then turned to Vince.

"Someone set up a relay which means unless Miguel set it up, someone else is going after Lolita." Vince got to his feet.

"Miguel didn't mention setting up a relay. Who do you think it is? Do you think they will help us?" Theron sat on the bed and pulled his boots on.

"I don't know, but I wouldn't trust it. Jean is trying to get around it. Then we will know more."

"I hate not knowing. Let's hope she can." Theron tied his boots and stood.

"Do you want to change the plan of attack?" Vince asked, following Theron to the door.

"Let's see what Jean finds. We can wait to attack the army if we have to, but Katie is another story."

"Agreed, nothing will stop me from rescuing her tonight." Vince ran a hand through his hair as they headed back to Jean.

"We will save your girl," Theron said, resting a hand on his shoulder as they went down the stairs. "And we will kill Lolita's army if it's the last thing I do." They reached the bottom and headed to the dining room. "Tonight, we will rescue Katie, kill everyone, and live happily ever after."

"What if we are walking into a trap?" There was a chance they had a traitor in their midst. *Maybe Lolita put the cameras on a loop while she prepared for the battle*. Vince wondered as they entered the dining room.

"I wouldn't call it a trap, but I've counted three people sneaking around," Jean answered, looking up from her computer.

"You got around the loop?" Theron stood behind one side of Jean and Vince stood at the other, allowing them all to watch the screen.

"Yeah, but they are all wearing balaclavas. I can't ID them."

"What are they doing?" Vince asked, scanning the screen. "Could they be lost tourists?"

"No, they are wearing all black and moved like professionals, plus it's not cold enough for face masks." Jean clicked over to a screenshot and zoomed in. It was fuzzy, but it was easy to see a tall lean man and a stout heavyweight next to him. They wore all black, with backpacks and moved hunched over like they were trying not to be noticed. "There are two of them." Jean moved the mouse and brought up another picture. "Here is the other one." The third man was dressed like the others, he was tall and thin but not skinny. Vince squinted, even though he had perfect vision, but it was no use, he could not recognize him with most of his skin and hair covered.

"Unless they take off their masks, we will never learn who they are," Theron said, pulling Vince away from the screen.

Jean clicked over to an email inbox. "I found Lolita's email. I will see if there is anything useful in there before I set up for tonight."

"Is there anything I can do to help?" Vince asked, looking at his knives, but he was too amped up to work on them any longer.

"Maybe. Did you bring Katie's laptop?" Jean asked.

"Yes, why?" Vince asked, moving to his knives, and stowing them in their places: one on each ankle, four on his belt and one on his left wrist.

"Can I borrow it? She has all the traffic cameras around the island set up to record. I might be able to ID the people on the island by tracing their boat."

"I'll be right back." Vince ran to his room, opened Katie's suitcase, found her computer, then brought it to Jean. Maybe he was acting paranoid, but he had a bad feeling about who was sneaking around the island.

"You're kidding me," Theron said, leaning over Jean's shoulder as Vince entered the dining room with the computer. "Thank Goddess we didn't wait any longer."

"What is it? What did you find?" Vince asked as he set Katie's laptop down next to Jean then plugged it into the wall.

Jean glanced at Theron with fear in her eyes, she didn't want to tell Vince something. "Jean found an invitation to a public execution scheduled for tonight in Lolita's outbox."

Vince froze and closed his eyes trying to rein in the anger boiling inside him. "Katie's?"

"As far as we can tell, Lolita plans to broadcast it on Facebook Live." A tear leaked down Jean's cheek, and Theron put a hand on her shoulder.

"We will save her. How much time do we have?" Vince paced the length of the table.

"It's scheduled to begin at midnight," Theron said.

"Then we have," he looked at his watch, "just under nine hours to rescue Katie."

Chapter 37

Lolita

"You haven't seen him?" Lolita spoke into her phone while looking out her living room window. The rain was coming down harder than before and the wind was forcing the trees to bend almost to their breaking point.

"No, I'm sorry," Geovanni said through the phone. "We will keep a lookout though."

"Thank you." Lolita wanted to scream but kept it inside. Where had Mark gone? A rowboat was missing, but she didn't know for how long. They hadn't taken an inventory since she left to get Katie which meant Mark could be on the mainland, or he could've dug a hole and was spending the day covered in dirt.

"Are you going ahead with your plans for tonight?" he asked.

"Yes, I will not let one vampire with bloodlust derail my plans." Lolita sank into her desk chair and thought about how much she had to do before the fun started.

"Good for you. You will have the humans of Europe enslaved and doing your bidding before the month is over, and I will be at your side to rule them." He laughed into the phone.

"Yes." She rolled her eyes but placated him. She needed him on her side for a while longer. "If you see Mark, kill him for me, would you?"

"I will, and I will notify you immediately."

"Thank you, Geovanni." She ended the call then reached her arms over her head in a long satisfying stretch. Geovanni was convinced that he would sit on her high council and rule at her side, little did he know she didn't plan on having a high council. She planned to appoint vampires who would carry out her will without question to positions of power. Most of the leaders supporting her would never take orders from her or anyone else. She would dispose of them one by one and replace them with her own vampires.

She got up and went through the door that connected her office with her bedroom. "Greta, I need the dress now," she said, going to her closet to retrieve Katie's crown. She snickered, how could anyone, especially a human, think she could be queen of the vampires? She picked up the gold, diamond, and ruby encrusted tiara and noticed the dried blood.

"Here it is Madame," her chambermaid said from the doorway.

Lolita turned and found Greta holding a garment bag. Greta had been with Lolita since she killed Greta's father. She had been slow as a human and easily manipulated. Now after hundreds of years as Lolita's servant she was more devoted to Lolita than she was to herself. Lolita gave her a tight smile, wishing the rest of her vampires were as devoted as Greta. "Good, lay it on the sofa. We need a bucket of water, a scrub brush, and a few towels." Lolita came out of the closet, unable to take her eyes off the crown. "And when you finish in the dungeon, I need you to polish this." She put the crown on the vanity then went to get Tonio. "Tonio, are you ready to visit your girlfriend?" She peeked around the corner and found him standing at attention with a goofy smile on his lips. "Well where's your leash, you know you can't go anywhere without your leash." He plucked it off the nail on the wall and held it out to Lolita. "Good boy." She clicked the leash onto his collar and picked up the garment bag as Greta came out with a bucket of water.

"Let's stop by the throne room before we go to the dungeon." Lolita led the way to the first floor and into the grand salon. It was a large room with wood paneling halfway up the walls and rose-colored plaster above it and covering the ceiling. Normally, there were three conversation areas, but her guards had rearranged it. Now it was all but an empty room, save for the Oriental rug lying on the hard wood floor and a gilded chair with purple velvet upholstery sitting at one end. The room looked perfect. Her plan was flawless, and it started with *the queen* on her throne with no subjects to do her bidding. Exactly how Lolita wanted the world to remember Katie.

"Lolita," Miguel said, rushing into the room and stopping in front of her. "Here you are. Any sign of Mark?" he asked, taking in his surroundings for the first time. "This is where you want to broadcast from?"

"Yes, we are getting ready for tonight." Lolita spun in a circle. She couldn't remember the last time she'd been so excited. Soon Europe would be hers.

"Are you sure this is a good idea?" His voice became hard and her smile faltered.

"Of course, it is a good idea." She rolled her eyes. *Miguel is becoming a problem.* "Tonight, I will dethrone the supposed *vampire queen* and crown myself the true queen of vampires." Lolita sat on the throne, imagining a room full of vampire leaders on their knees, accepting her as their ruler.

"And how are you going to do that?" Miguel softened his voice, but his face gave away his anger.

"By killing her of course." She raised an eyebrow, sometimes she thought he had forgotten everything from the early days. "Queens are not elected then dethroned to live a quiet life outside the public eye. Remember Marie?"

"But is it worth angering our creator?" Miguel let his arms hang at his sides. He was trying to be diplomatic, Lolita could tell, but it didn't matter, her mind was made up.

"She will go along with what I have planned." She shook her head. *Why am I explaining myself to him?*

"I want no part in this. Killing Katie will have irreversible effects." He turned to leave but Lolita moved to block his path. She was afraid it would come to this. Her only true ally was turning his back on her.

"You will help me, or I will kill you now." Lolita wrapped her hand around his throat before he could bat it away and shoved him back against the wall. "You have never been on board with my plans, but it's too late for you to turn back now. You will be at myside tonight then you may do what you wish, but make sure it's far from here. I will not allow you to undermine me any longer."

Unable to speak, Miguel nodded his head, she released him, and he backed toward the door. "Louis," she called.

"Yes, mistress?" he asked, appearing in the doorway.

"Please accompany Miguel to his room and keep him there until it is time for the ceremony."

"Yes, mistress." He moved to stand behind Miguel and caressed a cattle prod.

"Greta, Tonio, let's help Katie get ready for her big night," Lolita called, looking over her shoulder as she picked up the garment bag and headed toward the kitchen and the stairs leading to the dungeon.

Chapter 38

Katie

I lay on the filthy floor of my cell staring at the ceiling. Prepared for the avalanche of information that would flood my mind when I opened my senses. Hundreds of thoughts flooded my mind as my body stiffened. I tried to pull a single mind out of the many, but I couldn't lock one down. I closed it down and wiped the sweat off my brow. How was I going to do this? I sat up and tried to break it down. When I opened my sense up it was like opening a floodgate, so as soon as I opened it, I was overwhelmed with them. What if I only opened it part of the way? It was worth a try.

I opened my sense up the tiniest bit, but nothing came through. *OK, let's try halfway,* it wasn't as bad, not as many as when it was open all the way, but there were too many for me to concentrate on one. I opened it a quarter of the way. *Bingo,* I thought and began grabbing minds. I wasn't entering them, I just wanted to see how many I could hold before I couldn't stand the bombardment of thoughts and emotions any longer.

And fifty, I thought, opening my eyes, trying to keep a grasp of where I was. I had started with the vampires in the house since they were the closest, then I worked my way over to the asylum.

Fifty minds were hard since most of them were as hungry as I was. Which made me worry about the dream Jean had. The one where the army fed on each other and then escaped to the mainland. Was that why Miguel had helped Mark escape so that their supply of blood would run out? Was he trying to make Jean's dream come true?

I was about to grab another vampire when I heard the door open and three sets of footsteps descended the stairs. I let go of everyone then grabbed the ones coming for me. *Tonio, Greta, and the last one must be Lolita?* I felt them out and shook my head, Tonio and Greta weren't strong enough, even together, to take down Lolita. They would need something to cut her head off with and I doubt there was anything in the dungeon that would do it.

"Ah, there's our queen," Lolita said, stopping outside the cell. "And good, it looks like the drug has worn off. We wouldn't want your subjects to see you catatonic, now would we?" Lolita stood outside the cell tapping her long sharp, blood-red fingernail against her lips. "And as much as I enjoy seeing you covered in your own filth, we can't let your subjects see you like this." She laughed like she was telling jokes that only she would understand.

Confused I took my gaze off Lolita and looked at Greta and Tonio. The woman was holding a garment bag and Tonio held a bucket. I wasn't sure what was in it but the thought of it being water made me drool.

"Yes, this bucket of water is for you, but I wouldn't

drink it if I were you. None of the fresh water on the island is drinkable and I'm sure you would hate to mess up your new dress." She pulled a set of keys out of her pocket and motioned for Tonio to pick the water bucket up. "Tonio," Lolita said, forcing him to make eye contact with her. "I want you to force Katie to wash herself, do you understand?"

Shit, I thought to myself then. *Nod your head*, I thought using my powers. "You can't force me to do anything." I finally spoke even though I wanted to bathe almost more than I wanted food and water.

"Tonio, can you control her or not?" Lolita rolled her eyes at my outburst.

"You stupid…" I didn't finish my sentence. *Grunt yes to her*, I thought to him.

"Very good." Lolita unlocked the cell door. This was my chance. "Tonio take the water in, and Katie don't get any ideas. All the exits are guarded and locked, and I'm the only one with a key, so there will be no escape."

Well, there went that idea, I thought to myself. Would it be worth it to take all the guards' minds, overpower Lolita, and escape? What time was it? If I got out of the house would the army tear me apart? I decided to bide my time. I was getting stronger every minute since the drug had left my system and, with some luck, maybe Miguel would bring me more food and water. While I had been trying to figure out how to escape, Lolita had opened the cell and Tonio came in with the water. He put the bucket down and stared at me like he was trying to tell me something.

"Tonio, make her wash. You don't want to get into trouble, do you?"

Oh, I thought to myself. I unzipped my dress, let it fall then stepped out of it. I didn't enjoy being naked in front of people I hated, but I didn't want Lolita to know I broke the slave bond, plus I smelled bad. I unhooked my strapless bra and slid my underwear down my legs. I took the washcloth and dunked it in the water. I barely wrung it out before I squeezed it over my chest and let out a sob as the cold water cascaded down my body. Water had never felt so good. Once I was wet, I washed, trying to scrub the cleanest parts first. The water was cold, almost too cold to stand as goose bumps rose on my skin, but I would not let it stop me. I wanted to be clean more than I cared about the cold.

"Tonio, don't forget her back." He took a few steps closer to me then took the washcloth, dunked it in the water and scrubbed my back while I stood as still as a tree and directed him with my mind.

When he finished, Lolita held a brush through the bars. "Tonio brush her hair, it looks like she's been through a tornado." Tonio took the brush.

"I can do it myself," I said, crossing my arms over my chest.

"You can, but you're Tonio's slave and it gives me pleasure to no end to watch him, a grotesque creature, lower than a vampire or human, tell the mighty queen of the vampires what to do."

You will die at my hand if it's the last thing I do on this earth; I thought to her, and she winced, but said nothing.

"Tonio, make her kneel so you can brush her hair." Lolita demanded.

I got to my knees trying not to wince as the cold wet stone dug into my already bruised knees. I took a hold of his mind and made him gently run the brush through my hair, slowly working the knots out. In my mind it was me brushing my hair, not the creature who Lolita treated as a dog.

"That's enough, Tonio. Come here now," Lolita said.

I released my hold on him and she approached the cell door. I got to my feet and wondered if I would be fast enough to get through the door before Lolita closed it, but then what would I do? Even if I stole her keys and got past the guards, I would be naked on an island full of hungry and probably horny vampires.

She ushered him out and quickly hung the garment bag from a bar on the inside of the cell. "Here is your dress for the evening," she said, closing the cell door and locking it. "Put it on."

I unzipped the bag, thinking anything would be better than putting back on what was left of my dress, but after I saw it, I wasn't too sure. It was strapless, with a side zipper, it was short, so short I wouldn't be able to cross my legs while sitting down, and worst of all, royal purple sequins covered every inch. I pulled it out of the bag, purposely fumbling with it. The weaker Lolita thought I was the better. I finally got the dress on and zipped it up, but it was too big and fell around my waist as soon as I moved my arms.

"Seriously?" I asked, pulling it up and eyeing my dirty gown on the floor, maybe it would be better.

"Greta, did you bring your needle and thread?" Lolita asked.

"Yes, mistress," she said from behind her.

"Tonio, make Katie step over to the bars and Greta will fix it. I didn't realize how much weight she's lost since Spain." Lolita crossed her arms over her chest and paced the hallway.

I moved over to the bars because, even though the dress was eighties-prom-dress ugly, it was clean. "Did you find Mark yet?" I asked not sure why I was trying to have a conversation with my worst enemy, but it was better than wondering what Greta was doing to the back of the dress.

"Aw, Mark, your one-time lover. Did you like what Miguel did to him?" She stopped pacing and faced me. "You know he did it all for you."

Keep it together, I thought looking over my shoulder. *Don't let her get to you. Don't give her the satisfaction.* "Mark was an abusive asshole. I could not care less what you did to him but what will happen if he gets off the island and kills every human he comes across?"

"After tonight it won't matter." She looked at my shoes and back at me. "Don't suppose you want to tell me how he escaped?"

"He opened his cell door and walked out. Not much to tell. I thought you would have better security." Like I would tell her that Miguel left the keys.

"I could have Tonio force you to tell me." Lolita drummed her finger against her elbow.

I rolled my eyes. "Fine, but you won't like it." I scrambled for something. "I have no idea. I couldn't see what he was doing from my position. You drugged me. You should be proud of Antonio though, he protected me."

"There," Greta said. "Try it now." I stepped away from the bars and held my arms out. The dress stayed in place. "Thank you." I waited for Lolita's next question When she only stared at me, I asked. "Why the dress?"

"Because tonight the world will learn vampires are real and I will show everyone that a stupid human did not get the better of me." By the time Lolita finished, she was yelling so loud I had to put my fingers in my ears. She spun on her heel. "Tonio, Greta, come, we have things to do." She stomped down the hall and up the stairs.

This was it, I thought as I heard the door lock at the top of the stairs. *I would die at Lolita's hand unless I did something.* Miguel said Vince, and the others were coming tonight, but would they make it in time? I had to save myself but how? I could grab the mind of everyone but Lolita, but what good would that do me when she had the keys to all the doors? Would she be able to beat off all the guards if I forced them to jump her?

I closed my eyes and felt for the vampires in the house. Lolita was one floor above me, and I still couldn't get into her mind. Greta and Tonio were with her along with Christoph and Robert.

There were two other guards on the first floor whose names I didn't know. They were at opposite ends of the house, so I guessed they were guarding the doors. I sent my mind further out. Miguel was above me somewhere above the guards on the door, and Louis was with him. I pushed my way into Miguel's mind. He had a wall, but it was almost like he was waiting for me to come to him. As soon as I tapped on it, it shattered.

Miguel, can you hear me?

I felt him startle and look around. *Where are you?* he thought back.

In the dungeon, where else? Are you on my side in this or are you making a play to take out Vince? I asked, feeling him out. He was offended, like he didn't understand why I would have a hard time believing him.

I'm on your side, I've been trying to figure out how to get you out of here. He was being honest, and I didn't want to believe him, but I didn't have a choice if I wanted to live through the night. I could kill him after I escaped.

How is Lolita planning on killing me? Maybe knowing would help me.

I don't know how yet, but she is going to publicly dethrone you then execute you. We fought, and now she won't tell me anything. I'm trying to save you but I'm out of options.

I didn't know why I was surprised. Lolita would want to make a spectacle of my death. *Have you been in touch with Vince or Theron?*

Not since they arrived in Venice. As far as I know they are coming for you tonight. I haven't been left alone long enough to call them.

I slumped, relaxing, help was on the way. *I can help with that. Louis is with you right?*

Yes, he's a pain in the ass.

Give me a minute. I stayed with Miguel with part of my mind and found Louis before locking down my sensor. I took over his mind. *Close your eyes and don't move,* I commanded.

Not again, you fucking bitch, he thought as he struggled for control.

Just chill out for a minute, I thought as I took full control of him. *Miguel you're good to go.*

Thank you, he thought, and I watched through his eyes as he pulled his phone out and tapped out a message. *Lolita is planning on executing Katie at midnight. Please hurry, I don't know what else I can do to help,* he thought as he typed the message.

Wait, I thought as his finger hovered over the send button. *Can you send something to Vince for me?*

Yes, but/ this one is for Theron. Let me send it then we'll send one to Vince.

Thank you. I held back tears while trying to think of what to say. If things didn't go our way, it would be the last time I would communicate with him.

OK, why don't you take over and type? Miguel offered.

I shoved Miguel's mind into a corner and took over his body. *Vince, I'm texting you through Miguel. I'm alive for the moment, but I don't know for how long. If things don't go our way know that the best moments of my life were spent with you. I love you. Now come save me!* I hit the send button and gave Miguel his body back. *Thank you.*

Anything for you Katie. Can you keep Louis frozen for a while longer?

Yes, but hurry, I'm trying to conserve my energy. I kept Louis where he was and realized I needed to make him forget about this or Miguel would be found out, and I doubted Lolita would take kindly to me helping him or him helping me. *You will forget the past five minutes. If anyone asks you what you did while Miguel was in his room, you will say that you watched him get dressed and nothing else. Do you understand?* I put intent behind the words and let them sink in.

Yes, but she will make you pay for this, he thought back.

OK, you can release him whenever you're ready, Miguel thought, pulling on his tuxedo jacket and going to the mirror to adjust his bowtie.

I forced him to forget all about this, so play along.

I will, and Katie if we don't have time to talk, I'm sorry about San Sebastian.

I'm sorry too, I thought, letting go of his mind. I would never forgive him, but I believed he was trying to save me, in his own way. Plus, telling him to fuck off when I needed his help wasn't a good idea.

I wanted to pace around my cell, but I stayed where I was and thought about how I would save myself if Vince and the others didn't make it in time. Goddess, I missed Vince; he was the only reason I had survived as long as I had. The weeks he spent training me in Theron's compound had been so I could save myself and not have to rely on anyone else for help, but locked in a cell, surrounded by my enemies, I wasn't sure I could save myself this time.

Chapter 39

Vince

After the news of Lolita's email, Vince had gathered his weapons and retreated to his bedroom to meditate. He sat cross-legged on the bed and forced himself to visualize killing Lolita and saving Katie before it was too late. He tried not to think of anything else, if he dwelled on everything that could go wrong, he would lose his mind then take off for the island. It would be worth it to trust that the clouds would block the sun enough to keep him from burning.

He lost track of time, thinking of all the different ways he wanted to kill Lolita when someone knocked on his door, breaking his concentration. "Who is there?" he asked, unfolding his legs as Vinny jumped off the bed and stood at the door with his tail wagging.

"Theron," the voice said. "Vince are you all right? Let me in."

Vince stood then checked his watch. The sun would go down soon, excitement zinged through him. The wait was almost over. He unlocked the door and instead of inviting Theron in, he and Vinny went out. "I'm fine, I was meditating."

"Why did you take this room? You should have taken the master so you and Katie will have a space after we rescue her."

"I wanted to be alone and if I tried to take the master it would have caused a fight with Livius and probably Maria. I am not in the mood. Besides, after we rescue Katie, we are leaving." He thought of what the Goddess had said in his dream from the night before. "We have to save her Theron, or all will be lost."

"That's why we are here. We are getting ready for the conference call. I want you to be there."

"Let's go." Vince followed Theron through the house and into the dining room where the rest of their team waited.

"Nice of you to join us," Livius said from his chair at the head of the table.

"Shut it old man, I'm not getting into it with you again."

"You are the reason we are in this mess." Livius laced his fingers together and rested them on the table like he didn't have a care in the world.

"Yes, if you mean it was my mate who discovered that Lolita has an army and is preparing to take over Europe, then it is my fault." Vince slammed his hands on the table and stared Livius down. "Is there anything else you would like to blame me for?"

"No, I think that covers it." Theron interrupted,

taking the seat at the other end of the table. "Now that we are all here, let's get everyone else on the phone. We don't have a lot of time before we need to leave." He hit a few buttons on his phone then they waited as the vampires at the other houses joined the call.

"Now that everyone is here let's go over the plan one more time." He took a deep breath. "The vampires with me will go to the main house to deal with Lolita and anyone else there. Miguel will join our side once the fighting begins. After Lolita is dead and we rescue Katie, Vince will take Katie to the boat and wait while we go to the asylum and assist the other teams, if they haven't disposed of the army by then. Germany, Poland, and Romania will attack from the main entrance of the asylum. Netherlands and Brussels will go over the east wall, Sicily and Spain will attack from the west, and Great Britain and Macedonia will approach from the North. We need to watch our timing if we want to take them by surprise. If they have time to organize, we will not only be outnumbered but fighting a skilled team who fight the best as a group. If we can keep them from organizing, we will mow them down with few to zero casualties on our side." Theron waited, letting the plan sink in.

"Do we know how many guards will be at the house?" Vince asked as his phone vibrated in his pocket.

"Jean, what have you seen so far?" Theron looked at Jean, waiting for an answer.

"Nothing, since there aren't any cameras in the house, I have no way of knowing." She gave Vince a sad smile and shrugged.

"Jean will stay here, but she will be our communication hub.

She will feed each team intel on numbers, who needs help, and where each team needs to go next. Team leads, please don't forget your earpieces as they will be how you communicate with the rest of us."

Vince pulled his phone out of his pocket and looked at a message from Miguel. The first line of the message made him freeze. "Is there anything else?" He raised his eyebrows and looked around the table. He wanted to read the message in private.

"One more thing." Jean narrowed his eyes at him. "I believe someone else is going after Lolita, they were there earlier today. I couldn't tell who they were or what they were doing on the island, but everyone must be prepared for company."

"What does this mean for the mission?" Enzo, the leader of the Sicilian vampires asked.

"You need to be on the lookout for anything out of the ordinary. I'm trying to figure out who they are, but they were wearing masks, and it's taking forever to review the traffic cameras." Jean met Theron's eyes. "Just watch your back."

"If there is nothing else?" Theron looked around the room then at the phone.

"What do we do after we win?" Danielle asked.

"Celebrate however you wish, but I would suggest waiting until you leave Venice. Geovanni will not like the attention he will receive once we are done."

"Good idea," Enzo said. "He is ruthless."

"Anything else?" Theron asked. When no one answered he said. "Very well, let's get ready to roll." He ended the call and relaxed into his chair.

"I will meet you in the garage." Vince jumped to his feet with Vinny standing next to him.

"Vince, I know it's raining, and you want to rescue your human, but the sun isn't down yet. We still have fifteen minutes before it will be safe to leave," Livius laughed, grabbing his middle.

"Here, let me take Vinny outside before you go." Jean stood and walked to the courtyard door. "Come Vinny."

The dog looked up at Vince then at Jean. "Go, I will not leave without you." Vinny followed Jean out the door and Vince paced back and forth staring at his phone, scared to read the message Katie sent through Miguel. Letting out a breath he opened the message and forced himself to slowly read it.

Vince, I'm texting you through Miguel. I'm alive for the moment but I don't know for how long. If things don't go our way know that I spent the best moments of my life with you. I love you. Now come save me!

He laughed and felt a tear form at the corner of his eye. She was alive, and the same smartass that he fell in love with. Lolita had not broken her yet. She still needed to be saved, but at least he knew it was still a rescue mission and not a recovery one.

"There are a lot of things we could do to make the time pass more quickly," Maria offered, grabbing his waist from behind and running her hands down the outside of his hips, forcing him to stop thinking about Katie for a moment.

He froze and closed his eyes. This had to stop. He pulled her hands away from him and turned to face her. "Maria, my dear friend, the times we spent together in the past were fun, and I will never forget them, but they were in the past. I am in love with Katie, and I will not disrespect her by resuming my affair with you." He watched Maria's face fall, and she jerked away from him. "Please stay and help us. Do not let my feelings toward you change your mind about Lolita and what she did to you." Vince held Maria's gaze and watched the hurt turn to anger, then acceptance.

The door to the courtyard opened and Vinny bounded in, shaking the rain off his back, and covering them with dog scented water. "You guys better bring your rain gear, it's raining buckets out there," Jean said, wringing out the bottom of her white shirt.

"Lolita must pay for what she did." Maria nodded and walked away. Vince let out a relieved breath, she wasn't going to leave.

"Vince, bring our girl home," Jean said, running a hand through her wet hair then turning to Theron. "Be careful. Don't die or anything." She put her hands on her hips, trying to look tough, but Vince saw the worry in her eyes.

Theron moved to stand in front of her. "I didn't know you cared."

"I don't, I just want Katie back and for you to go

back to Crete." She stared at the floor then the ceiling, and Vince felt like he was eavesdropping on a private moment. He wanted to turn away but watching Theron and Jean dance around their feelings for each other was a welcome distraction.

"So, you don't hate me?" Theron took a step closer and moved a piece of hair that had fallen in front of her eyes behind her ear.

"Hate is a strong word, you're frustrating but you've helped me so much. I can't hate you." She finally looked up and met his eyes.

"Vince, Theron," Livius called from the stairs leading to the garage. "Come on. I thought you wanted to leave as soon as the sun went down.

Theron let out a sigh and turned away from Jean. "Let's go." He motioned with his hand, and Vince followed him to the stairs, nodding his head at Jean as he passed. "I'll bring her home."

Chapter 40

Katie

I was sitting on the dirty floor with my back against the wall, resting my eyes, concentrating on my breath, and saving as much energy as I could. I would need everything I had to live through the night.

The door at the top of the stairs opened, and heavy footsteps descended them. It was go-time. I got to my feet and maintained my calm. I was Asteria's daughter; I would not fail. Christoph and Robert came into view and eyed me warily as they stopped outside my cell.

"Stay out of my head," Robert said, holding a cattle prod toward me. "Unless you want five thousand volts running through you."

Are the keys to the front door on that key chain? I asked Christoph as he unlocked the door to my cell.

No, only to the cells down here, he replied before he realized I was in his head.

Frustrated, I let go of his mind. "I thought Robert told you to stay out of our heads," Christoph said, fingering the handle of the gun at his waist.

"No, he said to stay out of 'my head,' he said nothing about Christoph's. Besides, if I wanted to make you put the end of the cattle prod up your butt and push the button, I could and there wouldn't be anything you could do about it." I walked out of the cell with my shoulders back and my chin up like the queen I was, even if I was walking to my execution.

"Follow me," Robert said, leading the way upstairs, while Christoph followed behind me to make sure I didn't run away; not that there was anywhere to run. I felt out the vampires around the house. There were still guards at each end of the house, there were two with me. Miguel and Lolita were on the third floor with two more. *With Lolita on the third floor, now might be my only chance to get out of here.* I jumped into the guard's mind at the door closest to me.

Break through the door, I commanded, preparing to take over the minds of Christoph and Robert.

You're crazy. It's four-inch-thick steel. There is no breaking through it, the guard thought back to me. I checked with the guard at the back door and he confirmed the same type of door. Lolita had made this place impenetrable.

There went that idea. How am I going to escape? They led me through a commercial grade kitchen and down a narrow hall with windows on one side and paintings on the other. I looked outside, but it was dark, and droplets of rain covered the glass. I couldn't see much beyond the rain except for some foliage moving in the wind.

"Keep moving," Christoph said when I stopped and squinted, hoping to glimpse my rescuers.

"How thick is the glass?" Maybe I could break it with the cattle prod or the gun.

"It's bullet proof." Robert snickered. "Give it up there is no escape."

I shrugged; it was worth a try. The house was cozy, not something I would have associated with Lolita. The walls of the hallway were a bright blue and oriental rugs covered the old hardwood floors. The paintings were where cozy became macabre though. Where I would have expected to see oil paintings of Italian landscapes instead were grotesque, bloody paintings that my eyes didn't want to understand.

We came to the end of the hall, and Robert held a door open for me. I went in without complaint since my only other option involved the cattle prod, and I was tired of pain.

The room was long, almost as long as the hallway we had come down. The walls were a soft rose and gilded frames showed off more of the bloody paintings. There was a huge area rug covering a wood floor, with straight back chairs arranged in three rows all facing a lone chair at the far end of the room. It was more like a throne than a chair with its high back, gilded armrests and frame, and the back and the seat covered with a purple velvet. I looked down at my dress, purple, the color of royalty. Lolita had planned well. They led me down the aisle to the chair, and I stared at it not wanting to sit down.

"Sit here," Robert said, pointing to the throne and removing my manacles. "Put your arms on the rests." He pointed the cattle prod at me. "Hold still or don't. I'm itching to use this on you after everything you've done to me. One false move and I'll zap you."

I didn't see a way to escape and the damn prod scared me. I laid my arms on the rests. Christoph pulled two zip-ties out of his back pocket and secured my arms to the chair. It was too big, if I sat with my back against the back of the chair my feet dangled. If I moved so my feet rested on the ground I was sitting on the edge. It would be an uncomfortable night one way or another. Christoph went to the door and stood guard while Robert stood behind me with the cattle prod.

I found a semi-comfortable position and looked for a way to escape. Even if Vince and the others made it in time they would still have to get in and how would they get through the doors? *I hoped they brought explosives.*

I located Lolita with my mind and worked on the shield protecting her mind. If I could control her, all my problems would be over. I began kicking her shield, not too hard just an easy kick that wouldn't wear me out. It wouldn't do me any good to get through her wall then be too tired to control her. She started moving toward me, which made my work easier but also made me shiver with fear. If I didn't get through her shield, she would kill me, and I wasn't ready to die. I kept kicking, but it didn't feel like I was getting anywhere.

"There's our queen," Lolita said, stepping through the doorway. She had changed into a long, body-hugging purple dress that shimmered under the light of the chandelier. It had long sleeves and a sweetheart neckline. While mine was gaudy and cheap looking, hers made her look regal. Miguel was wearing a black tuxedo with a crisp white shirt. Even Tonio had dressed for the occasion, instead of only a loin cloth, he wore black suit pants and a black bow tie instead of his collar.

"But she is missing her crown." Lolita strutted down the aisle with Tonio carrying my crown behind her. She wore a hopeful smile, like she was presenting me with a gift she hoped I would like. I had almost forgotten about the crown Vince gave me before the party. "Now, hold still while I get this on your head. Tonio, keep her still. If you can't control her, I'll have Robert use the cattle prod on her." Lolita fitted it on my head and pinned it down with bobby pins.

I looked at Tonio who was staring at me pleadingly, almost like he was afraid of what would happen to him if Lolita learned that I had broken the slave bond. I wouldn't rat him out yet. Without a weapon I didn't have a chance against Lolita, even if I could keep Louis from hitting me with the cattle prod. Plus, I was zip-tied to the chair. "Good girl." She took a few steps back. "Tonio, stand at your queen's side."

Tonio moved next to me and rested his hand on my arm. His skin was clammy and slick to the touch, almost like he was covered in slime. I grimaced, wanting to pull away, but stopped myself. I had to pretend to be his slave for a little longer. Wishing there was a way out, I noticed Miguel setting up a video camera.

"Miguel, is the camera ready?" Lolita asked, pulling a compact mirror from somewhere and checking her face.

"Nearly, Lolo," Miguel said, mounting the camera on the tripod. *I will not let her hurt you,* Miguel thought to me, making eye contact for a second before returning to his task.

"Good, let's review the plan." Lolita faced me and put her hands on her hips.

"What are you going to do, kill me while the world watches?" I asked, keeping my breathing calm while continuing to kick at her shield. *Yes,* I thought as a hairline crack formed. I couldn't give up.

"I don't plan to kill you dear," Lolita said, smiling and licking her lips. "We will become one."

"How?" I asked as images of a girl on girl vampire porno popped into my mind.

"The only way possible, I will drink all your blood, thereby absorbing your powers and we will become one." She cracked a smile, and I thought she must have practiced the line because she didn't believe it.

"Why? You don't believe it will work." I kicked harder. *Mom, I could use some help here,* I thought as the crack grew another few inches then began to spiderweb.

"It won't matter, no one will know the truth but me. Having your ability to force vampires to do my will and read their minds will scare every vampire in the world enough to take my side." Thunder crashed outside, and I looked out the nearest window. Lightning lit up the night before more thunder shook the house. *Had I seen someone out there? Was Vince here?* I had to get into Lolita's mind.

"Do you think they're stupid, Lolita? That they won't make you prove it?" I needed to buy some time and keeping her talking seemed to be the best way.

"It won't matter you little twat. Your mother, Goddess, whoever, will need someone to take your place, and I am the perfect candidate. I will be the ruler of Europe and then the world with the vampires and a Goddess on my side. Who will stop me?"

"How are you going to make a deal with the Goddess when you don't believe in her?" The spiderweb was getting bigger, and I felt sweat beading on my forehead.

"I've seen the light." Lolita turned to Miguel. "You were right after all, Miguel, the Goddess exists." She walked to the middle of the room and turned back to me.

"And you think she will let you replace me?" Another crash of thunder made me jump, and I almost missed my kick. "Why would she do that?"

"Simple, we are both after the same thing." Lolita tilted her head from side to side, staring at me.

"What's that?" I wondered what she was staring at as her shield cracked more. A few more kicks and I would have her.

"Power."

"How are you going to make her more powerful? She's

already a Goddess." I kept Lolita talking as her shield crumbled, and I wanted to shout in victory. I was in. It was time to get the hell off the island. I was about to take her mind when another shield slammed into place. I wanted to scream in frustration, how could she have another shield? She was the strongest vampire I had ever dealt with.

"What makes any deity powerful? Followers."

"No," I screamed at her. I could not wait any longer. I was getting out of there. *Robert,* I thought taking him over and making Christoph freeze in place. *Try out that cattle prod on Lolita.*

Unable to fight me off he ran to Lolita with the prod held out. I pulled on the zip-ties trying to pull the arms of the chair off while they were distracted but they were firmly attached.

"Miguel help. Tonio make her stop" Lolita shrieked, running away from Robert. I would've laughed if I wasn't doing everything I could to electrocute her. "Christoph don't just stand there." Lolita ran at him for help, but I kept him frozen until pain exploded across my face, breaking my concentration. I lost my hold on Robert and Christoph. I shook my head, trying to lessen the pain and focus. I looked around to see who hit me and found Miguel standing next to me.

I'm sorry, I had no other choice.

"Bitch," Lolita shoved Miguel out of the way. "You think you're better than me?" she snarled holding the cattle prod an inch from my nose. "Your mother will forget about you a moment after you're dead. And you," she spun to look at Tonio, cowering behind her. "I thought you could control the human."

Unable to speak Tonio hung his head and shook it.

"Is there no one I can trust?" Lolita asked the room before pressing the cattle prod into Tonio's middle. He let out a yell then fell to the ground.

I wanted to take it from her and show her how it felt as I watched the defenseless creature twitch on the ground, but I was still tied down. I reached out to Robert and Christoph, but I couldn't feel them. Ignoring Lolita, I turned my head and looked beyond her, both vampires were on the ground, not moving.

I have to get out of here, I thought as Lolita shoved the prod back in my face.

"You forced me to kill two of my best guards," Lolita said as something touched my neck a moment before my muscles cramped and electricity shot through my body. The pain seemed to go on and on, even though it couldn't have been more than a few seconds.

I have a plan, Miguel thought to me when I could see again. *Be patient.*

After you hit me? Fuck you, I almost had her.

Lolita stepped away from me. "Miguel watch her, I have to fix my face after what Robert did. We go live in ten minutes."

Chapter 41

Jean

After everyone left, Jean went back to the traffic cameras, looking for a clue as to the identity of the men on the island. The closest camera gave her a distant view of Lolita's island and Jean thought she could see everyone who came and went but it was a busy lagoon and it was taking too long. The vampires would arrive at the island soon and she wanted an answer for them before the fight began. What if they were walking into a trap?

"What's your ETA?" she asked Theron.

"Ten minutes, have you found anything?"

"No, I'm still working on it." Jean glanced back at the screen to see a small boat leaving the island. "Wait, I might have something. I'll get back to you."

She paused the video then zoomed in on the boat. She had a full facial of the only person aboard, he didn't look like the one's she had seen on the island's surveillance footage, he was too thin but who else would come from the island during the day? The time stamp was from early that morning. She copied the picture and uploaded it into the facial recognition program. It wasn't the best, but it would work. After it uploaded, she traced the registration number of the boat. It was a rental. She looked at the clock then out the window overlooking the courtyard. It was too late to call the rental company, but she had other ways of gathering the information she needed.

The boat was rented to an Abe Frohman she found out after hacking the boat rental companies network. *Bogus name*, she thought and reviewed the record. He rented the boat the night before and returned it early that morning. She checked the facial recognition program, but it was still spinning.

She went back to the traffic cameras on the lagoon. *He had to go back. Why would he set up a relay then leave?* She didn't know when the loop had begun, but it went until three o'clock that afternoon. *Dah. They would have left the island before they took the cameras off the loop.* She pulled up the footage for two in the afternoon and watched.

There it is, she thought. Watching as a different boat left the island. She paused the video as the facial recognition program pinged. *Finally*, she clicked over to it. Jared Armstrong, the name sounded familiar, but Jean wasn't sure why.

She went back to the surveillance footage and zoomed in on the boat. She wrote the registration number down to check out later. It was raining on the video and no one was on deck, but she made out four people in the boat's cabin. She didn't know if it would be good enough to run through the recognition program, but she would try.

"Jean we are in position, what is the status of the other teams?" Theron asked.

"Let me check," Jean changed the channel on the radio and checked in with the other teams. They were almost there.

"It will be a few minutes. They will radio you when they are ready to move out."

"Thank you," Theron said as Jean uploaded the pictures into the recognition program and waited. She pulled up the real time surveillance camera, the rain was keeping everyone in doors. There was barely any traffic on the lagoon, but something didn't feel right.

"Jean, this is Zoi we are in position."

"Copy, hold until we hear from the other team."

Jean's eye flicked to the monitor. She needed to figure out who Jared Armstrong was. She looked at the clock. She had time. She typed in a web-address she had memorized years before and waited while the log in screen popped up. Her mom had told her she hadn't been tagged, and she had to find out if her friends were walking into a trap. Plus, her Mom knew where she was. What was the point in hiding?

Her credentials worked as Interpol's homepage welcomed her. She opened the search program and entered Jared Armstrong. His rap sheet opened, and she began reading. He was ex-German Army, information specialist, which meant he was a hacker like her. After he left the army, he followed the money which led him to the acquaintance of Alex Jorgenson. *Fuck,* Jean thought to herself. Jared would have the skills to set up the relay and hack Lolita's network.

He was on the top fifty most wanted list and he was probably working with Alex.

Alex wasn't dumb. If he planned to attack the island, he would do it during the day when the vampires had nowhere to hide. But what did they do on the island? She clicked on the live feed of the lagoon. It was hard to see anything with the screen covered in water, but it looked like there was a boat slowly moving around the island. She tried to zoom in on the craft but the moisture on the camera made it impossible to see anything more. A flash of lightning lit up the sky. She backed the stream up and froze the feed as the lightning flashed. *Yes,* she thought writing the registration number on the boat down then running it through the database. It was from the same rental company as the other boats and the same man had rented all three. *Sloppy,* Jean thought.

She knew where Alex was! She wanted to tear out of the house and arrest him, but she was on her own, and he had at least three people with him. She couldn't leave the others though; they needed her to stay and help rescue Katie and destroy the army. She stood and paced around the room. There had to be something she could do. She picked up her radio but paused before holding the button down. *Should I tell Theron about Alex?* They were in the middle of a mission and rescuing Katie was more important than Alex, but she couldn't sit and do nothing. She huffed out a breath, picked up her phone, and dialed a number she swore she would never use again.

Chapter 42

Miguel

Miguel took his place behind the camera and made sure he framed the throne the way Lolita wanted. He had to give Katie credit; she looked as beautiful as ever, even though she was covered in bruises, had only had a sponge bath and barely any food or water for the past three days. She sat with her back straight and her hands resting on the arms of the chair. She looked like a queen. *I will not allow Lolita to kill her.* He reached in his coat and adjusted the dagger hidden inside. It would be his only chance to save Katie, he just wasn't sure how yet.

Lolita had called the other guards to join them and to bear witness to her announcement. If he pulled his knife now, he wouldn't get anywhere but killed. He looked at his watch; it was almost time. *Vince you need to get your ass here*, Miguel thought. He glanced out the window, thinking he saw movement in the flash of lightning. *The doors! We were locked in, and it would take heavy-duty explosives to get through. Why didn't I warn them?* He did a mental face palm.

Someone pounded on the front door and Miguel jumped, wondering if Vince would have the balls to just knock on the door and expect to be allowed inside.

"Miguel," Lolita snapped looking up from the broad sword she was polishing, and he turned to look at her trying to keep his expression neutral. "Answer the door, I invited a few of the troops to join us." Lolita held the keys out. "I don't think Katie can take over older vampire's minds since she hasn't taken ours."

"Yeah, she probably needs more practice." Miguel took the keys and headed for the door.

"Hurry, we will begin as soon as you are back. Don't forget to lock it."

"I won't," he ran to the front door. *I finally have the keys, but it's too late to get Katie out,* he thought sticking the key in the lock and opening the door. *And now Katie will be surrounded by her enemies.* Miguel dropped his head and waited for them to enter, but when no one did, he looked up and found the doorstep empty. It took a second for him to realize the noise he heard over the din of the rain. Metal on metal and flesh hitting flesh. He squinted into the rain and saw Lolita's tattered soldiers fighting vampires he didn't recognize.

He slammed the door without thinking and took off for the grand salon. *Katie, help is here*, he thought forgetting about everything except freeing Katie. He came to a halt, almost running into Lolita when he entered the room. "Sister, we are under attack." He breathed out, trying to keep his attention on Lolita but wanting to run to Katie.

"By who?" she asked, setting the sword in an empty chair in the front row.

"I don't know but the soldiers you were expecting are fighting them outside right now."

"I will not lose again," she said, putting her hands on her hips. "Miguel begin the broadcast." Lolita moved to stand in front of the camera and smoothed down the bodice of her dress.

"Are you sure you want to keep going?" Miguel asked, hitting the power button, and looking through the viewfinder to ensure it was focused on her. "Maybe we should run while we still have time."

"Don't be ridiculous, there's more than one reason I had the soldiers come. I knew Vince would try to rescue Katie. Everything is under control, even if he does somehow make it through them and into the house, it will be too late. Now, count it down."

Miguel held up three fingers, then flashed two, then one while trying not to look at Katie. He hit the record button on the camera and pointed his finger at Lolita. There had to be something he could do, but what? He glanced around the room as Lolita began to speak, looking for anything that would help. If he could free Katie from the chair, they could make a run for it.

"Good evening fellow vampires. Tonight, the revolution begins. We will no longer hide in the shadows, afraid of being known to the humans. Tonight, we make the humans our slaves. It begins with this so-called *queen* seated behind me. She claims to be the human daughter of our maker, the creator of vampires, Asteria. She has gifts given to her by the Goddess, gifts that give her the power to not only read our minds but to control us, powers no human should be permitted to have. Therefore, while the vampires of Europe and the world watch, and with the Goddess's blessing I will drink her blood and absorb her powers thereby making me your rightful queen.

"With my go-ahead the leaders in Rome, Paris, and Barcelona will begin the takeover while Geovanni and I take Venice. Tonight, these cities will become ours, and by tomorrow night Europe will bow down before us if they do not wish for their citizens to perish." Panic took hold of Miguel as Lolita backed up to Katie, not turning her back on the camera.

"Join us, as our time to rule begins." Lolita looked down at Katie. "Do you have any last words?"

"You may win tonight, but humans are not meant to be slaves. They will not allow you to rule them, even if it means destroying the whole of Europe. You will pay for your crimes, Lolita, either in this life or the next." Katie met Lolita's eyes for a second then looked beyond her and into the camera. "Whatever happens to me, know that the powers Lolita will claim to have are a lie. The Goddess would never give the power she gave to me to someone with Lolita's ideals."

Lolita turned to face the camera. "Asteria, Titan, Goddess of the night, stars, and prophecy, bestow upon me the gifts you gave your human daughter and I will make you more powerful than any deity." Thunder rumbled as

Lolita finished speaking and a shiver went down Miguel's spine.

Vince, where are you? Miguel thought.

"You really think she'll choose you over her own flesh and blood?" Katie screamed, pulling on the arms of the chair as the smell of blood permeated the room. Tonio, recovered from the cattle prod, moved to his knees beside Katie and licked the blood dripping from her arm where the zip-ties had cut into her skin. Lolita's eyes went red, and she spun to face Katie. Miguel grasped his dagger. This was his chance.

"Guards, please restrain my brother, I fear he cannot control himself." Before he could make a move, Louis and Arnold were at his side, forcing him to let go of the dagger and watch Lolita hurl Tonio against the wall where he slid down and slumped, unconscious on the floor.

I'm sorry Katie. Can you keep them off me? I should've been faster.

Katie closed her eyes for a moment then opened them. The grip on his arms loosened. *Don't do anything until she is distracted then break away from them,* Katie thought.

Miguel met her eyes and nodded, wishing there was more he could do as he watched Lolita bend to Katie's neck. Lolita was done talking. Miguel tried to pull away from the guards, but they tightened their grip, making it impossible for him to break free.

Katie help, I can't get loose. I need you to make them let me go, he thought to her as panic pumped through his veins, he could not let her die.

I'm trying but they aren't listening, Katie thought, but she slurred her words, Lolita must have sliced open a vein causing the blood loss to affect Katie's powers. Miguel yanked, but it wasn't enough. He glimpsed Katie slumped in her chair with Lolita at her neck. He didn't know if she had given up or didn't have the strength to fight anymore. After everything Katie had been through, she never gave up, never stopped trying to get her life back. Even now dirty, half-starved, and dehydrated she only gave in because her body had nothing more to give. He had to do something. *Goddess give me the strength to save her.*

He wrenched his arm free from Louis, drew his dagger out and slit Arnold's throat in one smooth motion. Louis pulled out a pistol, but before he could get a shot off, Miguel brought the dagger down hard on his wrist severing the hand. Miguel stabbed Arnold in the heart then twisted the blade ensuring that the muscle was damaged beyond repair. Then he pulled the blade out and ran to where Lolita was drinking Katie's blood.

He glanced at Tonio still crumpled on the ground, and for the first time since he came to Venice there was no one between him and his sister. She was the one who saved him all those centuries ago. Without her kindness he would have perished before he became a man let alone a vampire, but as he watched her drink the blood of Asteria's daughter and thought of her plans for Europe, he realized she was not the same vampire. Before him was a true monster.

He plunged the knife between her ribs from behind and gave it a twist before pulling it out. She screamed, releasing Katie, and spun to him. "Miguel, what have you done?" she yelled as she staggered a step then fell to the ground.

"You have no respect for anyone but yourself, your plan would never have worked. I was only here to stop you and look at all the horrible things you forced me to do." Something jumped onto Miguel's back almost forcing him to his knees as fists pounded at the base of his neck. He looked over his shoulder to see who it was then reached behind his head and caught Tonio's hand, stopping the barrage of punches. He tried to pull him off, but the creature had his legs wrapped around Miguel's middle and had no plans of letting go. Unable to dislodge him, Miguel backed up to the wall and slammed Tonio into it over and over until his legs loosened, and Miguel dropped him.

Finally free, Miguel ran to Katie and cut the zip-ties holding her arms, put his knife down, and pulled her into his arms. "Katie, talk to me. You can't be dead." He took her wrist and felt for a pulse. He waited for the thump that would tell him she was still alive, but when nothing came, he picked up the knife and a tear tracked down his cheek. There was only one way to save her and it might already be too late. He sliced the vein at his wrist and held it over Katie's opened mouth. "Drink Katie, you must drink if you want to live." He didn't know if it would work and it was a risk even to try. He hadn't gorged himself on her blood first, which meant he might not survive the blood loss, but Katie was worth the sacrifice, even if it was too late for her. It was the least he could do after all the harm he caused her.

Chapter 43

Vince

Vince crouched outside the house where he thought Katie was being held. The rain was coming down in sheets soaking through everything, and he regretted wearing the leather pants, they were stiff and chafing after the rain soaked them. His whole body ached to move, ready to charge the front door, but it was no use. It was a steel fire door and it would take more than they had to get through it by force. One of Maria's vampires was trying to pick the lock while everyone else crouched in the bushes.

Jean set the security cameras on a loop before they arrived, but no one trusted the relay since they didn't know who had set it up. If it stopped working and caught them, it would ruin their surprise attack. A flash of lightning illuminated the house, and Vince squinted at a black square taped to the wall.

"I got an ID on one of the guys from earlier," Jean's voice said in his ear. "Jared Armstrong is wanted by Interpol for hacking into MI6 and planting a virus. He is also a known associate of Alex Jorgensen."

"Fuck, good work, Jean." Theron's whispered voice came over the radio. "I wonder if this has anything to do with Alex.

Notify the other teams to be on the lookout for anything out of the ordinary. The game just became more interesting."

"I'm pretty sure I've got eyes on something. It's under the picture window next to the front door," Vince said. "How's the door coming?"

"What is it?" Maria asked.

"I would bet that it is an explosive, but I am too far away to say for sure." Vince answered.

"Does anyone know how to disarm it?" Maria asked.

"Sorry the door is taking a long time, the rain is making everything harder," Maria's man said.

"Everything I have seen so far points toward Alex. Has anyone tried to get in touch with Katie?" Jean asked. "She might know of another entrance."

Vince did a face palm. *Katie are you here?* It should have been the first thing he did.

Vince? Is it really you? Katie's voice filled his head, and he felt himself relax a hair; she was still alive.

Yes, we are trying to pick the lock on the door, but it is taking too long. Is there another way in?

Katie was quiet for too long. *Katie can you hear me?*

Yes sorry, Lolita is beginning her broadcast. Hurry. I think there's a set of stairs that leads to the dungeon. That's how they got me down there when we arrived. God, why didn't I think of it before? She was rambling, and neither of them had time for that.

Are you still down there? Vince asked bringing her back around while running a hand through Vinny's fur.

No, I'm in the living room, zip-tied to a chair. Her thoughts sounded panicked. *Hurry Vince.*

"Vince are you there?" Theron barked into the radio.

"Yes, sorry I contacted Katie. She thinks there is another door that leads to the dungeon. I will find it."

"Be careful and try to stay out of sight," Livius said.

"Come on Vinny we have to find Katie." They sprinted across the clearing then hugged the house and stopped under the window. He looked at the black box with a steady red light on the side. "It looks like Alex and Lolita's relationship isn't going very well," Vince said afraid of touching the device. "It's C4, we have to get in and out before it blows this place sky high. Jean notify the other teams that the island is rigged to explode." Vince took a few steps toward the back of the house. "Alex is double crossing Lolita."

"Jean, tell the others to be on the lookout for explosives," Theron's voice came over the radio.

"Find Katie, Vinny," Vince told the dog. He put his nose to the ground, and they worked their way around the south side of the house until he whined and pawed at a section of wood paneling. Vince moved closer and risked knocking on the wood. The rain was coming down hard enough to disguise the hollow echo. "I've got something, everyone be prepared to move to the south side." Vince felt around the edges of the panel and found a hook.

"We've got incoming," Livius said through the radio. "Two dozen of Lolita's zombie vampires are headed for the front door."

"Fuck, Vince what did you find?" Theron asked.

"There is a hidden door I was able to get through. It leads to a basement. I'm going down now. I left the panel open you can't miss it. Should we take out the vampires before we go after Katie?" Vince ran down the stairs behind Vinny, stopping when he reached another steel door.

"I will stay and take care of these guys," Livius said.

"As will we," Maria said. "You and Theron go get your girl. If you can, wait to kill Lolita until I can watch."

He turned the handle, but the door did not budge. *No.* He pounded on the door no longer caring if they heard him.

"Looking for these?" A cracking voice asked from behind him. Vince whirled around, not recognizing the voice.

"Who are you?" Vince squinted, he should have known the vampire holding a set of keys, but it was too dark, and he was caked in mud. Vince reached out and took the keys. He didn't care who it was as long as he could get to Katie.

"Mark, I think we met in Spain." He took a step back as he tried the keys in the door.

"What are you doing here?" Vince asked, suddenly placing the vampire as Katie's ex-boyfriend.

"I escaped thanks to Miguel, I don't know why he let me go, but I couldn't leave Katie here even if she is a whore."

Vince narrowed his eyes at the new vampire, he could kill him in an instant, but he was out of time. "If you say one more disparaging thing about the love of my existence, I will make you suffer for a hundred years." Vince stepped into Mark's face, forcing him to take a step back and hold his hands up in surrender.

"Whatever, but I'm coming with you."

"Just stay out of my way," Vince said as the door clicked open. "I'm in. Theron are you coming?" he asked the radio as he ran down the stairs to the dungeon.

"Fine," Mark said, following him. It smelled rank and Vince hoped Katie had not had to spend much time down there. Vinny stopped at an open cell and went in. "Vinny, is she here?" Vince ducked his head inside and saw the dress Vinny was sniffing. "Come on boy, that is not her." Mark ran past Vince as he tried to get the dog to leave the cell.

"Did you find her?" Theron asked, catching up.

"No, just her dress." Vinny came out with his nose to the ground leading them to a set of stairs. Vince pulled his katana from his scabbard and ran up the stairs ready to take on anything standing between him and Katie. *We are coming*, he thought to her as he reached the kitchen.

Vince, she thought back to him, but she sounded weak and far away.

Chapter 44

Alex

Alex came in from the deck and wiped his mouth. "Damn I can't remember the last time I was seasick," he said, sitting down and taking a sip from a water bottle.

"The water is pretty rough," Jared said, moving the boat toward the lagoon, looking as green as Alex felt.

"Then let's get this over with." Alex looked out the window and tried to keep his eyes on the horizon, but the sun had gone down, and it was almost too dark to see anything through the rain. It had taken way too long to get a bigger boat. Jared had had to prove that he had a captain's license, which meant they had to go back to the hotel and Jared spent an hour making a phony license. By the time they were on their way again, the sun was setting, and the storm had gotten even worse.

Going after vampires in the dark made Alex nervous, even though he had no plans to set foot on the island. He needed to get a grip. All they had to do was get within a few hundred yards and push the button.

"OK," Todd said, looking at his phone then out the window. "We should be in range. Are you ready to blow the island to kingdom come?"

Alex belched and held his hand over his mouth, afraid he would vomit again. When nothing came up, he breathed through his nose and pulled the zip-lock bag out of his pocket. "Let's get this over with." He took the detonator with fresh batteries out of the bag and stood facing the island. "Burn in hell, Katie," he whispered under his breath and pushed the button as the boat bobbed up and down in the choppy water.

"Did it work?" Jared asked.

"The light went off, but I don't see anything," Alex looked down at the device and held the button down again.

"I was afraid this might happen," Todd said, looking over Alex's shoulder. "Can you drop the anchor?"

Jared spun and looked at him with wide eyes. "Are you crazy? Why do we need to drop anchor?"

"Because the storm is fucking with the radio signals the detonator uses. It needs an uninterrupted signal for two full seconds. Out here, bobbing around with the rain isn't helping."

Alex ran his hand through his hair. "Why didn't you tell us this before?" He glared at Todd. "Even if we anchored, we'll still bounce around on the water."

"I'm sorry," Todd put his hands up in surrender. "I didn't know it would be this rough. It should work. If it doesn't, you can drop me on the island, and I'll push the button myself.

"You say that now," Alex yelled. "You do not understand what's on that island." He spun away before he punched Todd. "The next thing you will tell me is that we will have to push the button for every charge we set."

"Normally, we wouldn't," Todd said, and Alex stared at him slack-jawed. "But with the storm we might have to move around the island to get all the charges to detonate."

"Fuck," Alex punched the wall. "So, you're saying we need to drop anchor, hit the detonator then pull the anchor and do it all over again?"

"Worst-case scenario, yes." Todd flinched as Jared and Randy shook their heads.

Alex closed his eyes and took a deep breath, exhaling through his nose. "OK, let's get started. I want to do the main house first. Let's be quick." Everything was falling apart. He had thought foolishly it would be an easy job when he arrived in Venice that morning, now it felt like he had used up all his good karma, and everything that could go wrong was going wrong.

Jared moved the boat as close to the island as they could without being noticed then set the anchor. Alex left the dry comfort of the cabin and went to the bow with one hand on the railing and one hand on the detonator in his pocket. He knew it was stupid to hold on to the metal railing as lightning lit up the sky and thunder rolled around him, but he didn't want to go overboard either. *If you're the God of thunder, you could chill out for a while*, he thought before holding the button down and counted *one-one-thousand one, two-one-thousand two.*

He stared into the darkness, waiting for the unmistakable sound of an explosion. He heard a rumble but with the sound of rain hitting the deck and the water he couldn't tell if it was thunder or the bombs until a flash of lightning illuminated the sky and he saw a thick plume of black smoke climbing into the night. *Die you bitch*, he thought and did a fist pump. *Both of you.* He went back to the cabin smiling, finally something was going right. "One down, two to go."

"Thank God it worked," Todd mumbled, and Randy nodded in agreement.

"Anchors away," Jared said, flipping a few switches and turning the key to start the engine. Nothing happened, and Alex watched Jared's face fall in fear. He turned the key again. This time the engine fired up.

"Lucky," Randy said, staring at Jared.

"I must have bumped the controls." Jared rolled his eyes as the boat began to move around the island.

Alex stared at the ceiling. If someone found them out there, it would be as good as admitting that they were responsible for the bombs. They needed to hurry and finish the job. "Move it, Jared." He looked out at the dark water surrounding them. "We need to finish this before the cops see the smoke." It would only be a matter of time.

"I'm going as fast as I can," he said, watching the GPS. "There's a lot of shallow spots. We don't want to run aground."

Alex drummed his fingers against his leg, his bad feeling was getting worse. He almost wanted to abandon the mission, the house was destroyed which meant Lolita and Katie were dead. Wasn't that what he wanted? The guys wouldn't go for it though, they wanted paid, and they had to finish the job to get the rest of their money. Plus, who knew what Zeus would say.

"OK, we should be in range of the main building," Todd said, looking through a set of night vision binoculars. "Let's set the anchor."

Alex zipped up his rain jacket and went out to the bow after Jared had sat the anchor. He pushed the button and a minute later a concussion wave rocked the boat, and he swore he heard screaming coming from the island. Relaxing he went back to the cabin. *Only one more, the boats, then I will be free from vampires fucking up my life.*

"One more. Let's get it done," he said, shutting the door and unzipping his jacket.

"Let's do it," Randy said, going to the galley and coming back with four beers.

"This has been the longest day," Jared said, turning the key. Alex rolled his eyes when the ignition clicked but didn't start again.

"Your joke is getting old, Jared." Alex took his jacket off and hung it by the door.

"Shit," Jared mumbled as the starter turned again but the engine didn't catch.

"Jared, now is not the time to fuck around," Randy said, pointing off the stern. "There's a boat coming our way."

Jared looked over his shoulder and adjusted the controls then tried the key again. "Fuck," he yelled when it didn't start.

"Move," Alex said, shoving Jared out of the way and checking the gauges. "We are out of fucking fuel." Alex slammed his hand on the wheel.

"What are we going to do?" Jared asked as Alex started loosening the laces of his boots.

"Good idea," Todd and Randy said starting on their own boot laces.

"What are you doing?" Jared watched Alex confused.

"Swim for it. We don't have a dinghy and without any fuel we're dead in the water. I'm not going to jail."

"But I can't swim," Jared's eyes went wide as Alex went to the door.

"Sorry man, I can't take you with me. There should be lifejackets somewhere." Alex held the door open for Todd and Randy. "Guess you should've made sure we had fuel before we left." Alex ducked out of the door and into the rain.

The boat coming toward them turned on their red and blue flashing lights and a spotlight was trained on them. *Time to go*, he thought moving to the far side of the boat following Todd and Randy.

"Hey Alex, we still expect to get the rest of the money for the gig," Randy said, stepping over the guard rail. "It's not our fault Jared didn't pull his own weight."

"Whatever," Alex replied, jumping over the guard rail and into the cold black water of the lagoon. When he surfaced, the spotlight was on him and someone was shouting at him in Italian through a megaphone.

He spun around in the water looking for a way to escape but there was nowhere to hide. He held his hand up blocking out the light and saw Jared, Todd, and Randy standing on the deck with their hands on their head.

"I don't speak Italian," he shouted after what sounded like twenty AR-15s were locked and loaded. He wanted to pull his gun from his waist band, but it was hard enough treading water wearing all his clothes, he didn't know if he could do it with a gun in his hand and he wasn't sure if he was ready to go down in a blaze of glory.

"This is Agent Vang of Interpol, you are under arrest. Swim to the stern of the boat, or we will bring in the sharks by chumming the water with your blood." A woman's voice called.

He looked over his shoulder weighing his options. He could swim for shore, it was less than a hundred yards and hope not to get shot, but then he would be on an island with a bunch of pissed-off vampires. *Do I want to die today?* he asked himself.

"OK, I'll swim around."

Chapter 45

Katie

It will work, I thought as soon as Lolita was distracted, I would force the guards to release Miguel and he would save me. I didn't expect to lose my power to control vampires when Lolita tore into my skin. Whatever strength I had was gone almost as soon as her teeth made contact, and I was so tired. I wanted to fight but my body wouldn't obey me.

My eyes found Miguel between long blinks that seemed to grow longer each time I closed my eyes. He was struggling with the guards, but it was too late. *Thank you for trying,* I thought to him. I let my eyes close, too tired to keep them open any longer. I couldn't breathe, I panted, trying to get a lungful of air, but I couldn't do it, I couldn't find my breath. The all-encompassing pain was too much. *Vince,* I wanted to tell him I loved him one more time, tell him I didn't give up, that everything he taught me was why I had stayed alive as long as I had. Tell him I was sorry we never got to go on a regular date. I wanted to tell him so many things, but I was too weak. All the time we spent training for me to kill Lolita and there I was dying by her hand. *I love you Vince,* I thought as I lost consciousness.

I didn't know how long I was out, but suddenly my mouth filled with the greatest liquid I had ever tasted. Coppery and sweet, thick like a soup, it is what I had always desired but never found on the menu. I opened my eyes and found Miguel looking down on me with red tears staining his cheeks; he smiled as our eyes met. *You will be one of us now Katie, I'm sorry I couldn't get to you sooner.*

His thoughts filtered through my mind and I blinked. This wonderful liquid filling my mouth was his blood? He was turning me into a vampire? I wanted to be revolted, to stop, I never wanted to become a vampire. I loved the sun too much to give it up for an eternity of darkness, but the blood tasted too good and deep down I had known it was only a matter of time before I became what I was intended to rule. *Thank you for saving me.* I wanted to smile, but I couldn't stop drinking. I needed more blood.

"You're welcome, it was the least I could do after getting you into this mess." He pushed a lock of hair out of my face. *Miguel admitted it was his fault?* Maybe some of it was, but my destiny would have caught up with me one way or another. I blinked, and my eyes grew huge as Lolita came into view behind Miguel holding the broad sword. I let go of his wrist to warn him, but I was too slow. He saw the panic in my eyes and looked over his shoulder, too late. The sword was already on its path and Miguel had no place to go. He pushed something into my hand a moment before his head left his body and fell away from me. I swallowed a scream, not sure if it was from fear or frustration.

"Go to hell, traitor," Lolita said as Miguel's body fell to the side.

It was time to end this. Holding in my rage, I staggered to my feet, hiding my hand behind my back. I was determined that Lolita would never hurt anyone again. I found my breath and lowered my center of gravity ready to fight her with everything I had.

"What did he do to you?" She grabbed a chair with one hand and used the sword in her other to keep herself standing. Her beautiful purple dress was stained with blood from her chest to her waist and the stain grew larger every time she moved. I wanted to thank whoever had wounded her for me.

"The only thing he could do to save me." Not knowing how long I had before I passed out and the change took me, I lunged at her, swiping at her with the dagger Miguel gave me before he died. I missed, and she sluggishly swung her sword toward me like a drunk playing ninja. "He changed me," I said easily dodging her attack.

"What?" she screeched, baring her teeth at me. She held the sword above her head and charged me. I brought the dagger up in time to block her, but the weight of the heavy weapon brought me to my knees. *Katie, we are coming*. Vince's thought filtered through my mind and I smiled. *Vince*.

"Why won't you die?" Lolita ground out, taking another

swipe at me, and forcing me onto my back. I had to move. I would not let her win. She struggled to pull the sword behind her again, ready to strike.

"You first." I rolled out of reach then sprung to my feet a half second before the sword hit the floor where I had just been. Before she had time to heave it again, I threw a roundhouse kick at her midsection, throwing her off balance. I followed up with a kick to her knee forcing her to lose her balance and fall to her knees. I punched her in the face and felt the satisfying crunch of bone as her nose broke. "Payback," I whispered dropping the dagger and wrenching the sword out of her grasp as she brought her hands to her face. She tried to scramble away, but I kicked her in the head before she could get too far. "Stay down." I took aim, bringing the heavy sword behind my shoulder.

"Katie," a voice I never wanted to hear again called.

"So not a good time," I muttered, stabbing the sword through Lolita's back and pinning her to the floor. "Mark, why are you still here?" I looked for the dagger, but it wasn't where I left it.

"I came back for you." His eyes flashed red, and he sprinted toward me. I glanced at the broadsword pinning Lolita. I would rather fight Mark with no weapons than give Lolita a chance to recover. I braced myself for impact, prepared to break his neck. I could finish him after Lolita was dead.

A second before he hit me someone streaked

between us, Mark screamed, and fell to the ground and Antonio sat on his chest. He thrust Miguel's dagger into Mark's chest.

"Thank you, Antonio," I said, touched that he helped me. He turned and growled at me while twisting the knife in Mark's chest. I retrieve my sword from where it pinned Lolita, but he growled again and ran between us swiping the knife at me. I dodged. "Antonio," I said in the softest voice I could manage. "Why are you protecting her? She's the one who made you like this."

He glanced over his shoulder at Lolita. With the sword still protruding from her chest she was trying to dislodge it from where the tip stuck in the floor. Tonio looked back at me with tears in his eyes, but the snarl he gave me made me understand, he would protect Lolita to the end. *The poor damaged vampire.* I wished I could save him, but it was too late, and Lolita had to die.

"Antonio, why help her" I asked, reaching out a hand. He slashed at me and I jerked away. I was about to force him to stop when a growl from behind me made us both freeze. Vinny jumped on Antonio, forcing him to the ground before I could stop him. I almost called Vinny off, but I was so happy to see my dog, my protector, all I could do was watch in awe.

"Argg," Lolita gargled as she moved to a seated position, with the sword still run through her middle.

It's time. I grabbed the handle of the sword, rested my foot on her back, then yanked, pulling it free. "Go to Tartarus you traitorous bitch."

"No, you can't kill me that wasn't the deal. You were supposed to die. That is what she told me." Lolita raged and unable to stand, she crawled away from me, but she was too weak to get far. I swung the sword around in an arch parallel to the floor and met almost no resistance as the blade melted the flesh, meat, and bone of Lolita's neck before coming out the other side with surprisingly little blood. I dropped the sword, letting it crash to the floor before her head fell from her body.

"Katie," Vince said, running to my side. Tears sprung into my eyes as he fell to his knees before me. I wrapped my arms around him, unable to speak and pulled him close, noticing for the first time that I could smell the blood coursing through his veins. "Vince," I cried, finding my voice, and watching Theron cut the heads off the guards Miguel had wounded.

"Are you OK? What happened? You are different." He released me and dragged me to my feet.

"I am vampire," I said, turning my neck to show him where Lolita had bled me out.

"How?" Vince asked, looking at the growing puddle of blood under Lolita.

"She sucked my blood, trying to absorb my power. I was all but dead until Miguel gave me his." I glanced around until I found what was left of Miguel lying a few feet away. His head was already turning to ash. "He saved me." Vince pulled me against his chest again, and I sagged in his embrace, feeling safe for the first time in days.

"Vinny," Theron said, pulling my thoughts away

from Miguel. "Stop, that's gross."

I went to my knees. "Vinny," I called as more tears spilled down my cheeks. Vinny turned and bounded over. Blood covered his muzzle, but I didn't care. I wrapped my arms around him and hugged him close, sobbing into his fur. He had saved me. Someone cleared their throat, and I let go of the dog, wiped my eyes, and stood.

"What do we do now?" I asked, giving Theron a grin and a one-armed hug as he joined us.

"First, we tell the world that Lolita is dead," Theron let go of me, picked up her severed head and stood in front of the camera. "If you didn't see the true queen send Lolita to her death, here is Lolita's head. If you were planning to go forward with her plan, I suggest you don't, as her army is being disposed of as I speak," He shook Lolita's head, then dropped it to the floor. "Now it is my greatest pleasure to introduce you to our queen. Queen Katie, ruler of vampires, long live the queen." Theron held his arm out to me, and I moved into the camera shot.

"Good evening. Please, I implore you to keep our existence a secret, at least for the time being. I will be in touch with you soon." I took the camera off the tripod and threw it against the wall. "What now?" I asked as Theron and Vince shared a look.

"Are you sure you're OK?" Theron asked, eyeing me up and down. When I rolled my eyes, he shrugged. "We have to get out of here. They rigged this place to blow." Theron moved to the doorway but stopped when something crashed in the hallway, Vince moved in front of me protectively and Vinny growled.

"Who is it?"

"Livius and Marios," Theron relaxed.

"Is it true?" Livius asked. "Jean said you are vampire."

"Jean knows?" My jaw dropped as I stared at Theron.

"It's a long story, but yes, and she was watching the broadcast."

"Yes, Livius, as of a few minutes ago, I'm one of you." I leaned into Vince.

"How are you still conscious?" Livius asked, looking me up and down. "If you were just changed, you should be dead to the world while the change takes place."

"She is my daughter," my mother's voice came from somewhere nearby.

I looked around frantically for her. "Mom? Where are you?"

"I am here." I pushed off Vince, following the sound. "Mom?" I asked again.

"Right here, daughter." I picked up Lolita's head by the hair and looked at it. "Thank you. The prophecy has come true, you were turned," my mother said using Lolita's blood-covered face. It was strange that she wasn't more upset. I thought she didn't want me to turn vampire. "You are truly the queen of the vampires now. Your first order of business should be to stop the attack on Lolita's army and claim them for yourself."

"No," Vince took a step forward and looked between Lolita's head and me. "We must destroy the army."

"Silence, Vince, this does not concern you." Asteria's voice became amplified somehow, and I felt every vampire in the room freeze. "You can feel them, can't you?" Mom cooed. "Feel their need to destroy. We could rule the world Katie and get rid of Zeus once and for all."

"That was never the plan." I wanted to let go of the talking head, but then I felt them. Lolita's army was behind the walls of the asylum and they were so hungry. If I gave them blood, they would do anything for me.

Yes, they are yours to command daughter, all you have to do is reach out and take them, Asteria thought as images of how easy claiming them and taking over the world would be. I blinked; it wasn't what I wanted. I had no desire to rule the world, all I wanted was to be left alone to live my life. That would not happen though would it? I was a vampire. Nothing would ever be the same again. She was right. I could take over the world easily, but what would it accomplish?

"I don't want to, Mom, I never have."

Mom clucked her tongue. "This was the reason why I created you. You are my way back to becoming the Titan I once was. You will do as I say. I will defeat Zeus and make him pay for forcing me to hide and lose my power all those eons ago. With Lolita dead, you are the only one who can help me gain the power I will need to best Zeus."

"What do you mean since Lolita is dead? I thought you

wanted me to kill her." A chill ran up my spine.

"I did want you to kill her until I realized that you and I do not want the same things. After she kidnapped you, I came up with a new plan. She wanted the same thing as I did: world domination. I convinced her to steal your power or use you and your power to take over the world. We had a deal. I would give her you and she would help me gain the power I needed to defeat Zeus."

"How could you do this to your own daughter?" I wanted to leave. I didn't want to believe anything she said.

"Very easily, I assure you. When you've been around as long as I have, you learn to hedge your bets. I knew I would win one way or another. Now let's get to business. Grab the minds of all the vampires you can feel and make them yours."

"No. I will not do your bidding." *Vince wake up,* I thought, dropping the talking head, and caressing his cheek.

"You will do as I command." Her voice was biting, and I felt her command wash over me as she tried to force me to do her will using Thrall, and I wondered if it felt the same as when I did it to vampires. If I did as she commanded it wouldn't hurt, everything would be warm and fuzzy and right with the world, but she would not draw me in. I mentally let her command slide off me and onto the floor.

"Did you forget Thrall doesn't work on me?" I

crossed my arms over my chest. It was time to leave, but I wasn't going anywhere without my vampires.

"What is happening? You are my child twice over, by birth and by blood. You will do my will." She tried again, and again I let her command slide off me.

I let my mind find the doorway in Vince's mind I created when he was training me. His mind as well as his body was frozen. He could see and hear everything going on, but Asteria had locked his movements and thoughts down like I had done to Thomas. *Vince,* I thought, thinking of a sword, and cutting through the bindings holding him captive. *Wake up, we have to get out of here.*

What about everyone else? he asked, and I smiled when he was able to reply.

"How are you doing this?" Mom was getting angry. *Stop!* she thought, and the command filtered through one side of my mind then exited the other. She was trying to make me freeze like she had done to everyone else.

"I will not be your puppet, Mother. Leave us now," I commanded.

"No!" she yelled, and I felt her presence sink into the floor as an explosion rocked the house.

"We have to go." Vince picked me up, threw me over his shoulder in a fireman's carry, and ran for the door as the ceiling fell around us. I pushed off his back as we ran, glancing back relieved to see the others running behind us. The spell Asteria had cast had been broken.

Rain drenched me in seconds as we exited the house, but I

didn't mind, I wanted to feel clean. Theron was on our heels along with Maria and her vampires. Livius had just come through the door when another explosion rocked the house. The concussion was so hard Vince lost his grip on me, and we all flew through the air.

I hit the ground hard, landing on my stomach, and I instinctively covered my head with my arms as debris from the house rained down on us.

"Are you OK?" I asked Vince once the debris stopped falling. I sat up and looked at the foundation where the house had stood a few seconds before.

"Yes," Vince turned over and sat up. "Are you all right?"

"Yeah, I think so." I got to my feet feeling light-headed as Vinny whined beside me. I looked around and spotted Maria and Theron. "Where's Livius?"

Vince got to his feet and squinted through the rain. "Livius?" he called out, searching the clearing. "Can you feel him, Katie?"

I closed my eyes and opened my senses. I staggered but Vince steadied me as the thoughts of all the vampires on the island invaded my mind. "Holy fuck." I closed the radius of my senses trying to only feel the vampires close by. I felt Maria, and Theron; they were pissed, and Vince was stressed out.

"Jean, the house exploded but we're fine, Katie is fine. We can't find Livius. What is the status of the others?"

Theron murmured into his radio, and I heard every word before I realized I shouldn't be able to. I wanted to hear what Jean had to say but finding Livius needed to happen first.

"He's dying, he's in the rubble." I finally found his mind, and I pointed at a pile of concrete about ten feet from where I stood.

"Will you be all right on your own?" Vince asked, taking my arm.

"Go find your maker." Vinny lay down next to me, and I sat next to him. I checked him for injuries, and sighed when I found none. "I missed you, buddy," I said, laying my head on his side to rest as we watched Vince throw pieces of concrete bigger than I was out of the way as Theron and Maria ran to help.

"He is here," Maria said, falling to her knees a few minutes later.

I forced myself to my feet and joined the others. "Livius, let me help you," Vince was saying as Maria and Theron stepped back from where the old vampire lay. He was on his back, staring into the night, his eyes wide and his mouth open. Livius's hands were around a two-by-four protruding from his chest.

"No, Vince. This is my time to go," Livius said in a whisper.

"But you can't, you have to live." Vince's back was to me, but I could hear and feel the tears in his voice.

"Livius," I said, kneeling next to Vince.

"Your Highness."

"Thank you for your help. You're a cranky old man with some interesting views about how people are treated, but I hope you have a safe journey to whatever afterlife you desire."

"Take care of him, Katie." Livius's eyes closed, and I felt his spirit leave his body.

"He's gone, Vince." I stood and put my hand on Vince's shoulder as he wept. I turned to the others. "Give him a minute." I walked over to Theron and gave him a hug. "Thank you for rescuing me."

"I'm sorry we didn't get here sooner," he said, squeezing me tight. "You are one of us now."

"No, I don't think I am." I didn't know why but something with the way Miguel and Lolita changed me made me different.

"What do you mean?" he asked, cocking an eyebrow at me.

"Asteria made all of you freeze back there and she tried to force me to do what she wanted, but it didn't work. I don't know, maybe it's because Lolita sucked me dry, but Miguel was the one who gave me blood. Whatever the reason, she is pissed." I looked at Vince. He was on his feet and walking toward us. "We can worry about her later. What is the status of Lolita's army and what do we need to do now?"

"Jean, give me an update on the others," Theron said into his microphone.

"They had the army trapped and were picking them off until the bombs detonated. One of them blew a hole in the wall killing half of them, the other half escaped and are roaming the island. I found the boat detonating the bombs.

My mother and the police are on the way. The other teams are hunting down the rest of the soldiers but we're running out of time."

"Good work, Jean."

"We should help them," I said, waiting for someone to lead the way.

"You are half-starved and in the middle of changing," Vince said joining us.

He was right, I was in no condition to fight, but I couldn't just stand around while the others did the hard part. "I could tell the teams where the soldiers are." I looked up at Vince.

"You will not be safe until you are off this island." Vince began to walk, pulling me along with him.

"Could you do it from the boat?" Maria asked from behind us.

"Yeah, as long as we don't get too far from the island."

"Let's get to the boat, and we will see what you can do," Theron said, breaking into a jog.

"Start around the island," I said, sitting at the bow of the boat. Vince was holding one of my hands and the other was buried in Vinny's fur. I held back a sob, I couldn't believe I was alive and with the two most important things in my life. The rain had slackened off and a full moon peeked out from behind the clouds as we ghosted over the water. We were winning, just a little more work, and it would be over.

I closed my eyes. "There is a dozen in the clearing thirty

yards from the shore headed this way. We can't allow them to leave the island."

Theron relayed the message over the radio and smiled. "Team one has them. There won't be anything left when they are finished."

Another explosion lit up the sky a few minutes later, and I felt the end of a dozen vampires. "Did Jean tell you who planted the bombs?" I asked, scanning for the next group.

"No, I forgot to ask her," Theron said. "Jean did you find out who was on the boat?"

"It was Alex and a few friends." I couldn't tell if she was happy or not. "They are all in custody. Alex tried to swim for it, but they caught him."

"Alex is in jail?" How were we going to get our revenge if he was in jail?

"Yes," Theron bit out, sounding as pissed as I felt. "But don't worry. I have nothing to do but wait for him to get out and as he grows older each day, I stay the same. His time will come."

"There's a group of six a half mile from here," I said pointing. It was getting hard for me to keep my eyes open. "I hope you're right. I would like to be there when that day comes."

Theron relayed the location then laughed. "Great, I'll call you. How many more are out there?"

I closed my eyes and reached out as far as I could.

"The only vampires I'm picking up are on our side." I leaned into Vince. "I think we're done," I said as the change took my consciousness.

Chapter 46

Vince

Vince buckled Katie's seat belt then tilted her head to rest on his shoulder as the flight attendant closed the door of the plane and with it the past nine months of hell he and Katie had gone through.

The bruises covering her body were already fading as her body transformed, and he couldn't wait for her to wake up and give him hell about undressing her while she was unconscious again.

After a long and bumpy boat ride back to the house in Venice, Jean had met them at the door.

"Tell me everything," she said, holding it open as Vince carried Katie in with Vinny not far behind. "Oh my god, Katie, is she all right? What is she wearing?" Jean had asked, following Vince, and almost slamming the door in Theron's face. Vince wondered why she was mad at him this time.

Vince wanted to ignore Jean but knew it would do no good. She would keep asking questions until he answered her. "Lolita is dead, by Katie's hand and Katie is in the middle of changing into a…" He wasn't sure if vampire was the correct word. He had never heard of anyone who had their blood sucked out by one vampire and replaced by another.

"A what?" Jean asked, bouncing around him as he lay Katie on the couch.

"I'm not sure, we will have to wait until she wakes up and see." He had laid her arms across her chest then turned to Jean. "Could you please get her a change of clothes?" She needed a bath, but he thought it could wait.

"Yeah, but when I get back, I expect details." Jean bounded out of the room. Vince rubbed his temples before he looked down and inspected Katie. They had tortured the poor girl given the black and blue marks covering the skin he could see. The thought of what he might find under the dress made him want to resurrect Lolita and have a turn at killing her. He would drag it out for years if he could.

"Vince, leave her," Maria had called from the dining room. "She needs time to heal, and change. Hovering over her will not make it happen any quicker."

Vince forced his gaze away from Katie, terrified that if he took his eyes off her, she would disappear. "What?" he asked, resting his arms on a chair but not sitting down.

"What do we do now?" Maria had asked, looking at a broken nail like it would never grow back.

"We won. Lolita and her army are dead. You can go home." Vince looked over at Katie; he could not believe he had her back. "Thank you for your help."

"And the ones who set off the bombs?"

"Arrested by Interpol," Jean said, joining them, holding a pile of clothes. "They are all under twenty-four-hour guard and will never see the light of day again. Oh, sorry, no offense."

"Do you know where they are being held?" Theron had asked, rubbing his jaw in thought.

Jean whirled around and pointed at him. "No, and even if I did, I wouldn't tell you. He's human, he needs to be tried as a human."

"Well, I am going home then," Maria said before approaching Vince.

"We couldn't have done this without you." Vince leaned in and kissed her cheek.

"I'm sorry you lost your maker tonight. If you need anything in the future, don't call me. When you need help, it always seems to be life or death." Maria kissed him back then nodded at Theron and Jean before leaving.

"Do you understand what Alex did to me and mine? How many lives he took?" Theron asked, banging his fist on the table.

"Hey, I get it, he killed my mentor. I want him dead too, but now that my mom has him, you won't be able to get close to him." Jean folded her arms over her chest.

"Fine. What are you going to do now?" Theron asked, leaning forward as if he was challenging her.

Jean looked from side to side and tapped her foot on the floor. "I don't know, I planned to go after Alex but since he's in custody, I think I'll travel for a while."

"Don't lie to me, Jean. What are your plans?" Theron

matched her posture.

"I was thinking of going back to Interpol until judgement is passed on Alex." She let out a breath and stared at the ceiling.

"Will you keep me informed of his situation?" Theron asked.

"Yes, but I'm not telling you where he is."

"Deal." Theron turned to Vince. "When are you leaving?"

Vince checked his watch; it was a two-hour flight to Sorento. It was just past one in the morning. He had to leave soon if he wanted to make it before the sun came up. "Soon, I want to get her out of that dress then we will go. What are you going to do?"

"Vinny, come here," Jean called, bending down when the dog left Katie's side.

"Since Alex is untouchable, I'll go home." Theron had looked down at Jean with sad eyes. "I have a compound to rebuild and an island to run."

"I will miss you, buddy. Maybe after Katie gets better, I can come visit." Jean wrapped her arms around the dog.

"You will always be welcome, Jean," Vince said, giving the girl half a smile. She was a pain in the ass but a loyal friend.

"Thanks Vince," she said, standing. "I have to finish packing." She gave Theron a long look before she went upstairs.

"Are you going to let her leave?" Vince asked, taking the clothes off the table, and going to Katie.

"What do you mean?" Theron asked, following behind him.

"I didn't think I would see the day you settled down, but if you leave without Jean, you are a fool." Vince set the clothes on the coffee table. He would not undress Katie with Theron watching.

Theron slumped. "I've tried to keep her around, offered her work, a place to stay, she hasn't taken me up on any of it."

Vince put his hand on Theron's shoulder. "Have you tried telling her how you feel?" Vince pulled back, afraid Theron would hit him, but he held himself back.

"Promise you won't tell anyone what I'm about to do?" Theron straightened and tucked his shirt in.

"Go get her." Vince slapped him on the back and watched Theron run up the stairs following Jean.

Vince did not know if Jean had left with Theron or not but based on the creaking of the bed he heard while changing Katie's clothes he thought Theron got what he wanted.

"Would you like something to drink?" The flight attendant asked, pulling Vince from his memories.

"No thank you. How long till we land?" He glanced at his watch.

"About an hour. If you need anything, just push the call button," she said then returned to her seat at the front of the plane.

"I have everything I need right here," he whispered to Katie, kissing the top of her head, then leaned over to pat Vinny.

Epilogue

Katie

I was sitting on a throne in a room similar to my mother's temple. The last thing I remembered was telling Theron and Vince where the last of Lolita's soldiers were.

I looked down. My skin was ivory, and all the bruises Lolita and her guards gave me had disappeared. I was wearing the gown I wore to Theron's party, and when I checked my hair, I found the crown Vince had given me resting on my head. I reached behind me and found my katana sheathed on my back, exactly where it belonged.

It was like the fight with Lolita had never happened. Except for the memories of the pain and humiliation she put me through. I would never forget her cruelty, and no matter what life threw at me, I would never allow myself to be as cruel as she had been.

The room was empty, and I wondered if my mother would show up and try to kill me. I sat there alone for a long time. I was tired, I could have stayed for the rest of the night, but I was there for a reason, and I doubted I could leave until I figured it out.

I rose and walked across the room, remembering what it felt

like to walk without being in pain. When I reached the doorway, I could go left or right. The hallways were made of stone and were dark. I pulled my katana out and started down the right hallway, prepared to fight as the light from the torches in the room I had been in faded, leaving me in the dark. It was so quiet, even my heels made no noise as I moved across the stone floor. At the end of the hall there was a big wooden door with wrought iron bands holding it together. I held down the lever and pulled it open. I peeked through, then stepped out onto Delos, the island where my mother's temple was located. The door slammed behind me, making me jump, and I turned to see who had closed it, but no one was there.

When I turned back a woman stood with her back to me. It wasn't Mom, her figure was longer and leaner than Asteria's. She wore all black and something told me I was there because of her. "Hello?" I asked, not wanting to startle her, but ready with my sword in case she attacked me.

She turned, giving me a smile that engulfed her face. "And you are the sister that mother refused to let me meet." She held her hands out, and I could not stop myself from sheathing my sword and taking her hands.

"I'm Katie." I was ready to jerk my hands out of hers at the first sign of danger, but I wouldn't need to.

"And I'm Hecate, your half-sister." She let go of one hand and pulled me along a path.

"Nice to meet you." I walked with her but couldn't

help looking over my shoulder. "Look, I really pissed off Mom earlier, and it probably wouldn't be a good idea for her to find us."

"You don't have to worry about her anymore," Hecate said, giggling. "That's why I'm here, silly."

"What are you talking about?" I asked, forcing her to stop walking and look at me.

"When you defied her by not taking Lolita's army as your own then killing them, you took what was left of her power."

I cocked an eyebrow at her. "Why would Lolita's army dying make a difference?"

"They gave her power, and she had been using a ton of it lately. When they died, she faded away, now she is, as she was, until you came along, only the dirt beneath our feet." She kicked a rock, and it rolled away.

"So, I don't have to worry about her plaguing my dreams?" I asked, thinking it was too good to be true.

"Nope, and the prison she was keeping me in is gone. I am free for the first time in centuries." She began walking again, pulling me with her.

"What are you going to do now?"

"There is a whole new world out there for me to explore. I want to roam for a while. Don't worry, I won't bother you very often."

"Great," I needed to call Tad, and tell him he was free too. I wondered if he would leave Kevo or if he would stay for fear of the world he had only seen from a distance. "Wait, what will happen to the vampires without Asteria?"

"What did the prophecy say?" Hecate pulled me around a corner of a temple, and we were no longer on Delos, but somewhere I had never been before. The sea was to the west, and behind me loomed a huge mountain. "You will bring the vampires back to where they should be. You are their queen. Mother gave you gifts no one before has had and because of her devious games she is trapped. You are in charge now. You are truly queen of the vampires."

I think my mouth fell open in astonishment during her speech because when I tried to speak my tongue was stuck to the bottom of my mouth. "So, it's over?" I asked, finally getting the words out.

"It's over. You and Vince can live happily ever after. At least until someone thinks they are stronger than you." She let go of my hand and kissed my cheek. "Look I'm going to go, but if you need me for anything, just think to me and I'll find you."

I blinked and felt the airplane touch down on the runway. I didn't know where we were, and I didn't care. I needed more sleep, I wasn't done changing, but I was close and when I finished becoming what I was destined to be, everything would be as it should. With Vince and Vinny at my side, and Lolita dead, I could rest and enjoy life, at least for a while.

"Katie?" Vince asked as I moved my head to a softer spot on his shoulder.

"We won, Vince." I smiled into his shoulder. "We won."

THE END

Wow, it's done can you believe it? I still pinch myself when I think about how far this story went and where it took me. I say took me because that is what it did. I had to give it a nudge once in a while but in the end, this was the story that needed to be told.

This could not have been possible without the help of some very special people. The first being you, the reader. If you are reading this then you read all of Katie's story, either through Kindle Unlimited, or buying a copy. It may not seem like much to you, but every time I sell a book, or someone reads the entire series I find the will to keep writing.

This book would not have been possible without the help of my sister, Leah, and one of my oldest friends Amy. They have been my beta readers/editors from the beginning. Their support, insight and advice means the world to me.

Along this journey I met some amazing people. My cover designer, Anelia Savova who produced all the covers for the series. Thank you! The cover is the first thing people see and you have proved how important they are.

Graham, my editor, thank you for all the help you have given me. I learned so much through you.

I want to thank my parents who believed I could do anything, even if I have a learning disability. If it wasn't for you, I would have never had the faith to write one book let alone seven.

Last but never least, to my rock, my best friend and my lover. Mike, thank you for letting me get a little obsessive while chasing my dream. Thank you for your support and believing in me.

About the Author

Joy lives in Moffat County, Colorado with her husband, two dogs (Ajax and Achilles) and a barn cat or two.

She has wanted to be a writer since the sixth grade. It took her a long time to get there, and while she still has a day job, she fulfills her dream early every morning when she sits down at her computer to write.

Books by Joy Mosby

Found by Vampires (Asteria's Daughter Book 1)

Trained by Vampires (Asteria's Daughter Book 2)

Hunted by Vampires (Asteria's Daughter Book 3)

Taken by Vampires (Asteria's Daughter Book 4)

Books by Ann McCune

(same author different pen name)

Knight Flyers (Knight Flyers Book 1)

Dream Defender (Knight Flyers Book 2)